Turncoat

****

Jon A. Connor

Murderous-Ink Press

Turncoat

A Murderous-Ink paperback
First published by
Murderous-Ink Press
Stevenage
HERTFORDSHIRE
England

Paperback ISBN: 9781909498082
Electronic ISBN: 9781909498099
Trade Size ISBN: 9781909498105

Acknowledgements

Thanks are due to the following people for their help and support:

Bill Butcher, an old friend and fine editor – Rodney Leighton, a true Canadian Loonie – along with John F. Haines and Steve Sneyd, both much underrated and unacknowledged creative people – for all their help in not only keeping me on-track and focussed, but for also making me play within the rules of literacy – and repeatedly telling me that 'handraulically' isn't a real word, even though I know it *is*, damnit.

Not forgetting my collection of nit picking beta readers – without whom there would be no quality to my writing at all.

And to my partner, Den, as always.

It never rains,
But it pours....

1

Tuesday Lunchtime

From across the hotel room he kept getting glimpses of the Glock G34, snug in the shoulder rig worn by one of the three Colombians. Even the well-tailored jacket couldn't successfully hide the bulge. Every time the guy shifted his weight slightly Eddie Caradine caught sight of the worn, matt black pistol grip out of the corner of his eye. It didn't help that the smell from his aftershave was mingling with that of his own sweat and jamming uncomfortably in his nose. Across from Eddie and his partner, Tony, sat the immaculately dressed character who'd introduced himself as Mr. Jose Martinez.

Jose? Renaldo? Fernandez? It was probably all a load of bollocks. But something was making him tense. Even cool, calm Tony was on edge. They'd worked this routine a dozen times in the past, without so much as a twitch. But something was well off this time. He felt his throat tighten and start to dry up. Something wasn't right, and it had to do with the two thugs Martinez had brought with him. They stood in the far corners of the room like statues – emotionally detached and radiating an air of cold professionalism. Protection was standard in this kind of business venture, and if you didn't protect yourself then you were already dead. It was obvious that Martinez wanted to come across as being impressive. But it was also up to Eddie and Tony to appear as unimpressed as possible.

No, he couldn't put his finger on it, but there was something about the way Martinez had been fucking around with them which made Eddie's head hurt like the onset of a migraine. That, and the fact Martinez never seemed to stop smiling all the time, which was really starting to piss Eddie off.

Martinez cleared his throat, then replied to Eddie's earlier question. "Don't worry. The goods are close to hand. More importantly, for me, you have the money?"

Eddie's turn to smile. "It's nearby."

Martinez tilted his head a little expectantly.

Trying to maintain his smile, Eddie continued, "Naturally we're going to need proof of quality before we're prepared to hand over such a large sum of money."

"You consider six hundred thousand to be a large sum?" Again with the bloody ingratiating smile. Eddie felt his anger start building again. Martinez was rapidly becoming the man with the punchable head. He paused for a moment, forcing himself to relax. Get too tense and everything they'd worked for could blow up in their faces.

"Six hundred? Big money? Not really. I just consider it good insurance not to carry cash on me, at any time. You never know when someone's likely to try and take it off you, do you? Still, as we agreed, we've brought a hundred thousand in cash – all used notes. The rest will be transferred to your accounts once we're happy."

Martinez spread his hands in acknowledgement. "I can appreciate your cautious attitude and, likewise, I hope, you can appreciate mine." Again with the shit-eating smile, despite Eddie's unsubtle jab.

The air in the room was becoming stifling and Eddie wished one of the hired help would either turn the air conditioning up, or at least crack open a window. It might be freezing and pissing with rain outside, but he could feel his shirt, where it was starting to stick to his back – something else he found bloody annoying, along with the suit he'd decided to wear. Tony also looked flushed and uncomfortable. It wasn't easy for him to just sit there and play support. But if they were going to pull it off then he was going to have to hold it together for a lot longer.

Suddenly Martinez said something in Spanish, or so it sounded to Eddie, and the thug he'd mentally named Mexican Pete moved in from the side. Eddie tensed as the bloke opened the wardrobe, then handed Martinez a Samsonite briefcase. Martinez laid it almost reverently on the low table, thumbed around with the combinations, then popped the catches – the noise of them snapping open sounded loud to Eddie. Martinez lifted the lid, then turned the case around so Eddie and Tony could see the contents. Inside was a neatly wrapped clear plastic bag containing a white, granular powder.

Tony sat back on the sofa and looked at Martinez, eyes narrowing a little.

"I'm no rocket scientist, but that doesn't look like five kilos of pure to me, no matter how fucking high grade the quality." He turned to Eddie. "I've had enough of this. Let's piss off and Carlos here can keep the bloody stuff. I'm sure we can find some other bastard nearer to home prepared to sell us some quality gear without all this bullshit."

Eddie hurriedly put his hand out, stopping Tony from getting up. Somehow things had veered completely off the script, and Tony seemed about to lose his bottle and blow it completely – even before they'd had a chance to get out of the hotel room. He didn't honestly expect the guy to turn up to the meeting with five bags of high grade gear in one case? He nervously licked his lips with the tip of his tongue. The stress was starting to leave a metallic taste in his mouth, which was always a bad sign.

In an effort to defuse the tension, he said, "Chill out a little. Jose is only being as cautious as we are, aren't you." He looked over to Martinez, and saw a simmering anger had crept into the smiley routine.

"If you do not want to do business, gentlemen, then say so now. I am a very busy man," he checked his Rolex, "And I have a flight to catch back to Cartagena."

Snap decision time. Eddie tried to smile. "The cash is only a five minute walk. I take it the rest of the coke is just as close? So, what I suggest we do is this. You, the two of us, along with Speedy Gonzalez over there," he pointed in the direction of the bodyguard who had a thin moustache, "We can step out for a little fresh air. You can show us yours, we'll show you ours, and that way you'll know we're on the up and still want to do business."

The two bodyguards looked across at Eddie suspiciously. The one now christened Speedy Gonzalez uttered a staccato "Que?"

Martinez started speaking rapidly in Spanish again. When he finished he looked over to Tony, his slippery timeshare salesman smile back in place. "When you're ready, gentlemen, we shall adjourn to the car park."

Eddie closed his eyes for a moment, grateful things were getting back on track, and silently hoping Tony would play along with the change to the script. They'd worked as a team for so long, Tony should know he could trust him implicitly by now.

Two heartbeats later he heard Tony saying, "Okay, but if I get frozen you can all fucking stand by." He stood up, wiped his mouth with the back of his hand, then declared to no one in particular, "All this rain is making me want to take a piss every five minutes." Without waiting, he hurriedly disappeared into the bathroom, closing the door hard behind him.

Eddie had felt his gut spasm as he tried to work out what the hell Tony was playing at, leaving him alone with the mark. They'd never split up before – not ever. They'd always worked on trust in the past, always instinctively covering each other's backs, regardless of how the deals went down. He looked sheepishly across to Martinez, and rubbed at his stomach. "I think the pizza lunch was a bit too rich." He grimaced, forcing a belch out for added effect. If this was Tony's idea of payback for him not bringing the money up to the room, then there was going to be one hell of a score to settle when this was all over, that was for sure. Only amateurs and the clinically insane would turn up with a holdall full of cash and not expect to get ripped off the first chance they got.

Martinez's smile disappeared and Eddie knew the two thugs were also getting edgy.

Come on Tony, what the fuck are you playing at?

Martinez made a show of looking at his watch again. "Your partner seems to be taking –" There was a flushing sound followed by the bathroom door jerking open and Tony, adjusting his suit, walked towards the hotel suite door. Pausing with it half open, he looked over his shoulder. "What the fuck's everyone waiting for?" Then leaving the door wide he started down the corridor, heading for the lifts.

*

As soon as they were outside the cold February wind came at them, bringing with it stinging flecks of ice. Eddie laughed to himself. If you asked any Mancunian bastard if it rained all the time in Manchester, they'd tell you to piss off. But there'd been times since he'd moved up North when he'd wondered what the sun actually looked like. Today was just heavy dark grey clouds and a nagging cold wind. Rounding the side of the building, they stepped off the pathway and onto the exposed tarmac of the hotel car park. Eddie guessed there must have been at least two dozen high end business cars parked around the perimeter. Towards the centre were clumped various people carriers, rag tops, and the occasional 4 x 4. Most of them were crowded up near the entrance, so drivers and passengers didn't have too far to walk before they were back in the warm protection of civilization again.

With Martinez leading the way, the four of them headed towards an impressive Lexus. At least it wasn't a bloody BMW. Almost every scrote of a dealer Eddie knew was driving a BMW of some sort these days. Either that or an Audi. Until they managed to get higher up the food chain and switched over to a fully equipped Merc. Or one of those new, lush Jags. Now, that really would be sweet.

Martinez pulled out a set of keys and depressed the fob, automatically opening the boot. Inside was spotless and empty except for a dull silver flight case, the sort professional photographers kept their equipment in. Another slim silver key and some more dickering with the combinations, then Martinez lifted the lid and stood to one side, letting Eddie and Tony see that the case was full of oblong plastic bags identical to the one still up in the hotel suite.

Snapping the case shut, Martinez said, "Now you have seen mine gentlemen, I would most certainly like to see yours." Eddie only just managed to suppress a snort of laughter, but a glance over to Tony stopped it in time. Tony looked like he was going to shit himself. This one really seemed to be getting to him. When it was all over the two of them would have to sit down and have a talk, because it was becoming obvious Tony had lost his nerve.

In a slightly hoarse voice Eddie said, "Ours is the blue Subaru over there. I'll get the cash then we can go back up to the hotel room. Bring the gear with you and we'll check the weight while you sort out the transfer details." All that honour amongst thieves was just bullshit for the movies.

A short walk, then Eddie popped the boot of the Subaru, grabbed hold of a large canvas overnight bag and unzipped it. He pulled open the top so Martinez could see the banded stacks of used twenties and fifties, before pulling the bag out and slamming the boot shut. Without waiting for the others he started walking back to the hotel, knowing they would follow close behind.

Later, when he looked back on it with the aid of twenty-twenty hindsight, he felt he should've seen the three thugs earlier. But with the weather and the poor light, he didn't see them until they'd already started to make their move.

The first was a white guy in a navy blue Crombie. His hair in dreadlocks, tied up in long rounded loops – something which Eddie thought looked stupid on most white people. As Eddie's group moved between two rows of parking bays, the white guy was coming in from their East, cradling an ugly looking snub nosed Uzi across his chest, military style.

The black guy with the close cropped skinhead was coming in from their West. He was carrying a massive automatic pistol down by his side – a Walther P99, with its distinctive two-tone colouring – waving it away from his body so not to get it tangled up with his coat. In a strange way it sort of matched the long, olive green Army jacket the guy was wearing, and for some reason Eddie focussed on the small Israeli flag embroidered up near the shoulder. You could pick the jackets up cheap from most Army & Navy Surplus stores. A fully functioning Walther was a lot more difficult to find.

But it was the tall bloke heading directly towards them who became the focus of Eddie's attention. Wearing a long serge overcoat and what looked like a fucking cravat. He was tall, stocky, with a determined expression and a cold smile. Plus he was carrying a sawn off shotgun with both hands, held at hip height, pointed directly at the on-coming group.

Eddie had already started to slow down, but to help emphasise the point, the guy with the shotgun shouted, "You! With the bag! Stay right where you are, fuckwits! Keep on moving and you're fucking dead! That goes for you three pricks behind him as well, especially you with the fucking Charlie!"

Eddie stopped, closed his eyes, dropped the holdall down by his feet and swore under his breath. "Oh Jesus fucking Christ! This day just can't get any fucking worse?" As if talking to himself, he tilted his head up towards the sky, and to no one in particular, he shouted,

"If you don't make a move now someone's going to get fucking hurt!"

At that point everything happened at once.

The guy with the shotgun looked slightly confused, but he continued moving forward, feeling himself safe with his two pals covering from the left and the right. Then, seemingly from nowhere, around the car park perimeter appeared a surge of Armed Response personnel. From one of the vehicles nearby came the sound of an over-amplified loudhailer: "Armed Police! Put your weapons on the ground and step away from them now!"

Shotgun looked directly at Eddie. "What the fuck is going on here?!" Only he never got to find out. From the hotel came the sudden explosive sound of Mexican Pete's Glock, followed moments later by a very surprised look on Shotgun's face. In slow motion he fell forward onto his knees, reflexively taking his left hand off the sawn-off to steady himself. But his right index finger, firmly hooked around the twin triggers, clenched in a spasm.

Flame and pellets exploded from one of the chopped down barrels, ripping into the black guy's thigh, knee and shin, effectively taking his legs out from under him. Another spasm sent pellets from the remaining cartridge bouncing point blank onto the tarmac, ricocheting back up like a psychotic swarm of tiny bees and setting off half a dozen car alarms.

Through the roar of his damaged hearing, Eddie could faintly hear some of the chaos swarming up around him. The bullet that'd killed Shotgun, had come from their hotel room up on the seventh floor. As he looked up, he could see the bodyguard's arm, trapped awkwardly between the window and its frame, unable to open the window fully due to the joys of Health & Safety.

The guy had still held onto the Glock even after five or six spider webs appeared on the toughened glass as rounds from the Armed Response rifles punched into the man's contorted body. He was dead before the backup team had climbed the stairs and kicked the door in.

Carefully raising his hands in the air Eddie slowly turned around, looking back at the others.

The black guy was rolling around on the wet tarmac, clutching his wounded legs and screaming his head off. Eddie thought he could see patches of exposed kneecap and shin bone in amongst the tattered remains of his black jeans.

On the other side, Dreadlocks had dumped the Uzi. It was probably under one of the nearby cars. Scene of Crime Officers would no doubt find it when they started their preliminary sweeps of the area.

He looked back again at the remaining three still standing.

At the back of the group, Speedy Gonzalez had grabbed Tony from behind, his right arm firmly around his partner's neck. Only Tony didn't seem to be resisting, or moving at all. Then, as Speedy pushed Tony away from him, Eddie watched his partner fall limply to the damp tarmac, the knife clearly visible as the South American dropped it and kicked it away across the car park.

Martinez was still staring wide-eyed, mouth half open, with a dark patch spreading across the front of his trousers where he'd obviously pissed himself. Over the discordant ringing in his ears, Eddie heard Martinez say in a broad West Midlands accent:

"Fuckin'ell! You two are coppers!"

There was little else Eddie could do. The operation was totally fucked up.

Worse, his partner had just been knifed to death in front of him, and the cold realisation of it, combined with stress, tension and shock, made him feel like puking the pizza back up. He closed his eyes to stop himself from crying out in sheer frustration and rage, barely able to hear the instructions the Armed Response Commander was shouting into the loudhailer. Eddie just wanted to walk over to the bastard, snatch the microphone out of his hand, and tell him that they'd just totally fucked his life up.

9

Trouble was, he was still under cover.

Keeping his hands on the back of his head, he carefully knelt down, then eased himself forward, face down on the car park tarmac. Putting his hands slowly behind his back, the only thing he could do was to wait for the Armed Response Team to start doing their job.

2

Tuesday Evening

The conference room of the South Manchester Divisional HQ, at
Elizabeth Slinger Road, still held the persistent aroma of long nights
and longer early mornings. Ghosts of inquiries past – when cigarette
smoke stung your eyes and bitter coffee screwed up your guts for days
afterwards. Even after a force-wide smoking ban and repeated
scrubbings by hordes of minimum wage cleaners, the room still had
an odour that crept up your nose and stayed there long after you'd
left the building.

Detective Inspector Mike Fennick caught it as he entered the room.
The whole scene was depressingly familiar. Fluorescent strip lighting
with establishment cream and green paintwork. Grand Designs, eat
your heart out.

Those who had already arrived were either sitting down or
gathered around the stainless steel coffee urn and obligatory plate of
biscuits. Above them, the clock on the wall read almost 6pm.

*Less than four hours after the collapse of Operation Gold Dust, and
they're already looking to start the witch hunt.*

Fennick kept the thought to himself as sat down at the conference
table. As he reached across to pick up a bottle of water and a plastic
cup, he said quietly to the person beside him, "Great you made it
back, I was beginning to feel like Daniel in the lion's den. I take it

things didn't change much after the rest of us left?"

Keeping his voice low so as not to attract attention, Detective Sergeant Steve Hansen muttered, "Still three dead, so no change there."

"Sarcasm ill becomes you."

Hansen grinned a little. "Marcus Swannick is out of emergency surgery and in the HDU until tomorrow. Looks like they've been able to save his leg, rather than amputate. I told one of the nurses they should cut it off first chance they get as it'll make him easier to catch the next time."

"I swear you get worse." Fennick poured some water into the clear plastic cup as Hansen continued.

"That's just for starters, here comes the main course. Mr. Jose Martinez is not even Colombian. Turns out he is none other than Paul Duffley, who is part of Renton Penstone's mob." Hansen adopted an atrocious Dick van Dyke cockney accent. "'E's a tasty Sarf Lundun geezah, with a large firm, an' quite a bit of previous as well, guv'ner."

Fennick grimaced. "Gawd bless yous, Mary Poppins." Hurriedly he sat up. "Looks like the debriefing's about to kick off. Try not to be too defensive if they start throwing questions our way."

Detective Chief Superintendent James Raynolds settled himself down at the head of the table. He reminded Fennick of a stereotypical middle-class bank manager, even down to the little salt'n'pepper 'tash and slightly greying sideburns. Raynolds had been head of Operation Gold Dust, and it was plain he wasn't a happy man. Hardly surprising. He was the one who was going to have to handle the media, take the flak, and try to salvage whatever glory could be pulled from a complete and utter pile of shit.

To Raynolds' right, tall and gangly Chief Inspector Leonard Stopes was representing the uniform involvement. Often unkindly called plod work, uniform had been invaluable when the operation had collapsed. They'd secured the perimeter, logged personnel movements in and out of the crime scene area, and kept the press at arm's length. They were also a partial defence against an ever-increasing sea of administrative paperwork when it came to things like house to house.

To Raynolds' left sat Chief Inspector Ramesh Bashani, head of the Armed Response teams, both in the car park and the hotel itself. Fennick nodded politely to him. They'd known each other professionally two years ago when they'd both been working in the south. Unkindly nicknamed The Major, he was one of the few Armed Response Team members who didn't come from any kind of military background. Bashani smiled warmly, then went back to reading the printout in front of him.

Down the table was Sergeant Lynn McKay. A youngish-looking tech expert, and one of the many women succeeding in the previously male-dominated specialism. She'd been the liaison for the Intelligence Unit that had supported Gold Dust. Down from her was DI Jack Telford, a highly experienced incident manager from the Major Crimes Team, who seemed to have a perpetually harassed demeanour, and an ugly taste in ties.

That left Fennick and Hansen, both included because they'd caught wind of the original lead over on their patch. That had led to another collar which, in turn, had then germinated Gold Dust as a full scale drugs operation. Out of professional politeness they'd been invited to the final stage, purely as observers, which was fine as it meant they were out from under their own DCI's feet for a while.

The only person missing from the debrief was Detective Constable Eddie Caradine. After he'd been located by the command team he'd been bundled off in an ambulance to be checked over and have some stray shotgun pellets removed from his face and neck. It should've been a simple A&E procedure, involving nothing more complicated than a pair of tweezers and a trainee nurse. But somewhere along the line Caradine had been dosed up with sedatives, and had to be ferried back to his flat in a taxi, in no fit state to be interviewed until the morning. Without the undercover DC, Fennick wondered how the debrief could be successfully concluded.

Raynolds loudly cleared his throat and what conversation there was around the table died.

"Lady and gentlemen. I don't have to tell you that the media will be all over this very shortly. Shotguns, submachine guns, police marksmen firing into buildings. No doubt some bastard in the hotel recorded it all on their smartphone and is probably in the process of trying to sell it to one of the cable news companies even now."

Nobody laughed. Over the years it had become common practice that any idiot with amateur video footage, regardless of what it did or didn't show, no longer automatically passed it onto the police as potential evidence. There was money to be had from TV news departments, all desperate to be the first to run exclusive pictures or footage.

Raynolds looked around the table before he continued. "As it is, everything has been delayed by DC Caradine being medically incapacitated. Now, I appreciate the more time spent in delays means more time for fine details to be forgotten. Which is why I want to start things off now, even though we're short of our star player."

Around the table heads bobbed in agreement. Even Fennick found himself nodding with the pack.

"Fine. Well, Gold Dust should've been a simple operation with no complications. They should have exchanged the money for the cocaine, given us the word when it was okay for us to move in, then left the hotel room so Armed Response could disarm the three of them and make the area safe. All with minimal use of firepower."

Again the collective heads nodded in agreement.

"Okay." Raynolds paused for a moment. "Then what the fuck happened to change the script? One minute we're ready to make the deal, the next we're down in the car park. We knew where their car was – we had both it and them on video *and* CCTV. We also had them in the hotel room with a kilo of high grade cocaine. So what the fuck were Caradine and Cooke playing at?"

Ramesh Bashani jumped in. "I have no idea what they were up to, but the change of plan left me with little time to split my team and get them into an advantageous position. I was lucky to have several qualified marksmen on the ground, otherwise we wouldn't have been able to deal with the bodyguard in the hotel room. Once he started firing into the car park, there was nothing else I could do but deploy active fire in order to protect those in the immediate vicinity. Thankfully the weather kept bystanders to a minimum."

Ramesh had been the only control officer actually out in the car park, so it had been up to him to make a snap decision regarding damage limitation when the shooting had kicked off. The others had been squeezed into a tiny back office which the techies had kitted out, effectively turning it into an Operations Control Room.

It was all Wi-Fi, Bluetooth – pinhead cameras and audio circuitry that could be discretely sewn into the lapels of a jacket. And, of course, it was no longer about the gathering of information, but the quality of it. Then compiling it and passing it on to the legal experts. It was, after all, the Crown Prosecution Service that would finally decide whether or not they had a winnable case when it came time to prosecute. Legal technicalities still held sway over factual evidence, and sometimes even served to undermine it.

Raynolds, McKay and Telford, along with Fennick and Hansen, plus Jill Gillian the interpreter, had all been shoehorned into the cramped space. Loaded with an impressive array of portable equipment, all part of the modern Police Ops circus, they'd even managed to bring in four large flat screens. Two had displayed static feeds from the hotel suite, focussed around the coffee table area. The other two had been feeds from Caradine and Cooke. When Cooke had used the toilet just before they left, the team had been treated to the sights and sounds of him urinating, then a view of him in the bathroom mirror while he washed his hands. Fennick remembered him looking uncomfortable and very nervous. Yet, even when he'd had the opportunity to say the magic word, he'd just dried his hands and left. Fennick had been sure Raynolds would call the Armed Response team in at that point, but he hadn't. Nor had he when reception from both of them had started to break up in the car park. Raynolds had hesitated, and that had helped fuel the confusion which followed.

But that was just the way Fennick saw it. Both he and Hansen had been transformed from observers to witnesses, destined to be dragged in front of various inquiry boards until their lords and masters were suitably satisfied.

Lynn McKay, her body language already aggressively defensive, spoke up. "If we'd known about the car park then we would have put directional microphones in place beforehand. There's only so much range you can get out of miniature equipment powered by watch batteries."

In a deliberate tone, Raynolds said, "No one is blaming anyone from technical support for the poor reception, because the car park wasn't in any projected scenario. I just wish we'd obtained more from the hotel room."

McKay snorted, her anger overriding respect. "At the initial briefings we specifically said we needed more time to prep the hotel room, rather than just rely on a couple of fixed cameras. We're tech ops, not bloody miracle workers."

Raynolds snapped back, "Alright! You've made your bloody point!" Then immediately regretted it. "Look, I'm sorry. No one is blaming anyone for anything at the moment." He turned and looked beyond her. "Jack, have we got anything on the three hijackers? The one who died looked like he was running things."

Jack Telford consulted his notebook then, in a steady tone, like a school teacher lecturing a class, he started in on what was obviously a carefully prepared report.

"First off, only two of the Colombians were real. The survivor is Alejandro Lucumi, and the other killed by Armed Response was Sebastian Tulio. They came into the UK via Holland, usually worked as a pair, normally as personal security guards. They're on the NAFIS database for various assault charges, but they've never been successfully convicted. Both are ex-military, but as far as we know there's no particular cartel affiliation. The third, Jose Martinez, is a British national by the name of Paul Duffley. Originally from Birmingham, but now usually London based, though with several addresses to his name."

He paused as if letting his students catch up with their note taking, before carrying on. "Duffley is a known associate of London based criminal, Renton Penstone, and despite the name, Penstone is as Essex as the day is long. We're assuming Duffley is working for Penstone, rather than freelancing in regard to this venture. It's a pretty good assumption that Penstone sanctioned the sale. He's been a high end London dealer and supplier for some time now. No recent record, but that's down to a good defence team and others prepared to take the fall for him." Again a short pause, even though no one around the table had written anything down. After an audible intake of breath he continued.

"Which brings us to the three armed hijackers. Marcus Swannick is in the Wythenshawe Hospital HCU, while they do their best to save his leg. He's a local villain, part of Peter Wainwright's crew, usually involved with prostitution and Internet pornography sites. The other is cooling off in one of the traps downstairs. He's Dillon Nichols, another of Wainwright's crew, though mostly petty stuff with a bit of dealing on the side. He's waiting for legal representation before we can proceed further. Forensics should have little trouble in connecting him to an Uzi, which the Scene of Crime team found under a nearby car. As far as they can tell, it's not been used for a while. The barrel has undisturbed rust, and three rounds at the bottom of the magazine were starting to corrode together. Not so Swannick's 9mm. That had been recently cleaned and oiled – a well looked after piece. The rounds in the clip also seem pretty new. They're checking to see if either matches anything we might have open at the moment, but that's going to take ballistics another day or so, at least."

He paused again, this time more for effect.

"Now to the second fatality. The man in charge of the hijacking was Edward Victor Carlton, originally believed to be in retirement."

Hansen tensed at the mention of the name, a reaction not missed by Raynolds.

"Would you care to add anything, sergeant?"

But Telford wasn't going to be upstaged by any interloper. "Edward Victor Carlton – also known as Tiewrap Teddy Carlton – was a long time enforcer, loan shark and general right hand man for Wilson Merrillies. Not quite a local hard case, Carlton worked more around the Ellesmere Port area. The nickname Tiewrap is due to his alleged use of large industrial cable ties. Placed around an immobile victim's neck and slowly tightened until they…." His voice tailed off to an embarrassed silence as he finally realised his mistake.

Face flushed slightly, Raynolds looked thunderously at Telford. "I'm sorry for interrupting you, Jack." He maintained the angry eye contact as he continued, "However, do you still have anything to add to that, sergeant?"

"No, sir. I was just going to say that I knew Carlton of old. He's never usually favoured firearms in the past, but then he's never been in charge of anything in the past either. Everything else is on file. It's fairly comprehensive since his supposed retirement."

Seemingly placated, Raynolds jotted something down in his notebook, then looked back up to Telford again. "Jack. I need you to keep me up to speed at all times. Anything new – literally anything – and I want to know about it. I've a full press briefing at nine-thirty tonight. Hopefully that should keep them busy long enough for them to miss the ten o'clock evening news. With any luck." There was another short pause while he organised his thoughts, then, "Okay. If no one has anything else to put into the pot?" He quickly looked around the table, noting the slight shake of peoples' heads. "No? Okay, I'd like to say thank you to Chief Stopes and Sergeant McKay for attending. If we need anything further then we'll contact you. Chief Bashani, I want you as deputy co-ordinator on this. You'll report directly to me. Jack, I want to see the forensics reports as and when they're in, plus the post mortem on DC Cooke as soon as that's ready. Push for it if needs be. I want to build up a good knowledge base as fast as possible, so we can get this whole thing cleaned up and squared away with the minimum of delay. Inspector Fennick, Sergeant Hansen, remain behind, I want a word with the two of you. Next progress meeting will be eight tomorrow morning. Again, thank you all for your time."

On his way out, Ramesh Bashani patted Fennick on the shoulder. "Catch up with you later Mike." Then without waiting for a reply he left the conference room with the others. As Fennick refilled his plastic cup, he noticed Hansen had started to tap his fingertips on the tabletop – getting twitchy for one of his smokes. Fennick had stopped ten years ago, though he always had sympathy for those who were still addicted.

Raynolds continued to write several more lines in his notebook, nodded to himself, then looked up.

"I've not discussed this with DCI Sugden, but I want to bring the two of you in to help with the investigation."

Fennick took a sip of water, and wondered if there wasn't a whiff of internal politics in the air. "Saying our DCI agrees, why should you want us to get involved, sir?"

"This investigation is bound to generate a lot of external interest, it always does when things go wrong. There's media speculation already – they cornered a couple of uniformed PCs before we managed to put out an official press release. I want the two of you involved so as to give us the benefit of an outsiders' view."

A little truculently Hansen said, "And if we find something you're not happy with, then what, sir?"

For a second Fennick thought Raynolds would explode, but he managed to keep himself in check. "Regardless of what you find, you'll report it to me and I'll deal with it accordingly. Whether I like it or not is immaterial. An officer has been killed in the line of duty and I want to know exactly why it happened on my watch."

Fennick tried to placate things. "I think what Sergeant Hansen meant was how much do we tell the public, if we're asked, and how much is going to be kept under wraps?"

Raynolds looked down at his open notebook. "I'll be the one handling the public and the press calls, so you don't have to worry about that." He let out another long, calming breath. "First thing tomorrow morning I want the pair of you to interview Caradine. I want to know why the change of plan and why neither of them saw fit to call us in when things started getting out of hand. But above all I want to know who the hell he's been talking to. It's obvious someone tipped these people off, and I want to know who."

Fennick was quicker than Hansen. "You suspect Caradine of being the leak?"

"At the moment everyone's a bloody suspect. Even you two."

Fennick kicked Hansen sharply under the table, cutting him off before he could reply. The last thing they needed at this stage was to start antagonising the DCS. Changing the subject, he asked, "You'll clear everything with DCI Sugden?"

"Don't worry about him. Just go and talk to Caradine in the morning. Or, if needs be, bring him back here, I don't care. All I want is his account of the fiasco, and I want it in by midday tomorrow. There's an incident room being set up. It's on the fifth floor. Once you've talked to Caradine, you can get yourself settled in there."

Raynolds slipped the notebook into his jacket, checked he'd left nothing else, then got up to leave. "I'll expect something by tomorrow lunchtime." Then he was out the door, heading back to his office.

Fennick looked down at Hansen's fingers resting on the polished tabletop. It looked like they were auditioning for a part in a finger-puppet version of Riverdance. Pushing his chair away from the table, he stood up. "Come on, Steve. Let's get you hooked up to a smoke before you kill something."

3

Outside, the back of the station was cold, wet and deserted. Patrol cars were mixed in with brightly marked police vans, while over the other side the on-coming shift were parked up under the harsh yellow sodium yard lights. To the left of the exit door was a large bike shed with a few cycles chained up in it. The command had still to give the die-hard smokers a dedicated shelter, so they had unofficially commandeered it. It wasn't much, but it offered some protection from the relentless drizzle.

Hansen ducked under the roof and took out a flat tin of small cigars. He thumbed a disposable plastic lighter into life and, after a couple of puffs, took a steady draw of smoke down into his lungs. Closing his eyes he felt his body relax.

Behind him, he heard Fennick mutter in a sing-song voice, "We are the Nicoteenies…"

Opening one eye Hansen glared at him defiantly before looking down, watching the glowing coal of his cigar struggle to survive the weather.

"Well, here's a pretty how-de-do, and no mistake."

Fennick dug in his pockets and located his smartphone. "Aye and here comes the rub." He tapped at the screen until he'd located DCI

Sugden's entry, looked at the various numbers, then checked his watch. Chances were Sugden had already left the office by now, and he had never been known to divert his office landline. Apparently that was doing humble dispatchers out of a job.

Fennick tapped the home number, heard it ring, then DCI Sugden's voice growled in his ear.

"If this is a dirty phone call, it had better be inventive." Without waiting for Fennick to reply, he continued, "I was wondering when you'd call. From what I've seen on the evening news it looks like you were ragged, bagged and royally shagged from the word go."

"That's one way of putting it, sir. However, it looks like DS Hansen and I are not going to be allowed to walk away from the wreckage. DCS Raynolds wants us to stay on as part of the investigation. So much so he's already assigned us for tomorrow."

"Has he now? That's nice of him. Hasn't said a bloody word to me though."

"Well, we've only just gotten out of a post op wash-up meeting."

"Wash-up? Tell me more, Michael."

He always hated it when Sugden called him Michael. It was always in the same tone of voice like his father used to use when investigating a suspected 'mischief'.

"There was just the seven of us. CI Stopes, CI Bashani from Armed Response, Jack Telford from the Major Crimes Team, a sergeant McKay from Urban Intel, plus Steve and myself. It was nothing much more than initial job allocation and task assignment. CI Bashani is deputy co-ordinator under Raynolds, and Telford's in as Incident Room Manager. Steve and I apparently provide the investigation with an outside viewpoint. Everything is still through DCS Raynolds."

"Everything?" From the receiver Fennick could hear the muffled sounds of Sugden's television and the distinctive signoff music as the local news slot concluded. Then Sugden's voice again. "Make sure the pair of you keep hold of your notes, just in case. Make copies if you have to."

"Why? Is something up?"

"For a start you've got one dead copper as a result of all this, never mind the villains shooting each other. Plus Armed Response opened fire in a public place. You can bet your last condom the human rights, and other 'concerned groups', aren't going to let a chance like that fade away. Not without using it to generate some kind of self-publicity. Police brutality and Big Brother – though I bet half the buggers couldn't spell Nineteen-Eighty-Four, even if you gave them a head start."

Before he could stop himself, Fennick asked, "How did you know about Cooke being killed? It's not been released to the media yet, as far as I know."

He could picture Sugden, feet up, sprawled across his worn out sofa, grinning like the Cheshire Cat.

"Mancunians. They're worse than fishwives when it comes to gossip, unlike proper Cheshire coppers. Right?"

Fennick groaned to himself. Yet more Force politics. "Okay, sir, understood."

"Right, remind me what the pair of you still have open at the moment? There's the B-and-Es over in Northwich,"

"Still collating statements. No witnesses, but looking at the MO it's a gang of three chancing it on a regular basis. Trouble is they're getting cockier with every success. Steve still has a couple of outstanding car-jackings, plus a domestic with the added attraction of potential ABH. The injured party's going to be in hospital for a while yet, and the woman who put him there is in remand. At least this time the bloke's coming forward and admitting he got the shit kicked out of him by a woman. Not forgetting I'm likely to be invited to the IPCC as part of the Complaints Commission investigation. Hopefully we should have this fiasco wrapped up in a couple of days, but there's obviously no guarantee of that."

"Aye. Well, keep me in the picture as and when you turn something up. Oh, and one more thing. Make sure you put your expenses through on their budget, not mine. Don't want the pair of you thinking you're MPs and claiming twice, now do we. Talk to you tomorrow." With that the line went dead.

Silently shaking his head, Fennick dropped the phone into his pocket. At least Sugden would be happy it was all happening on someone else's patch. Turning his back to the wind, he asked, "How do you know Vic Carlton?"

Hansen dropped the remains of the cigar on the floor and rubbed it out with his foot.

"I knew of him, and in the past I've had to interview some of his handiwork. It's one thing half strangling someone with a length of hard plastic until they agree to pay the interest, or the protection, or whatever. But afterwards it takes a sharp knife to cut someone free, and there's not many places you can cut without seriously hurting the victim. Cut your own throat, or choke to death. Not much of a choice." Hansen shoved his hands in his pockets and hunched his shoulders against the weather. "He should have been put away long ago, but we could never build a solid case against him. And with his reputation, backed up by Winston Merrillies, no one was ever going to come forward and testify against the bastard."

"So before my time then?"

"Sort of. He hasn't been active for about four, maybe five years now. Sold his books to several thugs he'd been grooming for the part. There had been a rumour of a falling out between Merrillies and Carlton, but nothing anyone could officially pin down."

A gust of wind whipped along the open shed. It brought with it heavier rain, which drummed loudly on the corrugated roof. A quick glance at his watch, then Fennick said, "Sod this. Let's see if the desk sergeant can find us somewhere to stay."

Back in the warmth they headed to the front desk and finally located their target. She was a slim, amicable, woman who'd kept a touch of grey in her hair rather than dying it out.

"I wouldn't hold out much hope. It's mid-week, so most of the station house will be booked out until Friday."

Fennick smiled optimistically at her. "What about something in the local area?"

"This close to the airport? Look, if the station house can't place you then I'll ring around and see what else might be available. There's a list of approved hotels somewhere around here." From under the front desk she picked up an A4 ring binder. "Here we go. As soon as I find something I'll send one of the PCs to find you. Where are you likely to be for the next hour or so?"

Hansen jumped into the conversation. "Probably the canteen." Turning to Fennick, he added, "It'll be easier to locate us there, rather than the incident room, seeing as that's still being set up at the moment."

"Fine. I can't promise anything mind, but at least it'll be warm and dry."

*

Once through the double doors Hansen headed towards the servery while Fennick made himself comfortable at one of the deserted tables. The canteen wasn't much above the basics. Pastel coloured utility furniture, strip lighting and a selection of posters screwed onto emulsion washed walls. Still, it was better than some he'd been in when he'd worked down south. A minute or two later Hansen returned carrying two teas. Placing them on the melamine table, he sat down and pulled a Kit Kat out of a pocket. Opening the wrapper he snapped the biscuit in half and offered the other half to Fennick.

"Thanks." Fennick took a sip of his tea and wrinkled his nose a little. At best it could be described as warm and wet. Anything other than that was being overly generous.

After a short period of silence, Hansen said, "What are we doing here, sir? I mean, we were only supposed to be here for the day. Get to see a result, and then back home again. I also get the feeling there's history between the DCS and Eddie Caradine. Hardly surprising, given Caradine and Cooke's reputations."

Fennick looked over the rim of his mug. "I only know some, and most of that's hear-say. It's common knowledge their nicknames were Butch and Sundance. They got results, but most of the other teams considered them a right pair of cowboys. I only met them for a couple of hours, but Caradine gave me the impression of being the wilder of the two." Fennick paused to break off a piece of chocolate. Still chewing, he said, "I know their clean-up rate protected both of them in some circles."

Hansen nodded, indicating the approaching desk sergeant. "Looks like we've at least got an early result on the accommodation."

She looked slightly pensive as she put the booking information down in front of them. "I've found you a couple of rooms at the Grafton Hotel. It's not much, but it's clean and tidy and it won't make too big a hole in your expenses."

Fennick looked down at the address and sighed a little to himself. The Grafton wasn't what he'd call a result at all.

*

Up in the Gold Dust incident room, CI Bashani watched the last of the IT support team leave, and members of the investigation team start to log into workstations. Grabbing some stationery from a pile of supplies he sat down in front of his own screen, his mind wandering as he tried to psych himself up into making a start. He really was getting too old for this kind of crap. Every year he'd tell himself it was going to be the year he retired. Once his kids finally left for good then he'd take himself and his wife off to the south coast. Or Cornwall. That had always seemed nice. Somewhere with a little bit of sea and some sand. Somewhere that was bloody warm and sunny for a change. He'd only taken the Manchester position because it supposedly offered a better promotion route and pension prospects. Then the recession had started to bite – pay freezes and budget cuts – and it had kicked the *tatti* out of his savings and group pension funds. One day, though. One day.

Breaking out of his reverie he powered up the workstation, then logged himself into HOLMES2. A few intro screens, then he pulled up a template and started modifying it to suit the initial investigation requirements. Designated statement readers and the office manager would amend it further, but for now he needed something familiar to help him relax before going home. The system was already loaded with information previously indexed when Gold Dust had been sanctioned as an operation. It just needed importing and tidying up. Loading and linking the sections now would help to save time in the morning.

Around him the activity began increasing as others got down to typing up initial reports. Already in were statements from the hotel staff, from the few bystanders who'd been in the car park, and from many of the hotel guests who thought they might've seen something important. At this stage it was impossible to say what information would turn into leads and what might turn out to be dead ends. Everything handwritten still had to be typed in manually rather than scanned, then added to the database, before the analysts could start. Not forgetting, in accordance with Data Protection procedures and protocols, forms stating that the information had been correctly inputted, would also need to be inputted. And filed. Ad infinitum.

A young DC carefully placed a sheet of paper on his desk. "It's the contact list, sir. The office manager says could you please check through your details and let him know if there are any changes."

A quick flick across the columns – nothing to change. His gaze drifted down the list of names until it stopped at DI M. Fennick. He hadn't seen Mike and Jan in a long time, and there was some catching up to do since their Hertfordshire days. Least of all, how Mike had managed to avoid being charged with assault.

*

In Raynolds' office the main lights were turned off. Light spilled softly from the uplighters, and from a swan-necked brass reading lamp on the uncluttered mahogany desk. Under the light was the first of Jack Telford's update briefs, giving Raynolds enough immediate material for the 21:30 press briefing, and a list of additional tasks still awaiting completion.

He sat back, rubbing his eyes and pinching the bridge of his nose in an effort to relax before facing the cameras and bloody journalists. He still had twenty minutes before he was due down in the Media Room. With his eyes closed, he went back over his mental checklist for the umpteenth time. He ticked off the points he wanted to emphasise, those he wanted to play down, all the while making doubly sure whichever direction the bastards came for him, his arse was well and truly covered. And with one undercover officer killed, along with the two civilian fatalities, he was going to have to keep a very tight control on things. Otherwise they would be like a pack of sheep-worrying dogs tossed a sacrificial lamb.

Breathing deeply, he opened his eyes and re-read Telford's brief. Most of it was what Jack had given at the 18:00 meeting, though there was some additional information regarding DC Cooke. The Pathology report stated he'd died almost instantaneously when the tip of the knife pierced his heart. Left-hander Alejandro Lucumi had been carrying the thin stiletto in a custom made sheath sewn into the sleeve of his jacket. Then it was a simple case of slipping the weapon free, then sliding the wickedly thin blade into Cooke's back, the slant of the thrust and the razor edges of the blade ensured it would fatally damage vital organs, regardless. He remembered making eye contact with Lucumi as the Colombian was being driven away from the scene. There had been no emotion. No anger, no triumph, no remorse. Just a cold, flat, soulless void – as if he were totally dead behind the eyes.

In fact Lucumi had remained silent ever since his arrest. An interpreter had tried for several hours to get him to admit to his own name, but he'd just sat there; unmoving, uncaring. Raynolds had even brought in a psychologist to check if Lucumi had managed to put himself in a trance by self-hypnosis. Wasn't that supposed to be a conditioned defence against professional interrogation these days? There were dozens of questions he wanted to ask – and not just in regard to the killing of DC Cooke – which he felt sure Lucumi had the answers to.

Paul Duffley, on the other hand, had been quite the reverse. He hadn't stopped talking since he'd been brought in and processed. The trouble was it was all shite. Demands for specific up-market solicitors, phone calls to inform dependents and family, along with wild claims of police brutality if he caught someone giving him so much as a dirty look. Raynolds had told the cell sergeant to shut him down for a while. Let the tosser fester for a bit. Once he realised he was just pissing people off, then he'd be more amicable when it came to interviewing the bugger. They already had enough on him to put him away for a decent stretch, regardless of how lenient the judge might be. But if they could use him to get intelligence on other activities, all the better. Mice to catch rats. Maybe. The problem was, once one had managed to become King Rat, it took quite a lot to actually pull the bastard down.

Raynolds shuffled some of the paperwork around until he came to a photocopy of the file on Duffley. A quick leaf through showed a blank MG6E sheet. So far nothing had turned up which could damage the prosecution's case. But it was still early days. There was also the matter of getting Caradine's initial statement down and on record, so the IPCC wouldn't kick up a fuss. At least having him medically off limits for twelve hours gave the team breathing space to get organised. It also helped to keep him out of harm's way, and the media spotlight, come to that.

He sighed and pushed the papers away from him, then picked up the silver framed photograph he kept to one side of the reading lamp. It was a studio shot of himself, his wife Patricia, and their son, Nathan, when he was a few years younger. Now he was about to graduate from university to make a career out of something. Raynolds thought hard for a moment, but couldn't recall the last time Nathan had mentioned anything about career aspirations. For the umpteenth time he told himself he needed to talk to his son. There again, the way he'd been feeling about life and work of late – not strictly apathetic, more just a general world-weariness – maybe it was time to jack it all in and retire? But he knew he couldn't afford to, at least not in the present financial climate.

He put the photograph back then looked at his watch. Time to greet the lions. He went over to the coat stand, slipped into his uniform jacket and checked himself in the full length mirror on the back of the office door. Since he'd become a desk man he'd dispensed with the clip-on and had taken to wearing proper ties. It was mostly out of snobbery. That, and the fact they photographed better in publicity and presentation shots. He fastened his jacket, and looked himself over in the mirror one last time. No doubt the psychologists would say the uniform was his protection against the pains and inadequacies of the real world. A pseudo-protective shell, from which his ego could happily dictate to his underlings with impunity. And you didn't need a university education to recognise bullshit when you smelt it.

He closed his eyes, building himself up once more, but as he opened the door and stepped out into the corridor, the desk phone started ringing. With an angry grunt of dismissal he waited until the eighth ring, at which point his voicemail kicked in, then closed the door behind him. Whoever it was, he would pick the message up later.

4

Wednesday Morning

In the muzzy glow from the street lighting outside the bathroom window, Eddie Caradine leaned his body, zombie-like, over the toilet bowl. One arm outstretched so as to support himself against the wall, it took him about thirty seconds to finally realise he hadn't freed himself. Having pissed in his own boxer shorts, he was standing near naked and barefoot in a cooling puddle of his own urine – his boxers clinging wetly to his thighs and groin. Through the fug in his head he regretted doing the vodka on top of the hospital sedatives. His tongue felt dry and numb, and his head felt as if someone had their hands against his temples, trying to squeeze his brains out like a teenage zit.

A blind scrabble through the contents of the bathroom cabinet had turned up a strip of old Co-Codamol tablets. He remembered getting the prescription strength painkillers from a little scrote of a dealer, after the last time he'd tried to patch things up with Simone. Everything had gone horribly wrong. Come the finish, she'd ended up slapping him hard across the face. He had reacted instinctively and punched her – thankfully pulling it at the last second so she'd only ended up with a badly bruised nose and 'panda' eyes for a couple of days. He'd gotten the Co-Cos for her to ease the pain for a day or so. But every time he'd rung her old number it'd gone straight to voicemail. Even her few friends had eventually refused to answer his calls.

Despite all the hassle and stress, he was sure he still loved her, and he figured he'd find a way of getting her to take him back. Once all this crap was over he'd see about a transfer to somewhere else – something more conventional which Simone would be willing to accept. She'd never been happy with him doing the dangerous stuff, even though she knew he enjoyed it. He was bloody good at it, too. In fact, despite all the amber flags on his personnel file, he had received several commendations early on in his career. But Simone always wanted him to change departments every time something heavy got splashed up on the evening news. Or at the start of a new assignment, where he needed to be away a lot, doing surveillance and getting himself established. She'd become more insistent about it until finally, after the arguments had become explosive, she'd kicked him out. Or he had left. One of the two. Anyway, doing undercover work wasn't going to be the same any more. Cookie had always been there to cover his back, and he knew he'd never really trust anyone else like that. Not again. Not with his life.

Popping a couple of the plain white tablets into the palm of one hand, he turned the cold tap on and cupped the other into the stream of water, then tossed the painkillers into his mouth. Quickly sucking up water from his cupped palm he hoped he could swallow without triggering any gag reflex. The way he felt at the moment, if the tablets stuck in the back of his throat he would puke his guts up for sure.

He turned the tap off, shut the bathroom cabinet door, then started wondering why he was still standing in a puddle of his own piss. Clumsily he peeled off the wet boxers and peering around the dimly lit bathroom he located a crumpled towel. He'd thrown it back into the bath after the last time he'd actually taken one, which had been Monday afternoon. He picked it up and half-heartedly used it to rub his groin and legs dry before finally dropping it onto the floor in a half-hearted effort to soak up the rest of the urine.

He wandered out of the bathroom and through the bedroom, picking up a discarded pair of jeans and oversized sweatshirt as he went on through into the lounge. Finally dressed, he crossed to the wardrobe style doors which hid the tiny kitchenette. Opening them wide revealed a small sink, a two-ring hotplate, and a microwave. All the modern comforts of home. He grabbed the kettle; half filled it, and stuck it back on its stand. As it started to boil he rinsed out a mug, dropped two teaspoons of coffee and three large spoonfuls of sugar into it, then followed it up with boiling water.

Under the TV, the display on the DVD player showed 04:30 a.m. as he sat down on the sofa, carefully sipping at the hot drink and trying not to burn himself. He was going to need all his wits about him later on, especially when the post-op inquiry started to get going. Perhaps the Co-Cos, the caffeine and the sugar wouldn't be enough. From the low table in front of him he prodded at the collection of remote controls before he picked up one more battered than the rest. Peeling back the sticky tape which held the broken battery cover in place, he lifted the lid and took out a little Ziploc bag of powder.

Just a little lick. To help with the healing process.

*

Steve Hansen slowly started to climb back to consciousness. Strange beds and unknown surroundings always meant he had a lousy first night's sleep. He'd finally awoke just before half six to find himself lying diagonally across the hotel double bed. Sometime during the night the covers had been pushed to one side, and now the sheets were damp from sweat caused by the heating still full on. Not because he'd been cold, but because he'd been unable to find a way to turn the bloody thing off.

He slowly worked himself free of the top sheet, gathered it up into a large ball and tossed it to one side. He slid off the end of the bed, padded naked across the nylon carpet and threw open the curtains. February was a really depressing month, especially this early in the morning. Outside was still dark and cloudy, though the lights from the traffic moving along the M60 didn't seem all that sparse. Welcome to Manchester: a city that never sleeps. He opened the window as far as he could, letting the chill air cool the room and his body for several minutes before he turned back to look at the dishevelled bed. Bloody depressing or what? Glancing at his watch didn't help any. It was that stupid time of the morning. He could drag out his shower and shave, dawdling around for the extra half hour, or he could remake the bed and try to catch another ten minutes sleep. But he knew, as soon as he tried to settle back down, his mind was going to wander and he was going to end up thinking about Felix again.

*

Mike Fennick woke slowly; languidly he turned over, stretching under the bedclothes, savouring the last fleeting moments before having to start in on what he knew was going to be a long and probably painful day. It was late by the time he'd returned home. He'd taken one look at the name of the hotel and immediately recognised the franchise. He also knew from past experience how the chain always strived to live down to its well-deserved reputation. Even though he expected their part in the investigation to last only a short time, he decided that he would rather long-haul the distance from home to the Greater Manchester South station than risk staying at the Grafton. It meant early starts and late returns, but then, what else was new?

Beside him, Jan started to gently snore, her face turned towards him on her pillow. She had been out at one of her evening group meetings and had probably come in around midnight. Whatever time it'd been, he couldn't remember her getting into bed beside him.

They had been together for nearly ten years, and neither had ever mentioned the M-word during that time. He thought about it for a moment and wondered why they both shied away from becoming what his mother would have called 'legal and decent'. Maybe there was still an appeal to the debauchery supposedly inherent when the two of you are 'living in sin'.

But if there was then it was somewhere in the background, buried under all the bills, sacrifices, commitments and responsibilities they both helped to carry in order to keep their relationship working.

Looking at her face he could see where a crease in the pillowcase had gently worked itself a little way into the corner of her slightly open mouth. The result was a wet patch slowly spreading as she continued to dribble in her sleep.

If only his phone wasn't still in the pocket of his trousers.

Careful not to disturb her, he eased out of bed, lifted his dressing gown off the nearby chair and put it on. From the wardrobe he collected underwear, socks, a fresh shirt and a plain tie. Sticking his shoes in his dressing gown pockets, he picked up his suit off the back of the chair. For a moment he reconsidered capturing Jan with the camera in his phone, but then decided his testicles were best kept where nature had originally placed them. Silently he closed the bedroom door and headed into the large, open-plan living area.

They both agreed they'd been very lucky to get the 'modern style' warehouse loft conversion when they did. True, it had a twelve foot high ceiling, and the mass of historically preserved cast iron supports and crossbeams reminded him of a giant Victorian railway station. But the solid concrete floor required to support the listed metalwork meant they were pretty well insulated from any potentially noisy neighbours below.

From the basket by one of the large windows came a slightly startled "Mr'owl?"

Belladonna, Jan's large pitch-black cat, rudely awoken by his movements. They glared at each other for several long seconds before the cat's head slowly disappeared back down into the basket again. If ever there was a way of measuring evil, then on a scale of one to five, the cat was sure to register a six.

Mike smiled as he went into the guest bedroom and turned on the shower in the en-suite bathroom. All things considered, life could be a damn sight worse.

*

Hansen was already standing at the Grafton Hotel's entrance by the time Fennick drove up. The weather was still foul, though given the choice Hansen found it more preferable than waiting in the reception area. Fennick's car was warm and still smelled of air freshener. Comfortable, with the radio tuned to Piccadilly, but turned down low and in the background. As he clicked his seatbelt home, Hansen dispensed with the usual morning pleasantries.

"So what's first on the agenda, Boss?"

Out of the corner of his eye he could see Fennick frown a little. He wasn't the Senior Investigating Officer on this one, and it was common knowledge he always disliked being called Boss, but Hansen felt a little payback was in order for being abandoned in favour of the joys of home comforts.

"If we see any place that looks good for a breakfast then we'll stop. If not, it'll be straight to Caradine's flat. According to the hospital, he should be fit enough to give a statement."

Hansen nodded, then let the radio fill his attention for a while. They were already losing time by collecting information from Caradine at his home. Why hadn't he been interviewed directly at the scene? His injuries were, according to the ambulance staff, more ugly than life threatening. He could've been taken back into the hotel before going to the hospital, or taken straight to the booking station and the on-call doctor. The wounds were messy and uncomfortable – ugly where some of the pellets had lodged under the skin – but it was nothing to stick him in an ICU for. Having him booked and processed under his assumed name would've at least meant he could keep his cover intact and probably uncompromised.

Fennick glanced over at Hansen. "What's up?"

"Sorry?"

"You're too quiet, so what's up?"

Hansen shifted a little in the passenger seat. "Nothing… Something… I don't know. Could we just go and take Caradine's statement? The sooner we do, the quicker we can get back to our own patch."

Keeping his eyes on the congesting motorway, Fennick smiled. "You're not telling me you're missing Molly already, are you?" Molly was DCI Roger Sugden's unofficial nickname when out of sight and earshot. Around several of the Cheshire stationhouses it was rumoured if you spoke his true name three times while looking in a mirror then, like the Devil, he would appear behind you.

"No, it's not that, it's just…" Hansen looked out the window at the cars travelling alongside them. "It's just a feeling, nothing more."

"Christ! First Sugden won't tell me anything, and now you go all Mystic Meg on me."

A little aggressively Hansen said, "Look, it's something you said last night about the pair of them being a right couple of cowboys. And I don't like the fact one of ours got killed in the process…" His voice seemed to trail off and he went back to looking at the cars in the adjacent lane again. "I also don't like the fact we thought it was going to be some standard business with a Colombian wholesaler, when clearly it wasn't. Okay, if we can connect something back to Ren Penstone, then fine, but how the hell did that connection get missed in the first place? And that's before we try and sus out how Wainwright, or Merrillies, or who-bloody-ever got wind of it all. And why did Alejandro Lucumi and Sebastian Tulio kick off the way they did? I can understand the shooting – you can put that down to protecting your team. But why kill Tony Cooke?"

"And you figure Caradine and Cooke for some of that?" Fennick sounded concerned.

"That's it – I just don't know. And I don't want to go making Caradine fit if he's had nothing to do with it. Does that make sense?"

Fennick nodded, more to help settle Hansen, rather than in total agreement. "Okay, we'll go talk to Caradine first, but if there's time then we'll be stopping off for brunch – I can feel my cholesterol level falling already."

They followed the M60, then onto the A57 towards Rusholme and Longsight before taking side roads and backstreets, until turning into the bottom of Carpenter's Road.

Fennick let the car slowly crawl towards the five story block of flats where Eddie Caradine was living. In the half light of morning he could see that more than a few of the cars parked up by the kerb had For Sale signs clearly on display. With cheap SIM cards, it was easy to run a kerbside dealership and not get done for illegal trading. Given the on-going recession, the dodgy traders were coining it in. Finally he found a space close by and parked up. With a touch of luck it wouldn't get keyed before the interview was over.

Caradine was on the top floor, and coupled with the surprise of the lift actually working, there was also a distinct smell of disinfectant in the background. It was good to know people were actually doing something about the quality of their lives, rather than just sitting around blaming the police, the rich, the councils, the government, or whoever they thought was the cause of all their woes were this week. But it took a concerted effort, and some places were happy to shut their front doors and let the low-life get on with it.

At Caradine's flat Hansen pressed the doorbell. From somewhere inside they could hear the muted sound of a buzzer. A pause, then the sound of movement from behind the door as Caradine opened it. He was wearing washed out jeans, local market trainers, and a baggy grey sweatshirt with some kind of American university emblazoned on the front. As he stood looking at the two of them, both Hansen and Fennick registered the slight contraction of his pupils and the vague furtiveness as he looked towards the lifts. The left side of his face was still patched up with several two-inch square pads of cotton dressing, held in place by strips of papery sticky tape. As Fennick looked closer, he could see dark spots where some of the pellet wounds had seeped through before they'd finally stopped bleeding.

Automatically Hansen started to flash his warrant card, but Caradine just turned round and headed back into the flat. "Come on in. It's not as if I haven't been expecting you. Just didn't expect you this early."

The front door led straight into the living room, and walking around the sofa towards the open kitchenette, Caradine said over his shoulder, "Tea? Just about to make one for myself."

Fennick shook his head. "Not for me, thanks. We don't want to keep you too long. Just wanted to see if you felt up to giving us your account of what happened yesterday."

Unperturbed, Caradine looked expectantly over to Hansen, who had already taken a notebook and pen out of his jacket pocket. "No, I'm fine as well. But thanks for the offer."

While Eddie threw a teabag and boiling water into a cup, Fennick and Hansen settled down in the two easy chairs either side of the large sofa.

Sitting in the middle of the sofa, Caradine cleared a space on the coffee table and put his cup down. Deliberately he looked expectantly from one to the other, then back again, and Fennick started the interview.

"DCS Raynolds has decided to keep us on while the Gold Dust investigation gets underway. We're here to get your account of yesterday afternoon, though we both appreciate it's not been the easiest of twenty-four hours. However, the sooner it's processed then the sooner we should be able to close things."

Eddie let out a short, barking, "Ha!" then grabbed a battered packet of cigarettes and a disposable lighter off the coffee table. Without asking or offering, he lit one up, sat back, and exhaled the smoke loudly. Fennick continued unperturbed.

"As I said, we know it's not been easy, but best to get this down now while it's still fresh in your mind." Deliberately he looked over to Hansen. "Sergeant?"

Hansen cleared his throat as the smell of the burning cigarette made him realise he hadn't had one himself since leaving the Grafton. "Can you give us your movements for the last twenty-four hours?" He tried to make it sound as casual as possible, not wanting to create any animosity early in the interview. "Start from the time you left this flat, or went out to meet anyone. Did you stay in Monday night? Or did the two of you go down the pub, or out for a meal? Anything like that?"

Caradine looked suspiciously at Hansen. "Hold on. Am I a suspect or something? Are you making out I had something to do with the whole thing going tits up? Because if that's the case then this stops right now, and we can start again when there's a Federation rep here with me."

Hansen sounded a little exasperated, "No one's setting you up, or accusing you of anything." Then, to reassure Caradine, he added, "C'mon Eddie. You know the score, probably better than we do. We've got to be seen to be squeaky clean, and that means eliminating everyone involved in the operation. It's just routine statement gathering. Plod work, for fuck's sake."

Caradine gave another short laugh of contempt, but after a moment's contemplation he launched into a detailed rundown of his movements, starting with the Monday prior to Operation Gold Dust.

Keeping a casual ear on the conversation, Fennick didn't seem to hear anything which sounded even a little off, and as he recounted it, Eddie Caradine sounded confident and unhesitating – the account clear and concise, seemingly free of any obvious inconsistencies. Fennick let his gaze wander around the tiny, one bedroom flat. It had been bigger at one time, but 'Property Developers' had thrown up dividing walls in their efforts to minimise space and maximise their income. So maybe Caradine wasn't the tidiest of people and the flat wasn't in what you might call a comfortable district. But then being undercover often meant you had to rough it in order to maintain your credibility.

He also remembered a seemingly casual conversation about a week ago, in the run-up to the operation itself. When he and Hansen had been invited back to the operation as observers, it had felt like some kind of *This is how we do things in the City* thing. Typical sort of stunt DCS Raynolds was noted for. Raynolds had also suggested that he and Fennick should "touch base with the guys at the sharp end." So they'd both met up with Eddie Caradine and Tony Cooke on the Saturday evening prior to the final takedown. They'd all gone to a backstreet Chinese which Cooke said was well off their regular patch – far enough to stop them being seen and recognised while they were still working the operation. Fennick had to admit to a touch of admiration when it came to undercover work. It wasn't always successful, and it came with the risk of being exposed, but at least they were actually doing something constructive.

During the evening, Raynolds had come on like some Army Field Marshall who thought the war was already won without even going into battle. His attitude had clearly rankled Caradine, though it'd been Cooke who'd become the more introverted as the night went on. Fennick mentioned it when they were down to coffee and fortune cookies. Tony had brushed it off, saying although he wasn't superstitious he still didn't want to jinx the operation by being too cocky.

But no matter how often Fennick replayed that evening over in his head, he couldn't remember anything which might have indicated something was wrong. They'd both seemed like honest guys about to set up a heavyweight dealer and supplier.

Bringing his mind back to the present, Fennick listened to Hansen reading Caradine's statement.

"So you're saying you stayed over at Cooke's flat the night before last. The pair of you ordered a takeaway pizza and watched a couple of films. After that, an early night, with an early start in the morning so you could be fitted out with surveillance kit."

Caradine kept nodding his agreement. If he didn't agree with it all then he wouldn't sign it, and no signature meant no validation – which meant it could, and probably would, be contested later.

Hansen finished, then looked up and stared hard at Caradine.

"Are you absolutely sure you never talked to anyone about any of this?"

Caradine closed his eyes, deliberately taking a deep breath before replying. "We stayed in, watched two or three crap movies, then Cookie went to bed and I slept on the couch. In the morning we got fitted with fibre optic cameras and mics, then went up to the room at the hotel to wait for the bastards to turn up. I only stayed at Cookie's place because it was nearer to the exchange point."

He snatched his packet of cigarettes up and angrily lit another one, his third in quick succession since Fennick and Hansen had arrived. It didn't help that Hansen's own nicotine threshold was starting to wear thin.

In an attempt cool tempers down and regain Caradine's confidence, Fennick said, "Off the record, what do you think went wrong with the operation?"

Caradine looked down at the filter tip trapped tightly between his two fingers. "I don't know. The Colombians were definitely out to fuck us over, though I don't think they'd tumbled to the fact we were undercover. At least not until the shooting started in the car park."

"So why go down to the cars? I thought the plan was to run the deal from the hotel room?"

"Because we had to make Martinez show us the rest of his gear. The same way he thought he had to make us show him the bag full of money. That's the way it works in these sorts of deals. If we'd gone swanning in there with the cash in a bag we'd've looked like a right pair of fucking amateurs. Straight off they would have suspected something was wrong, and going by what happened outside the hotel it wouldn't surprise me if they hadn't thought about shooting us right there in the bloody room. We said at several briefings we weren't happy bringing a load of loot into the hotel – especially when almost all of it was counterfeit shit pulled in from that raid up in Edinburgh a year or so ago. But we were overruled by shiny-arse Raynolds." Caradine's contempt for the DCS was obvious as he met Fennick's gaze. "So Cookie and I took the initiative and decided to leave it in the car." Calming down again he looked back at the remains of his cigarette. "As it turned out, it really didn't matter one way or the other. We were both set up by somebody else who ambushed us in the car park, so someone's been talking to someone they shouldn't have."

There was a touch of accusation to his voice which rubbed Hansen up the wrong way.

"It certainly wasn't us. We were dragged into this right at the end and, to be bloody honest, we have a whole shit load of better things to do than fuck about in the rain, watching a simple operation turn to utter rat shit."

Fennick immediately stood, breaking the aggressive tension building between Caradine and Hansen.

"Okay, well, I think we've got enough here to take back with us. If you'd just sign the notebook we'll get your account onto the system and that should keep Raynolds happy. For a while, at least." He waited until Caradine scribbled what looked like a signature under the last line.

"Okay, no doubt you've been through similar post-operation

routines before, but," Fennick paused for a moment, wondering if Eddie Caradine was actually taking any of it in. He appeared to be distracted, looking intently down at the low table and nudging several of the remotes around with a finger. Doggedly Fennick carried on. "But you're now being placed on post-operation leave. However, you are to ensure you are available for interview at any time until the investigation is closed. No doubt the IPCC will be in touch, and you may want to talk to the Federation and have them assign you a dedicated legal rep for the duration of this investigation."

Caradine still kept his gaze on the coffee table. Fennick nodded to Hansen, and without saying a word, the two of them left Eddie alone with his thoughts.

5

Sitting on a bench by the first floor escalators of the Arkendale shopping centre, seventeen year old Mikka casually looked up at the back of the CCTV camera again. She'd made sure she was tucked in close by the plants, so as not to draw attention to herself from anyone heading down to the ground floor. Carefully she looked along the direction of the lens and imagined the arc of vision the operator could probably see on the screen in the control room. The cameras were prominent and easy to spot, so it was simple to work out where the security pictures criss-crossed the main traffic areas of the shopping centre floor.

Down below, on ground level, their cover was more accurate and security had most of the central walkway under surveillance. But unlike the first floor cameras, those on the ground floor didn't have to deal with the big hanging displays from the outlet stores, advertising sales or special offers which seemed to last forever.

Pulling the peak of her baseball cap further down over her eyes, she stuck her hands into the pockets of her overly large jacket and looked out across the mass of moving people. They were always an unpredictable problem, along with the other obstacles to worry about. People were gathered around promotion stands, or the walkway stalls selling *Ye Olde Fashioned Sweeties* at ridiculously high prices. And who the hell buys those ultra-cheap watches which never seem to last more than a couple of months at best? Even the highly visible security guards had problems walking their rounds when the lunchtime shoppers came crowding in around midday.

Planning. They'd always stressed that at school. Whatever the plan, it stood a much better chance if you spent time planning. She'd never worked the Arkendale Centre before – too many nosey truant officers for one thing – which was why she'd come early in the morning. And it had paid off as now she had a better idea of what the security teams couldn't see. It wasn't much to be honest. Most of the shops had little or nothing useful, and none of it was going to be easy. Not the way most of the good stuff was security tagged. And it would still be risky because she didn't know all the escape routes intuitively.

The bad weather hadn't helped, either. It had pushed more shoppers and street people into the mall, so security appeared more awake than usual. Her uneasiness was also due to a gang of hoodies hanging around the upper level like dog shit on a carpet. The wankers seemed to wander around from one end of the walkway to the other, turn around, then aimlessly head back again. If they started kicking off then she could probably use it to her advantage. Just straight in, snatch something close by, then out again while everyone else was trying to see what all the fuss was about. But it looked like the tossers couldn't even get that right.

Listlessly she got up and joined the trickle of people heading down the escalators to the ground floor, then out through the plate glass doorway and down the steps outside. They had tried to make the ground between the car parks and the shopping centre look nice. Some designer had landscaped it with low hedges and park benches here and there. The shrubs always looked a bit scraggly and depressive after Christmas, though they still stopped enough wind from making you too cold.

She sat down on one of the deserted park benches close to the main pathway. Seconds later she had fished a cigarette from the packet of ten and lit it up. There were still three left. Once she'd smoked the last she'd decided she'd go to Tesco or Asda – somewhere big like that – and lift some anti-smoking patches. Apart from the sodding cost of the bloody things, several of the crew at her previous squat had started wheezing and getting short of breath whenever they'd had to do a runner. She wasn't going to get caught just because she was still on the fags. For one thing the Welfare would try to send her back home again, which was something she feared, enough to lose sleep over.

She hunched up in her coat and took another long drag on the cigarette, cupping her hand to protect it from the weather. Then she tensed. Behind her, through the hedge screen, she could hear loud voices getting nearer. Then off to her left, half a dozen hoodies appeared. They seemed more intent on talking and arguing amongst themselves than having any obvious interest in her, but it always paid to be cautious. She continued to track their progress in her peripheral vision. Suddenly one of them, towards the back of the gang, looked her way for a second or two and she felt her body go rigid with tension. But he continued on, looking around aimlessly as he walked and not really noticing she was there. He was more intent on arguing with the hoodie alongside him, emphasising something by jabbing the other in the chest several times as they carried on walking past.

She closed her eyes for a moment, cigarette still halfway to her lips.

Don't start a fight. Don't start kicking off right here...

But they just carried on walking, ignoring her and heading towards the car parks – the one out in front turning to shout at the pair arguing, telling them to "Just shut the fuck up!"

She opened her eyes at the sound of his voice, and caught a glimpse of his face when he turned round again. Hard and angry, but still a baby face all the same. He reminded her a lot of Danny Aziccio, and the memories came back.

Danny had been the last straw. He'd been tormenting her for some time and, like most bullies, he'd built up a little gang to follow him around. He'd not been much older than her at the time, around fourteen, but always acting like he was a child. She'd said as much to his face, and he'd told her he wasn't a child anymore because he'd gone through puberty, and for 20p she could see the hair around his dick. Then he said he would give her 20p if she would suck it. She'd spat in his face then ran, hiding herself away in the depths of the estate where Danny and his gang couldn't find her.

Then one evening, a week or so later, they'd caught up with her. Eventually they'd chased her out onto some wasteland, shouting and calling out until she'd finally turned around to face them. Danny had carried on dancing around in front of her, taunting her, calling her names like skank, and whore, even though he probably had no idea what they really meant. Just throwing out words in the hope they would somehow hurt her.

In retaliation she had made a fist, as if she was going to try and punch him on the chin, then angrily stuck her hands into her jacket pockets, silently glaring at him instead. He'd just laughed at her. Even turned around to his gang behind him, laughing and pointing at her, while they were all laughing with him. Then he'd stuck his chin out towards her, his face a little flushed, and through half suppressed laughter he'd told her to do her best. She'd taken her hands out of her pockets, still keeping them shaped into fists, and pulled her right arm back as if she were some cartoon character about to throw a crazy punch at someone.

While the others behind him watched on in amusement, it looked as if she'd just stepped towards him then taken a swipe at his chin – but only brushed the side of his face with her knuckles. It was at least five seconds before Aziccio realised he was bleeding. The Stanley knife blade had been securely pushed into the potato before she'd left home, hidden safely in her pocket for protection. She'd gripped it in her fist and had slipped the razor sharp steel between her knuckles just before she took her fist out of her pocket. The simple, quick, girlie swipe had opened up a three inch long slash down Danny's podgy left cheek.

As he put both his hands up to try and stop the blood, she'd stepped forward onto her left foot and swung her right foot hard into his balls – dodging backwards as he started to fall forwards onto the ground. With him gasping and writhing down by her feet, one hand holding his cheek together and the other clasped to his damaged testicles, his mates had just stared at him then ran off. When the last had disappeared she'd gone through Danny's pockets and found his phone, along with half a dozen little bags of what looked like Charlie, and a large amount of cash. She knew the gear wasn't his. He'd been some dealer's runner for a while, which was how he'd kept his gang around him. She looked across the wasteland but the rest of Aziccio's gang had vanished. No doubt one or two would head back to the dealer, to see if they wanted to recruit a new runner boss.

She'd used Danny's phone to call 999, telling the operator she needed an ambulance as she'd been involved in a gang fight and was cut up pretty bad. While the operator kept asking for her name, Mikka just told her she was on the wasteland at the back of the estate, then she'd laid the phone near the bleeding dickhead – the voice of the operator sounding tinny and distant, still squawking "Can you give me your name please, love? Hello? Can you give me your name please?" from the phone. She'd picked up the little bags of white powder and the large roll of cash, walked to the nearest bus stop and caught the next bus to anywhere but back home.

*

Chief Inspector Ramesh Bashani yanked the chair out from his desk, sat down heavily, then pulled himself towards his computer screen. Two minutes later he was still having trouble concentrating and organising his thoughts. The anger was a result of the 08:30 morning brief. Jimmy Raynolds had been his usual slope-shouldered self, refusing to take any action on unless there was a publicity opportunity attached to it somewhere. And Jimmy's barely veiled criticism of his Armed Response Team had pissed him off no end.

For one, he couldn't see how he could've prevented Sebastian Tulio from opening the bloody hotel window and snapping off several rounds into Vic Carlton. What if the bastard had carried on firing indiscriminately into the car park and killed innocent bystanders while the Armed Response team were trying to break the door down?

As luck would have it both Gillett and Decker, his two marksmen, were fully range certified, thankfully managing to keep the rounds grouped to just the one window. It was also a good job the Colombian had jammed his shoulder in the small gap between the window and the frame. If the bugger had ducked back into the room then they might've lost the chance to neutralise the bastard without the risk of yet more casualties. Or worse, the whole thing could've turned into one of those bloody awful siege situations.

And what about the fiasco in the car park? If Carlton hadn't let rip with his shotgun and taken down Swannick, then it could have turned into a Wild West shootout – probably ending with a lot more than just Carlton and DC Cooke dead.

He looked down at his hands on the desk top and tried to ease the stress he felt. Best to just suck it in and forget about it. Raynolds wasn't worth the blood pressure, and Ramesh had already decided to make damn sure he was going to be called away somewhere – any fucking where – when it came time for the 15:00 afternoon press briefing. If Raynolds really wanted the glory that badly then the bastard could find someone else to play whipping boy.

Around him he saw that most of the investigation team were also settling at their desks. They were staring at monitor screens or hanging off of telephone headsets. Pens poised over memo pads or fingers over keyboards – ready to take down anything and everything that might be useful. The familiarity of it all was, in some respects, comforting. The trick, as Bashani knew, was in keeping the momentum going after the first forty-eight hours.

In one corner of the room several DCs were logging CCTV material from the hotel and surrounding area. Ramesh could see washed out images of vehicles and people, all moving in double and treble quick time. Number plates would be identified, logged, then checked against the DVLA records. Each person would be frame-grabbed and compiled into a gallery, to be used in matching drivers to vehicles, or just simply eliminating them from the inquiry itself.

Part of the morning Team Brief that Raynolds had presided over earlier had been a composite video, compiled and patched together from various cameras and locations. It showed two cars and a white van as they headed along the motorway to the airport, turned off at the Polaris Hotel, then parked up for twenty minutes before the two undercover DCs, along with Lucumi and Paul Duffley, had appeared from around the side of the hotel. It was the best they could do for a timeline, even though the short collection of clips only really covered a sixty minute period. Trying to work it further back had failed due to the lack of adequate CCTV coverage.

Bashani jotted some thoughts down on a large yellow post-it note. He wasn't sure why, but somehow there seemed to be far too many high rollers involved, and that sort of thing always made him feel uneasy.

He pulled his keyboard nearer and started searching for the latest material to be entered – but he knew full well he wasn't likely to find much this early on. As he glanced across at his overloaded in-tray, he could see Jack Telford's pale green 'Breaking News' folder sitting on top of the pile, still waiting to be circulated. That was the trouble being saddled with the Second-In-Command post; the bloody paperwork. Budget approvals, expense claims, travel requests, facility requisitions – and already a complaint about police harassment. It was all there, dumped in his trays and waiting for his initials or counter-signature. He'd already been briefed about the complaint, and without bothering to read it he took the pink folder from near the top of the pile and slipped it down to the bottom. Not so much a case of ignoring it, more a case of re-prioritising the workload.

The complaint had come from Gordon Lemon, who was Paul Duffley's solicitor and legal mouthpiece. The fact Lemon probably charged his clients fifty pounds just to sit down in his office was an obvious indication he was being financed by someone other than Duffley himself. Smart money was naturally on Ren Penstone, though without any actual physical evidence, his involvement was nothing more than just informed speculation. And it would be a little unusual for big time villains in the larger cities to go stepping outside their comfort zones without some kind of 'gentleman's agreement' with the local lags.

That was one of the questions Bashani had hanging in the back of his mind. It seemed that Ren Penstone had been looking to sell large amounts of high grade narcotics through Duffley, and as far as everyone on the team could tell it was going to be the start of a regular supply line. So why all the subterfuge? Unless he'd been looking to start expanding and moving up North? Perhaps he believed the violent reputations, which some Colombian cartels generated for credibility, would help smokescreen and protect him while he established his operation?

There again, Manchester was getting quite an international reputation itself these days. What with an on-going history of Yardies, Russian Mafia and Indo-Chinese gangs, it could certainly give London a good run for its money. It wasn't something Bashani would happily sit around and brag about to old colleagues from down South, but at least he felt they could call on each other's experiences – provided the Met weren't in the public dog house again.

He pulled the circulation file off the top of the stack and flipped it open. Chepstow had yet to come back with forensic reports for blood and tox. The facilities at Martlesham were dealing with the Uzi and the 9mm pistol, but checking the striation marks against the National database took time. It wasn't like that CSI on the television, where you press a button and get a printout in a matter of minutes. Far from it.

Flicking over the page Ramesh found copies of the morgue release forms. After the initial post mortems on Cooke and Vic Carlton, their bodies had been released for collection by respective family members, and in Vic's case a nominated 'Next Of', within the next forty-eight hours.

And that was it. Mike and DS Hansen had yet to come back from interviewing Caradine, which left Ramesh with only a few options when it came to getting out of the incident room and away from Raynolds for a while. It was going to be either Dillon Nichols, who was still down in the traps, or Marcus Swannick in the HCU at the Wythenshawe Hospital.

No competition when you thought about it logically.

He hurriedly knocked out an e-mail to the rest of the team, telling them he was going to be out later to interview Swannick, and as it was a hospital visit he would have his mobile turned off.

Yes, when you factored in all the advantages that particular requirement provided, then there really was no competition at all.

*

Eddie left his car parked up in the rented garage at the back of his flat, and caught a bus heading towards town – or at least into the nearest shopping area. He needed time to think. It'd been a shock opening up the back of the remote again and finding the little bag almost empty. He wasn't hooked on wiz. Far from it. Certainly not like the tweaker freaks he sometimes had to hang out with during his working days. But it had been a surprise to find he'd actually dabbed his way through the last couple of grams without really remembering doing it. Nobody else but himself to blame, in this case. But the stress of the last few days had not been easy, so it stood to reason he'd need a little bit more of a boost than usual.

He could stop using it any time he wanted to. It was just that when you needed to be up with things twenty-four seven, he sometimes needed a little chemical help from time to time. Not all the time. Just sometimes. But he shouldn't have had the lick earlier. He should've waited until after the two Cheshire yokels had been and gone. The sergeant had been the more devious of the two, going back over the questions again and again, only rephrasing them differently every time. Almost as if he thought Eddie had been some kind of thick scrote they'd just pulled in off the back of a stop and search routine. One giving it with the questions while the other did the observation. He'd just shut his body language down and did his best to answer the questions in a regulated, emotionless tone. Except when the arsehole had gotten under his skin and he'd thrown out the comment about who might have leaked the operation. They were the bloody outsiders after all, so who's to say one of them hadn't lined up a little extra to add to their pension fund?

The bus pulled into the stop opposite the frosted glass window of a pub halfway down Collis street. Automatically Caradine got off and waited for the bus to pull away again before checking out the front of the pub. No need to look at his watch, the door was already off the catch and invitingly half open. Still protected by the bus shelter, he carefully eased the surgical tape and peeled off the white gauze patches, feeling the growth of stubble under his fingertips. Balling up the dressings, he dumped them in the nearby rubbish bin as he headed towards the pub doors. Just before the entrance it had taken a deep breath and a slow count of ten to compose himself – dropping back into character like a method actor, just before he made his first entrance. Psyched up and ready, he pushed the door wide and walked into the aptly named Cat & Fiddle.

It was the pub he often went in when he wanted to meet up with people – usually when he was doing some business, fishing for information or tip-offs. It was a huge conversion of a place, with a cavernous ground floor scruffily lit by 40 and 60 watt bulbs. Their low light was added to by several fruit machines which ting-tang-tinged in competition with the digital jukebox.

The other advantage was that most of the regulars were middle-aged petty villains and chancers, more in tune with the working class career criminal, rather than being some professional gangland watering hole. People kept themselves to themselves, hunched over their pints and newspapers – perfect for whenever Eddie wanted to become invisible. Whether he sat at the bar, or did business at one of the tables, nobody gave a toss.

Except that, in the Cat & Fiddle, he wasn't known as Eddie. Everyone who knew him around this area called him Shaun. For a one-off operation away from his usual patch, such as the likes of Gold Dust, he had been Aaron Deedering. Cookie had been Carl Scully. They had spent months establishing their identities in preparation for that Op. They'd put so much effort into it, not knowing it was going to be a fucking monumental cock-up that would end up getting Cookie killed.

He folded his arms and rested them on the bar top, nodding his head to catch the attention of one of the barmaids as she leaned back against the till. When she finally looked his way, he said cheerily, "Pint of Stella and a large Glenfiddich, love."

The girl had flashed him a bored smile, pushed herself off the back counter just using her arse, then set about his order. As she drew the pint of lager, she made a show of moving the glass up and down provocatively, so as to create a head of froth. It was probably the sort of thing she did on a Saturday night to excite the punters, and short measure the pint, though it had little effect on Eddie. While he waited, he pulled out a small packet of chewing gum from his jeans pocket, unwrapped a piece and started chewing on it. The smoking ban was sometimes a real frigging pain, but pubs enforced it just in case there was a council inspector doing the rounds.

Finally she came over and set the drinks down in front of him. Eddie quickly took the gum out of his mouth, snatched up the whiskey and took a large mouthful, feeling himself start to relax as it burned its way down into his stomach. Putting the gum back, he located a crumpled tenner in a pocket and handed it over.

"Cheers, love." Then, when she'd remained silent, he'd added, "Been a bit of a long day already."

Her only reaction had been to silently hand Eddie what little change was due, then she'd gone back to her previous position, wiggling her arse until she was comfortable against the back shelf again.

He took another large mouthful of scotch, then picked up the other glass and sipped the top off the cold lager.

From his left came the sound of a man's voice. "Did you hear about Dusty?" The landlord, who Eddie remembered as being called something weird, like Archibald Mackinley Fouches, looked towards him while waiting for a pint of Irish stout to settle in the glass.

Blindsided, Eddie had just said, "Who?"

"The guy you used to come in here with from time to time. Big Sid Miller."

"Oh. Yeah?" Eddie remembered Miller as being another strange piece of work. An overweight, middle aged, gun and knife dealer, who'd always made it a policy not to sell any weaponry to kids. If they looked too young then Sid wouldn't deal with them until they'd shown him some form of ID with a date of birth on it.

The landlord gave Eddie a long, hard stare, distrustful and calculating, automatically assessing him. Eddie carried on chewing the gum, waiting for the landlord to continue. It was always the same. Over the years, Eddie had become so used to it. He'd even found himself doing the same kind of snap evaluation before deciding how far he could trust someone.

The landlord looked down and checked the pint of stout. "Yeah. Well, he's dead."

Eddie stuck a hand in his jeans pocket, pulled out a disposable plastic lighter and started to tap it on the bar mat in front of him. "How the fuck did that happen?"

"Autoimmune hepatitis. Gave him liver failure. They let him out of Risley a couple of months ago so he could get better treatment. Only he was one of the unlucky bastards and it didn't work. Always used to see the pair of you in here, regular, before he got banged up. I'm surprised you didn't know about it."

Eddie looked down at his pint and self-consciously shuffled his feet. "I haven't seen him for a long time now. I always said I would keep on visiting him, but we just seemed to lose touch. You know how it is."

The landlord's stare intensified, as if he was trying to figure out if Eddie might've had something to do with Dusty Miller getting sent down. He hadn't. Dusty had been more valuable outside than in, even though he wasn't an official, on the books informer. Still, the scrutiny had made Eddie feel nervous and uncomfortable.

Then, suddenly, the landlord had leaned towards Eddie and dropped his voice down to a confidential level.

"Life can be a real fucking bastard sometimes, can't it? You know there's no cure for it, and you've got no fucking idea just how long you're going to last." Shaking his head philosophically he went back to pouring a second pint of Beamish. "Of course, if the government legalise the assisted suicide thing, then you can bet your life they'll stick a fucking tax on it!"

Eddie managed a nervous half smile, then downed the last of his whiskey, quickly followed by the last of his pint. It was cold, and made his teeth ache. All the tension had gotten to him and despite the chewing gum, he was in serious need of a ciggie. But lighting one up would have to wait for a while. At least until after he'd sorted out some other business.

Over in the corner furthest away from the fruit machines, sat a skinny little guy Eddie knew only as The Poet. His skin looked pale and unhealthy, and there were traces of glue sniffers' acne around his thin lipped mouth which, thankfully, managed to hide most of his badly damaged teeth. His face was framed with shoulder length greasy black hair and there was a wild, animal furtiveness about his eyes whenever he looked up. He was wearing a worn and faded greatcoat and was hunched over one of the small pub tables. Scattered on the top were a dozen or so pieces of cheap lined paper, and under his protectively bent arm he was fanatically scribbling and writing on the top sheet of a thick A4 pad with a fairly new pencil.

Eddie walked over and sat down beside the guy, catching a whiff of his strong stale odour. He watched as the pencil point jumped and skittered over the paper, then he started to read some of the pages lying on the table top. They were a crazy mixture of text and poetry – lines from adverts and popular TV shows, chunks from Shakespeare and what looked like pornographic novels – while in the margins were odd thumbnail sketches of demons being eaten by Easter bunny rabbits. The poor sod should have been institutionalised for his own good years ago. But word on the street said he was one of Peter Wainwright's charity cases, physically and financially protected, which was why nobody took advantage of such an easy target.

Eddie dug a pair of fairly new twenty pound notes from his back pocket. He made a little show of tilting his head from side to side in appreciation, before finally tapping the end of the twenties on one of the sheets.

Without pausing to ask questions, The Poet put his pencil down, took the money and squirreled it into a pocket, while from another he took out a new and remarkably clean business envelope. He carefully folded the paper Eddie had tapped and slipped it into the envelope, laboriously sealed it, then pushed it towards Eddie. Then he picked up his pencil and went back to frantically sketching and writing yet more craziness down onto the lined paper as if his life depended on it.

Eddie stuffed the envelope into his pocket and headed back to the bar. The place was starting to get busy with lunchtime drinkers, popping in for a swift one while doing the sandwich run. Eddie ordered another pint of lager, took a mouthful, then picked it up and headed off towards the toilets.

As he opened the door, the smell of industrial cleaner and stale piss caught in the back of his throat and almost made his eyes water. After a couple of tries, he managed to find a cubicle which still had a working lock. He closed and bolted the door, put his pint on top of the cistern, then took the envelope from his pocket. Ripping the top open he upended it, shaking it several times until the small clear plastic bag fell into the palm of his hand. Without a second thought he set the plastic bag down beside the pint glass, then spent a minute or so tearing the envelope and its contents into a confetti of small pieces, scattering them into the toilet bowl as he went. He watched as the fragments absorbed some of the water, before he picked up the plastic bag of grey-white powder.

Carefully opening the Ziploc seal, he shook some of the contents onto his palm, then tipped the rough measure into his pint. Watching the liquid dissolving the meth amphetamine he was pleased to see very little debris sinking to the bottom of the glass. That was the good thing about The Poet; you rarely got rubbish gear from him. It was usually cut with sugar, which helped to get the kids started in on the stuff. Not that Eddie was an addict – not like the kids. It was just, recently, he'd needed the wiz a little more, mainly as a pick-me-up to keep him going when he felt worn out or a bit depressed. Cookie had shown him how to use it sensibly, and Eddie knew enough habitual dealers so getting a little here or there wasn't a problem. And he was only using it about two or three times a week, tops. When he wasn't stressed out. And then, only to keep himself going…

Out of habit he licked the residue from his palm, picked up the foamy pint and guzzled half the speed and lager mixture down. A pause to belch loudly, then the rest of the mixture was downed just as fast, before he pushed the lever and flushed away the waterlogged paper.

As he started walking back through the pub he could feel his heart rate pick up and his general mood changing as the wiz kicked in. By the time he pushed open the front door and stepped out onto the pavement he was even smiling a little maniacally, like some comic book killer. Purposefully he started back up Collis street, the buzz off the new gear giving him energy. Time to start finding out which bastard, or bastards for that matter, had been messing with his plans, and trying to set him up for a fall.

6

"Jimmy! Good to talk to you rather than having to leave a wretched voicemail message again." Gordon Lemon's over-enthusiastic voice made Raynolds wince. If anything, the solicitor sounded more pompous in the earpiece of the smartphone than the bastard did in person. Several years ago, when he was changing his service provider, Raynolds had thought about changing his personal number and keeping it strictly private. But, in the end, he'd never bothered doing it. Which was why, at times like this, he often wished he had. There again, whatever he did, the likes of Lemon were bound to pick it up from somewhere – if not from him, when he was in one of his more amicable moods.

Forcing a smile, he said, "Gordon, how nice to hear from you. It's a social call, rather than business, I hope?"

Over the line Raynolds could hear noises as Lemon settled himself down in his obscenely expensive office chair – the polished leather sounding like a case of terminal flatulence.

"It's a bit of both, Jimmy, I'm afraid. Bit of both."

Raynolds squeezed his eyes shut for a moment. *Get to the fucking point!* Then, taking a calming breath, he said, "Well, give me the good news first."

Again the sound of chronic wind breaking from the chair, and Raynolds pictured the bespoke suited legal expert, grinning contentedly, flicking through the pages of the diary app on his desktop touchpad. "I was wondering if you would be free, Sunday after next, to make up a four for golf?"

"Shouldn't be a problem if we can agree on a time." Raynolds checked his own desktop computer diary, then, "Say a ten o'clock start? Who else is coming along?"

"Ten should be fine. It'll be myself, plus a couple of new members who fancy working on their handicaps. Don't think you've met them yet. In fact, we don't seem to see much of you at the club at all these days, Jimmy. Got to keep yourself fit and active, otherwise who knows? Suppose you heard about Archie Spindler? Stone cold dead. Heart attack in his sleep. Maureen says she never felt a thing – probably the best night's sleep she's had in a long time. Woke up the following morning and there he was, cold and stiff beside her. He was about your age, I think. Used to be a regular at the club as well, until his business started slipping in the recession."

Raynolds tapped his foot against the carpet under his desk, waiting for a break in the flow of gossip so as to try and wedge in a comment or two himself. Finally he got his chance.

"Well, so much for the social catching up, which is always appreciated, Gordon, however…." He left the sentence deliberately unfinished, knowing full well Lemon would seize control of the conversation again.

"Oh. Yes." Lemon paused then dropped his voice down a tone so as to make himself sound more authoritative. "I had some trouble when I tried to see a client of mine yesterday. Not only was I made to wait a considerable length of time, but I found out after I finally saw some paperwork that he'd been held for quite a while without being interviewed, or even charged."

Still trying to sound amicable and concerned, Raynolds said,

"Refresh me, Gordon. Which client of yours are we talking about? As far as I know we haven't pulled in any sons of the ruling classes for being over the limit, or for indulging in some recreational weed or ecstasy."

Lemon's tone cut through the forced levity. "This isn't funny, Jimmy. My client, Mr. Duffley, was arrested at two-thirty yesterday afternoon. By the time he was allowed to notify me it was gone nine pm, and even by then he still hadn't been properly charged."

Raynolds put a colder tone into his voice. "Gordon, we have your client, Mr. Duffley, clearly visible on surveillance video. Not only is he in the process of brokering a deal involving a significant amount of a Class A controlled substance – to whit, cocaine – but he's also involved in the murder and shooting of two people, one of whom was an undercover police officer."

Lemon barely paused. "My client has informed me he was only involved with the proceedings under duress. The two Colombian gentlemen had threatened the lives of various members of Mr. Duffley's family, stating they would be brutally murdered should he fail to help them with the disposal of their narcotics."

Raynolds was rapidly losing patience. "What the hell are you trying to pull here, Gordon?"

"I'm not trying to pull anything, Detective Chief Superintendent. I am merely pointing out that my client is, in fact, a sad, unhappy and unwilling innocent in this whole sorry affair. And, considering that the surviving Colombian has remained silent throughout the proceedings so far, I would think that alone would make my client a very valuable witness for the prosecution of the surviving instigator."

"Who the hell told you about Lucumi remaining silent?"

"It really doesn't matter as he's also being represented by us. Well, our associates at Maplethorpe and Gittings. But regardless of that, I probably picked it up listening to the idle conversation between police officers while I was left hanging around the front desk, prior to seeing my client. The point is, my client is at risk, and if he is going to be of any value to the case then he'll need to be protected."

Raynolds did his best to control his anger. "You're losing it, Gordon. You know that? You are really fucking losing it."

"Am I? Well, we'll see what your superiors think."

There was a loud click as Lemon broke the connection, and after a second or two Raynolds tossed the smartphone across his desk in disgust.

*

Looking down at his all day breakfast special, Fennick imagined Jan's disapproval.

I dread to think what your cholesterol level is going to be after you've eaten that lot.

The waitress returned with coffee for Fennick and black tea for Hansen. In a voice bursting with indifference, she asked, "Can I get you anything else? Bread and butter? Toast?"

Fennick, quickly swallowing the remains of a piece of sausage, shook his head, adding, "No, we're fine," Just in case she failed to get the message.

With another surge of apathy she walked back behind the serving counter and sat down on her stool by the till. Fat Freddy's was one of those greasy spoons which always seemed half full no matter what time of day it was.

Fennick went back to attacking the sausage, then looked out of the window at the street beyond. With the initial interview complete, they'd left Caradine's flat not long after 09:30, and after a five minute break for Hansen to recharge his nicotine batteries, they'd started back towards the station. Not long into the return journey, Fennick – true to his earlier word – had discovered Fat Freddy's. The choice made easier by being able to park nearby.

Inside was warm and seductively inviting, with a homely childhood atmosphere of hot chip fat and industrial strength tea from a massive stainless steel urn. But on closer inspection the fixtures and fittings seemed tired and worn out. A lot like the waitress, in fact.

Fennick looked down at the remains of his all day breakfast plate. An egg, some bacon and several stray baked beans stared back up at him, accusingly. *It might be fried, but that doesn't mean it's all bad for you, does it?* He looked over at Hansen's plain omelette and wrinkled his nose. *Anyway, what the eye doesn't see, Jan can't nag about.*

They ate in silence for a few minutes, Fennick basking in the guilty pleasure, Hansen eating out of necessity, before Hansen put a hand in his jacket and pulled out his notebook. Flipping the pages over in quick succession he read through his shorthand, then looked up at Fennick.

"Was it just me, or did it seem like Eveready Eddie was hyped up on something?"

"It was probably the after effects of whatever the hospital prescribed for him. It wouldn't hurt to check with them though, see what they actually wrote up for him."

Hansen's pen made several twitching motions as he jotted the task down. Setting the pen aside, he picked up his mug of tea and took a swallow. The look on his face told Fennick he was still coming to terms with the new healthy living kick.

Some more flicking through his notes, then Hansen shut the notepad and put it back into his pocket. "Whichever way you look at it, I've got a strong suspicion he's right."

Fennick looked up. "Who?"

"Eddie Caradine."

"About what?"

"About the whole thing. It doesn't feel right at all."

Fennick balanced the last of his fried egg on top of the final fragment of bacon. "You mean everything seems to points to a leak of some kind?"

Hansen carefully organised himself before voicing his feelings, aware of how sensitive the subject had become. "It's not just that. It's everything else about the whole operation. Why make out you're a Colombian dealer when you're not? Why the need for deception if all you wanted to do was set up an outlet? Unless, of course, Penstone was trespassing? And that's before we start looking at the who, what, where and why of Vic Carlton's involvement. Someone'd clearly tipped him off, so why the hell didn't he go back to his old firm to get some muscle, rather than hiring a couple of Peter Wainwright's men?"

Fennick pushed his empty plate to one side and picked up his mug of coffee. "And there was me thinking you didn't want to get involved with this one."

Hansen worried at his bottom lip. "Okay, officially it's not our case, as such, and all Raynolds wants us to do is gather info for his team. And there's also our own outstanding caseloads to consider as well. But there's just too much to this which makes me want to see it properly closed."

"You're saying you want us to conduct some kind of parallel investigation?" Fennick pursed his lips. "Molly would go ballistic, and as you say, it's not as if we don't have a full in-tray waiting for us when we get back."

"I know, I know. It's just Caradine. It seemed to me as if he thought we were the source of the leak because we're the outsiders."

There was no question in Fennick's mind as to where the leak had come from. Somewhere within the GMP itself.

Hansen looked down at his lukewarm tea. "The way things are at the moment? Taking into account this is now a media-fuelled high profile case, I don't doubt there's at least three or four personal agendas involved somewhere in all of this." A short pause as he fidgeted with the salt pot. "Something must be going on, otherwise why did Molly call last night?"

"I called him, remember?"

"But he was waiting for your call, wasn't he."

Fennick sighed a little. "That was probably due to the local media crap on the TV." Hansen knew from the tone of Fennick's voice that Fennick now had his own doubt niggling at the back of his mind. Fennick sucked at his front teeth for a moment. "Okay, I tell you what. We go back to the station, input the statement from Caradine, then see what else has turned up. If there's nothing new, and Raynolds isn't around to reassign us to something else, we'll use our initiative and see what we can put together ourselves."

Hansen smiled. "Now that sounds a much better proposition."

*

Gary Tang sat at the kitchen table in his one-bedroom flat, rolling himself another straight cigarette. He licked it, smoothed it, and put it inside the tobacco pouch with the other four he'd just rolled. He was having a good day, and the way things were likely to shape up at the clubs later on, it could only get better.

His mobile buzzed again with another text message.

What chances of City for the cup? It was signed Scooby.

Scooby was a regular customer, usually looking for a weekend supply. He was always good for a handful of E, some wiz and some ice. Plus Scooby always paid cash, up front without fail, and didn't dick around either. Unlike some of the other shitheads he usually had to deal with. Tang thumbed back a reply.

The first Dale of Arken in the 11:30, running good to firm.

It meant Gary would be on the first floor of the Arkendale Shopping Centre, around 11:30, and there was a good chance he would have what Scooby was interested in. True, it wasn't much of a code, but with some of the wankers he was dealing to, it paid to keep things as simple as possible. The last thing he needed was some prat, totally ripped to the tits and off their face, burbling into his voicemail and leaving behind a mass of incriminating evidence. Hence the texts only phone service.

In this business, it paid to trust no one. He'd learned that to his cost the last time. Fuck Symonds. He wouldn't have gone near the bastard if he'd known Symonds was going to turn him in to save his own arse.

Gary had returned to the flat around nine that evening, put some bags and twists together, stocking up with merchandise before he set off clubbing. Several of the bouncers would look the other way for a couple of hundred apiece, and he'd easily make that back after the first circle of the dance floor. Second and third time round was where the profit came from. Yet he hadn't even made it to the first venue when he'd seen Symonds heading towards him. Gary had even crossed the road to make sure. The bastard had crossed over as well, and still kept heading for him. It was the last thing Gary needed, especially when he'd been carrying quality gear which Symonds couldn't hope to buy. But by then it was far too late; he'd locked onto Gary like some kind of crack-seeking missile. Only when he'd gotten up close he'd started to kick off – like big time – his breath rancid and minging as he'd ranted and shouted in Gary's face. The other pedestrians had immediately moved away from the pair of them as the one-sided argument flashed up.

He'd tried to push Symonds away, but the bastard just kept getting right up in his face, coming in closer and closer every time, until finally Gary had lost it himself. He'd just hauled his fist back, then snapped it forward, smacking Symonds square in the face. Symonds had gone down like a sack of shit, which had actually made Gary feel a little better. He'd been about to walk off, leaving the bastard bleeding on the pavement, when the two undercover arseholes came out from nowhere and fronted him up. They'd flashed their warrant cards in his face, shouted a load of crap at him, then he'd been bundled into the back of an unmarked and driven down to the

Linster Square nick. It wasn't until later he'd realised they'd left Symonds to fend for himself, still lying on the pavement with a split lip and a bloody nose.

Once down the nick he'd been made to empty his pockets out, and with the amount of the class gear he'd been carrying, he'd figured he would be looking at doing some serious time for dealing. So it was no big surprise when they'd finally stuck him in a holding cell overnight. Left to his thoughts, he'd decided there was no way he was going to grass up any of his suppliers and run the risk of any of them getting off. For one, he had seen what 'Mad' Merrillies had done when someone had pissed him off. Far safer if he were to throw the Babylon a couple of rich kid users, especially if it got him time off his sentence. Stitch up a couple of wannabes whose parents could easily afford the legal, and who would probably get off on some technicality or other.

But then the undercovers had rocked up in the cell the following morning and had quite literally made him an offer he couldn't refuse. Gary could walk out of the nick that same day, all paperwork shredded, provided he agreed to set up a meeting between the two coppers and a big supplier.

He'd told the pair of them he needed time to think about it and consider what would be his least life threatening option. That, for once, had actually been true.

But the arseholes had only given him less than half an hour to decide, otherwise they'd bang him up good and proper, regardless of who he eventually gave up.

Alone in the cell, Garry had tried to work out if there was some way of stitching up Wilson Merrillies without any of the crap coming back on him. But the more he thought about it, the more he remembered what he'd seen happen to some poor sod called Nadjier, who had obviously crossed Merrillies up.

Over the years, Wilson Merrillies had earned his reputation by working his way through various outfits until he'd been able to head up his own. From that vantage point he'd strong-armed various takeovers until he was one of Manchester's statesmen of crime. He didn't take any shit from anyone, and made sure everyone he felt needed to, knew exactly how things stood. Gary had been buying gear from him for a while, but on this one occasion things had become seriously fucking heavy.

It had been just before midnight when he'd had gone over to a garage and repair shop up near The Narrows. It was a place which Merrillies owned and regularly did business from. Gary had been met in the front showroom by the man himself. If anything, that should have triggered alarm bells, but Gary had been too focussed on getting the new gear so he hadn't thought anything of it. Merrillies had been all smiles and good humour at first, even offering Gary a beer – none of that supermarket crap either. Then, after a couple of minutes of idle chit-chatting, they'd exchanged Gary's carefully counted packet of cash for a cheap plastic holdall that contained a generous variety of quality gear.

He'd been about to go when Merrillies had invited him into the garage workshop out the back.

"I just need a second pair of hands. Shouldn't take long, just the two of us."

Gary had thought he was going to shit himself as he desperately tried to figure out if he'd managed to somehow piss Merrillies off in any way. But Merrillies wasn't about to let him go. Even put an arm around Gary's shoulders – all pally like – and guided him through the side door, into the large area at the back.

He'd had continued shepherding Gary over towards the massive car lifts and inspection pits, and he'd been torn between dropping the gear and doing a runner, or just coming right out and asking Wilson what the fuck it was he'd done wrong. But, more importantly, what did he need to do in order to try and make things right between the two of them again.

Then, across the workshop, Gary saw Nadjier. He was a tall, coffee-skinned, Asian-looking guy, who'd been stripped naked and suspended upside down by a chain and pulley contraption hanging from the roof. Gary had seen mechanics lifting engines out of cars using the same kind of stuff. Only instead of the end being wrapped around a heavy engine block, it had been wrapped around Nadjier's ankles. His hands were bound at the wrists with dull silver masking tape, and his arms were hanging down below his head, though his fingertips were still a foot or so above the workshop floor. The same tape had been used to seal his mouth shut as well and, understandably, there was a wide eyed and terrified look on the poor bastard's face.

But it wasn't until the two of them came alongside the large workbench did it finally dawn on him. He wasn't going to become the victim, he was about to become an accessory in one of Wilson Merrillies' discipline sessions. He'd swallowed hard, several times, in an effort to stop himself from puking. If he refused to be a part of what was going to happen, then he knew he would find himself in exactly the same position, quite literally, awaiting Merrillies' sick pleasure. As he struggled to keep control of himself he realised Merrillies was still talking behind him.

"Gary, I want you to meet Nadjier. Nadjier used to look after a group of girls for me. Eastern European ladies who are over here for work experience, as it were."

He'd only been vaguely aware of what Merrillies was up to behind him, rummaging around the workbench searching for something. Sounding only slightly distracted, Merrillies continued his one-sided conversation.

"Only Nadjier decided he would do a little business expansion himself." Merrillies raised his voice and called out over Gary's shoulder, "Didn't you."

Nadjier, eyes wide, tried to protest despite the masking tape.

Merrillies carried on, regardless.

"Personally I don't mind a little entrepreneurialism. It shows initiative for one thing, and foresight for another. But what I do mind is greed. A little skimming is to be expected – you can factor it into the business model as part of your overheads. But, when it gets to the point of being too much, then we have to look at a reiteration of the company's mission statements. Don't we, Nadjier."

Again the muffled protests, which became even more frantic as Merrillies moved around Gary, the end of a heavy electrical jump lead gripped firmly in his hand by its large crocodile clip. In a casual manner, Merrillies had simply reached up and connected the powerfully sprung clip to the chain cutting into Nadjier's ankles. Following the cable back to the workbench, he realised that the other end was securely screwed onto one of several heavy duty lorry batteries.

"Now Gary, you might want to stand back as this next bit is a little messy." Merrillies had then reached down by the side of the bench, picked up a bucket of water and thrown the liquid over Nadjier's naked body.

Muffled cries had turned into muffled screams and Nadjier's jerking around had set him off swinging from side to side. Merrillies stepped up and stopped it, then looked back at Gary, a wide grin on his face, forcing him to stare directly into his soulless eyes.

That was the point when Gary Tang realised that all the urban legends about the man were true. Wilson Merrillies was a 24-carat, solid gold, psychotic fucking head case. Even though his face had taken on an excited expression of anticipation, it was heavily mixed in with a very cold sense of power and pleasure – almost a corrupted, sexual tension – and Gary'd felt his guts start to cramp up again.

Happily cruising in his own world, Merrillies continued talking as he went back to the bench and carried on connecting a second lead to the remaining free battery terminal.

"You see, Gary, this isn't just about stealing from me. Stealing is bad enough, but it's not just about that. Oh no. Nadjier had set himself up with several girls, whom he'd repeatedly assured me, had done a runner down to London." There was a moment's silence as he checked the connections again, then carefully pulled on a pair of thick rubber kitchen gloves. Gary had tried long and hard to forget the image of Merrillies, standing there, wearing a pair of bright yellow Marigolds on his hands, a cold hard look of disgust on his face.

"No, Gary. What this is about is the fact that this insignificant fucking prick thought I was fucking stupid enough to believe him!" Merrillies' voice was getting steadily more aggressive as he started to work himself up. "Not only that, but he honestly thought I wouldn't find out about him doing more than a little bit of business on the fucking side!" He turned to look at Gary, his face starting to flush with rage as little white flecks of spittle foamed at the corners of his mouth. "Can you imagine it, Gary? Can you *fucking* imagine it?!"

No matter how hard he'd tried since, Gary doubted he would ever forget the whipping Merrillies had given Nadjier. He'd picked up the second cable and had run his hands down its length until he'd found the makeshift insulated grip. From there the thick cable continued for five or six feet before the sheathing had been stripped away. The remaining length of copper strands had been separated, then platted together again into a flexible copper cat o'nine tails.

With the cable gripped in one hand, Merrillies had positioned himself in front of the hanging body, almost as if he were getting himself comfortable on a golf course, casually flicking the cable behind him. Then, with his arm out from his side, he brought it forwards then back in one sharp jerk, whipping the braided copper ends viciously so that they curled around Nadjier's back and landed across his chest. It had happened so fast that later Gary thought he'd heard the whip-crack just before he saw the mass of tiny sparks jump and burn at Nadjier's wet skin. Nadjier had convulsed and twisted around like a fish, dangling from an angler's line – while behind the masking tape he'd made noises Gary never, ever, wanted to hear again. Merrillies' second stroke had broken the guy's skin, and it wasn't long before Nadjier was bleeding from literally dozens of vicious cuts and welts on his chest, back and thighs.

Twice Gary had been told to throw cold water over the poor sod in order to revive him, and when Nadjier started to puke Merrillies had told Gary to pull the masking tape off his mouth.

"Don't want the fucker choking to death now, do we Gary."

After a while Gary had found it easier to concentrate on watching little chunks of Nadjier's vomit mix with the cold water on the floor – watching it slowly trickle over the side and into the concrete inspection pit.

Eventually Merrillies had felt the retribution had run its course and the 'injustice' had somehow been rectified. He'd thrown the makeshift electric whip down near the workbench, then walked up to Nadjier and removed the crocodile clip. He'd then coiled up both cables and set them to one side, telling Gary to unhook the chain keeping Nadjier suspended. Gary'd let it slide through his hands, unchecked – the noise of the links running over the blocks was deafening in the hollow silence, only ceasing when his body collapsed onto the floor. He lay there, twitching and jerking uncontrollably, eyes rolled back in his head and his mouth silently open, while Merrillies had peeled off the blood flecked rubber gloves and tossed them onto the workbench. Turning back to focus on Gary again, his face had seemed calm and benevolent – almost as if the bloody violence and brutal violation of another human being had somehow never taken place.

"Don't know about you, Gary, but I've got to be off."

Gary had looked back down at Nadjier, still bleeding and twitching in the dark, the bruises and ugly cuts in sharp focus. Then he'd felt Merrillies' hand on his arm, turning him around and pointing him towards the back door.

"Don't worry about him, Gary. The cleaners come in early. It's their job to clean the crap up around here." It had seemed as if he'd been talking about a pile of greasy rags, or some discarded cardboard packing. Gary couldn't help wonder just how many people this certifiable nutter had done over or killed before now.

In a numbed, half-dazed state, he'd started walking towards the exit, his mind thinking over a list of people he'd once known, and had all disappeared without a trace. Then he'd heard Merrillies coming up behind him, calling out to him in his emotionally cool, slightly menacing voice.

"You don't want to forget this, now do you, Gary?"

He'd been on the verge of pissing himself, but when he'd turned around, Merrillies was holding out the cheap nylon sports bag full of the gear he'd just bought.

Sitting in the cell with those memories had been enough. There was no fucking way Gary Tang was ever going to give up Wilson Merrillies, regardless of who did the asking.

Thirty minutes later the two coppers had turned up to see if he was prepared to play ball. Gary had tried his utmost to sound genuine.

"What if I were to put you onto something I'm only just getting into myself? It's likely to be a pretty big deal." He had no idea what the hell he'd been talking about, but he figured if he could just keep his story believable, then it might buy him some time. Enough so he could do a runner down south, or out to East Anglia. He had relatives out that way – an 80-odd-year-old aunt out in Great Yarmouth, or Lowestoft, one of the two. He hadn't seen her in years, but she should still be good for a couple of weeks at the very least.

"How big a deal?"

Oh, fuck, keep things simple. "Not entirely sure at the moment – very early stages – but it's likely to be a regular supplier, bringing it in direct," *What the hell was that about?!* Trouble was, once you started with the bullshit, there was no way of stopping it. It just got bigger and all the more uglier. Yet the thought of doing some serious time, and ending up as some tattooed animal's cell bitch, had kept pushing him further into fantasy. "Yeah, possibly even three or four times a month."

One copper had looked sceptical. "What kind of gear are we talking about here?"

"Ice, E, crystal, Afghan skag…" *Christ, where the fuck had all that come from?*

The two coppers had walked over to a corner, huddled together and whispered to each other, leaving Gary to sweat some more while they talked things over.

When he'd looked up again, one of them broke away and came over to him.

"Okay, Gary, from now on you're going to be setting things up for a couple of players." He'd passed Gary a sheet of folded paper. "Aaron Deedering, and Carl Scully. There's some background info which should be enough to get your story straight. Tell the supplier that they're old mates of yours, moving up from the West Country – around the Plymouth area. You've got three days, otherwise we'll come looking for you, and this time it won't just be for possession with intent either."

Then the pair of them had walked out and buggered off. Just like that. Gary had even stayed in the holding cell for another hour, before the booking sergeant stuck his head round the door and told him that if he didn't piss off, they'd charge him rent.

After the first day of no luck, Gary had been sweating worse than a fat tart's crack. In an effort to cut the amount he was holding he'd put the word out he was having a sale and had then hit the clubs. The idea was to get rid of as much as he could, as quickly as he could, then do a runner with whatever cash he'd made. So he'd been doing a fair bit of business when, out of the blue, he'd been approached by a guy calling himself Jose Martinez. Gary had sold him a little bagful, and when

Martinez handed over the cash, he'd also handed Gary a business card. Plain white, with black lettering, it just had the guy's name and mobile number. Then Martinez had said he was looking to start supplying gear at competitive rates, and even offered Gary a small sample bag of his own merchandise for free. The only stipulation was that he would need to shift a lot of the stuff in order to make it worth their while. Martinez would become his sole supplier.

There had been absolutely no way Gary was going to stop buying from Merrillies – the bastard would go mental, at the very least – so the following morning he'd phoned the coppers' number. It had gone through to voicemail. So he'd left a quick message, saying they should meet up as he'd located a big supplier who was interested in supplying them with whatever they fancied. Just so long as they could handle the stuff in large amounts.

Which was how Operation Gold Dust had been born.

Gary had gone on to hook Martinez up with 'Aaron Deedering' and 'Carl Skully.' And, thank fuck, after their first meeting, Gary had been virtually side-lined. Finally he'd been pushed out of the proceedings completely when they'd started talking kilos of the stuff on a regular basis.

Now, having seen the news reports about what had gone down at the hotel, he was overjoyed everyone had considered him too small a player. Not only that, he could go tell his clients the stuff was difficult to get hold of, and jack the price up accordingly.

He looked up at the clock on the kitchen wall. Time to be making a move if he was going to keep his appointment with Scooby.

7

Wednesday Lunchtime

Fennick checked the dashboard clock as he parked the unmarked car in the station car park. For some reason he'd yet to work out, the atmosphere between himself and Hansen had started to feel odd while they'd driven back from Fat Freddy's. Hansen had been uncharacteristically introspective and distracted.

In an effort to lighten things up, Fennick said, "We've got about an hour and a half before Raynolds is due back on stage for the in-house twelve forty-five brief. I'll head on up and sort out our desk if you want to grab another smoke before we start?"

Hansen nodded absently. "A few more minutes isn't going to make much difference. There's nothing from what Caradine's said so far that moves this case on. Well, no burning revelations that will make Raynolds' day."

"True enough." Fennick waited a second or two, but Hansen remained silently unforthcoming as they got out of the car. Fennick wondered if it was the right place to start probing and try to find out what was clearly up with his DS. But a strong gust of cold wind scythed across the car park, aiding his decision. Later, when the surroundings were more conducive to conversation. "See you in the incident room in five then."

Fennick crossed the tarmac and disappeared into the station while Hansen pulled the collar of his jacket up and made his way over to the makeshift smokers' shelter. A few more minutes to try and get his head back together wouldn't hurt. Especially as he'd started to feel the old tension inside himself again. This time with a vengeance. It had been there, subconsciously pushing at him, since the early hours back in the hotel room. A slow and relentless building up of pressure. It was part of the reason he didn't want to face the crowd milling around in the incident room. Not just yet, at any rate. He'd nothing against them personally, and chances were he probably knew more than a few of them socially, as well as professionally. It was just that, at that moment, anything more than Mike's company felt strangely invasive and claustrophobic somehow. As if the others were going to be silently judging his actions and trying to find fault with them. He'd tried to dismiss it before, telling himself the feelings were totally emotional and irrational, but it was there, in the background, all the same.

He pulled out his wallet and thumbed around in one of the pockets, tentatively easing out the small passport-sized photograph of Felix. It had been the last he'd sent, attached to an e-mail, just before Felix and his team had gone out on patrol. Between his thumb and forefinger, Felix looked back up at him. Eyes squinting slightly in the sharp sunlight of dawn, he was standing, looking into the lens, his distinctive Caribbean face lit up by a wide grin. He was dressed in full desert combats and was holding an SA-80 rifle held close across his chest, barrel pointed down at the sand. The weapon appeared small against the broad camouflage jacket, and dwarfed by his large, long fingered hands.

Felix's sister, Cathy, had phoned their Ellesmere Port flat the evening of December 23rd – it had been around five to midnight. She had said how sorry she was to pass on bad news, but Felix wasn't going to be coming home. She'd then started crying over the phone as she explained how her younger brother had been killed during a night skirmish, deep in the Helmand province. He'd died on the 19th, but their parents had already flown back to St Lucia by then for

Christmas, and their mother hadn't updated the next of kin details. Luckily, when the Army Welfare Service hadn't been able to contact them easily, one of the on-duty clerks had remembered that Cathy's details had been on a previous list.

Steve had thanked her and numbly put the phone down. He didn't remember walking into the living room, or sitting down in the chair. Felix had been due home – their home – on the 22nd, and when he'd not turned up on the doorstep, Steve had started to get concerned. He'd desperately wanted to contact the AWS himself, only the trouble was that Felix had never told the Army he was gay, or that he had a civilian partner. Steve had come out to the world just after he'd left school, and after university he'd joined the Police on the back of a recruiting drive in either Attitude or GT Magazine. It hadn't been easy back then, even with the support of the Cheshire LGP Association, but he'd successfully passed the training, stood his ground, and had made the Force a serious career.

With Felix, things had been a lot different. On his first and only attempt after leaving college, his father – in a fit of violent rage – had disowned him completely, kicking him out of the house without any consideration, despite the mute support of his mother. Felix had gone to Cathy for comfort and a roof over his head while he thought about how he was going to live the rest of his life. Within a couple of months he'd signed up for the Army – putting his sexuality into denial, both to the outside world, and then to his colleagues and commanding officers in the Reds and Royals. Even after the Forces had adopted a more open minded policy, Felix hadn't been prepared to fight decades of ingrained prejudice, regardless of what support there was from various agencies within the Army itself. As far as his commanding officer and compatriots were concerned, Felix was just a 6ft 2 inch sergeant, whose judgement was respected and trusted in the field, and who was usually to be feared on the rugby pitch.

Yet despite their long and stable relationship together, with no Civil Partnership in place, the Army didn't even know of Steve

Hansen's existence.

The cold wind brought Hansen back from his reverie. Behind him the door banged open and he hurriedly pushed the photograph back, before slipping the wallet into his trouser pocket. Two uniforms and a WPC walked out, preoccupied with their own chatter and handing around a packet of cigarettes.

Rather than get involved, he dropped the stub of his small cigar onto the tarmac and scuffed it out several times with the toe of his shoe before heading towards the heavy back door. As he passed he forced a sociable nod of greeting to the three fellow smokers, before letting the wind bang the door closed behind him. Time to get back to the grind.

*

"Thought you said you were giving up?"

The whine in Jason's voice made him sound like a petulant child, even though his driving licence said he was twenty. With his slightly gimpy left hand he offered Mikka a cigarette. As usual he only had a few left, but he felt compelled to offer the packet to her all the same. She took one that didn't look too crumpled and lit it up, watching from the corner of her eye as Jason smiled a little shyly. Despite his seemingly never ending complaining, the three of them – Jason, Mikka and little Mousey – had bonded quickly into a mutually supportive team.

Jason was tall, thin, and had those large eyes you see on the cards and posters in gift shops. His long face always seemed to have a naturally pleading look to it. Love is... Never having to run away from home. Even now, as he went back to watching the shoppers walk past the bench where they were sitting, he looked like he should have a paper cup in his hand. Shaking it incessantly and looking forlornly at the passers-by in the hope they would give him some loose change. Only he was getting too old, and too street damaged – no longer cute enough for that kind of scam to keep on working for much longer.

Looking beyond him, she made a quick motherly check on Mousey. The small child held tightly onto Jason's arm with one hand, while the other was deep inside his coat pocket. Poking up around his sleeve was the stitched face of the threadbare soft toy which he could never bear to be parted from. Mikka had no idea what it used to be, only that it needed regular repair to stop it falling apart; quite a lot like Mousey.

He'd appeared out of nowhere at the squat one day, just before Bonfire Night. Small and hurt, Mikka first thought he was about 4 or 5 years old, until she had found the little stash of possessions he kept in a small backpack. She'd unpacked it while he'd been asleep and washed it for him, discovering it was an old Paddington Bear bag. Inside had been a few pages from a school notebook with some drawings on and the cut out photo page from a passport, which gave his name and date of birth. His proper name was Paul Spencer, and he was going to be 9 years old in a few months' time. The papers had been a lucky find as he'd rarely said a word to either Jason or Mikka since the night he'd arrived.

Both she and Jason always made sure the squat was locked down tight. It was too good a find and they'd deliberately kept its location a secret from anyone who'd asked.

Then, that night, they'd come down from their attic hideaway to watch the rockets exploding overhead, and had discovered Mousey. Somehow he'd found his way in, around one of the wooden boards Jason had fixed up. From the outside the plywood sheet seemed just like all the rest. Unless you knew how to move it, it looked like it had been nailed against the back door of the terraced house.

Mousey was sitting cross-legged at the bottom of the carpet-less staircase, wearing the backpack and tightly clutching the stuffed toy to his chest. At one time it had probably looked like a large brown mouse, years ago, when it had been new. There was a long, shallow gash across his forehead, which had started to scab over. It made Mikka wonder if he'd been bricked, or had run into something without seeing it – which would've helped explain why his clothing was dirty, bloody and torn. The following day Mikka had gone out to Help The Aged and then on to the PDSA, nicking some clothing which looked about his size, so he had something clean to change into when he'd finally felt safe enough to start going outside again.

Mousey had proven useful, once she had put a bandana on his head to hide the cut while it healed. He could wander into shops and stick things in his pockets – and because of his size people didn't notice him much. If they did, then she and Jason were always somewhere close by, ready to play angry Mum and Dad – Jason grabbing Mousey by the hand and walking off with him, while Mikka apologised about their son's terrible habit of picking things off shelves.

He was also good at running interference if it looked like either Mikka or Jason were going to get caught. He'd somehow developed the knack of distracting security guards when they started getting suspicious, giving the other two enough time to vanish into the crowds.

Beside her, Jason made a low grunting sound to attract her attention. "Look who's coming our way." He held his good hand up near his mouth and let the end of the cigarette do the pointing for him.

As she watched the sporadic flow of people walking in and out of the car parks, she spotted the familiar face of a dealer heading towards the entrance of the shopping mall. All three of them had kept themselves relatively clean – nothing stronger than tobacco and sometimes a bottle of alcohol now and again. But they knew enough crack heads and tweakers to make it worth their while to keep tabs on some of the smaller street dealers. The three of them had seen this one from time to time, and knew he wasn't likely to cause them any trouble if he found them selling a twist or two on his turf. Especially as the gear was probably originally from him in the first place.

It'd been Jason who'd come up with the scam that had seemed, to Mikka, to be perfect for quick money, provided they didn't overwork it and get recognised. Any dealer was going to be carrying protection, either tooled up or else have someone around to keep an eye on things. Targeting them was just asking for trouble. So you didn't go after them, you went after the users instead, and Jason had the routine down perfect in no time.

Street dealers would either move around or stay near one particular place. If you waited long enough you could always see when a deal went down. When you did, all you needed to do was hang around until the user moved off, then you could start to follow them. Usually they wanted to get back to their crib and get high again. But somewhere along the way there was bound to be an ideal spot to mug them. Jason was good at memorising routes and shortcuts, even in the dark, sometimes running along parallel streets in order to get ahead of the user, then bounce them for their gear as they came towards him from the opposite direction. Hit a couple of users and they usually had enough gear to sell, whatever they'd managed to get.

Having worked the routine several times before there was no need to say anything more. As the dealer walked by, first Mikka, then Jason, closely followed by little Mousey, slipped off the bench and started heading back into the shopping mall again.

*

Raynolds took another deep breath and slowly re-read the email again. The Assistant Chief Constable had written, personally:

In view of the obvious intelligence potential that Mr. Paul Duffley has to offer, not only in regard to the use of independent Colombian nationals and their roles in the trafficking of Class A narcotics, but also other diverse areas of interest/intelligence in regard to various ongoing operations in London...

Raynolds had known what was coming next, but like an insatiable masochist he drew the inevitable out for as long as possible. Eventually he got down to the part which hurt the most:

So, therefore, Mr. Paul Duffley is now considered to be a valuable source of information, from which will hopefully come a series of successful prosecutions, and possibly the uncovering and eventual breaking up of another major drug importation route into the UK.

Henceforth, all interviews will be conducted on the understanding that Duffley is a witness for the prosecution, rather than just a perpetrator. With that in mind, while it is appreciated that he is also wanted in connection with a string of potentially minor offences, these should be disregarded and excluded from all formal interviews at this time in order to facilitate better co-operation.

Even though the signature said ACC Richardson, Raynolds knew it had probably been dictated to Richardson by one of the Met's hierarchy. Bloody typical. Not content to see him hung out in front of the press, the bastard was more than happy to pass up the chance of closing a national case. But then Richardson had always been an arse kissing wanker.

Lost in thoughts of revenge, Raynolds failed to register the first knock on his office door. He needed to think over the consequences in regard to making sure Duffley was looked after, but that was going to have to wait. The second knock was rapidly followed by the third, which didn't warrant the anger Raynolds put into bellowing "Come in!"

The door opened and Jack Telford appeared almost timidly standing in the doorway. "Should I come back later, sir?" If Telford had a forelock he would've been rapidly tugging on it.

Raynolds screwed his face up in a grimace and pushed the mouse to one side. "No, Jack. Whatever time is going to be a bad time, until this whole bloody mess has been cleaned up. What have you got?"

Telford waved his green 'latest news' folder like a flag of truce as he stepped into the office. "Got the report back about the drugs consignment." He paused halfway to Raynolds' desk, looking expectantly at the DCS.

Raynolds glared at him. "And?"

"And it seems most of the bags are rubbish. Seventy five percent is a mixture of sugar and baby formula. The stuff on show in the hotel room was good, as was one of the bags they picked up from the car. The rest was just crap to fool the buyers."

"But the kilo from the hotel suite will still be enough to make a conviction stand up in court if we need to?"

Jack nodded silently.

Raynolds smiled at the titbit of good news. "Has Duffley come up with a statement yet?"

"No. The only thing he's said to anyone is that he's not going to say anything until his legal rep turns up. Gordon Lemon. He's the lawyer who put in the complaint about – "

Raynolds cut him off. "I already know all about Mr. Lemon and his fucking complaint." Raynolds clicked his computers' mouse and the copier in the corner whined into life.

"Some fresh information for you to put into the investigation. It seems Duffley is now considered a valuable asset in the war against crime." Telford looked confused until Raynolds resignedly explained: "The bastard's done a deal, Jack. He's now so Teflon coated that no amount of shit is going to stick to him, regardless of what we turn up."

"Oh." Telford paused and tried to think of something to fill in the embarrassed silence. "In that case I'd better tell the boys to put the rubber hose away then."

Raynolds shook his head a little. "Not funny, Jack." He looked down at the sheets of paper laid out on his desk in front of him. He thought he'd been ready for the 15:00 press brief, but the email changed everything. "On your way back to the incident room, Jack, tell Margo Weiss to come down and see me. We need to re-jig this press call so it doesn't look like Duffley is getting away with murder, even though the bastard actually is."

*

As Fennick entered the incident room, he felt the emotional buzz he always did at the start of an investigation. Only this time he had the luxury of not being the Senior Investigating Officer. As with any high profile case, various elements of the SIO role had been divided up between the hierarchies that sat above the role of humble Detective Inspector. The more limelight, the more the brass came out of the woodwork. Except the way this one was going some of them had already slithered back behind its protection again.

He looked over to the incident display boards. Already up was a series of photos. Some were police booking shots, others had obviously come from surveillance operations, taken at various stake-outs and kept on file. They were arranged in groups; Duffley and the two Colombians in one, head shots of Tiewrap Teddy Carlton, Marcus Swannick and Dillon Nichols in another. To the side was one each of Wilson Merrillies, Peter Wainwright, and Renton Penstone. All three were connected to their known associates via red, black and green marker pen lines. There wasn't much else on the boards, except for a load of question marks.

As he studied the unfamiliar faces, his mobile phone started up. DCI Sugden. The bastard couldn't even wait for an update to be passed to him. Tapping at the screen he said, "Hello sir."

Sugden's bass-edged voice boomed, "Haven't you closed that case yet?"

Fennick was about to say something verging on the derogatory, but bit his tongue while Sugden carried on regardless. "So what's Caradine got to say for himself?"

"Nothing much really. He stayed with Cooke the evening before the operation was due to happen. He says they got a takeaway and some DVDs, but – "

Sugden broke in. "Any receipts? Address of the takeaway?"

Defensively Fennick said, "We're only just back at the I.R., sir."

"I'll take that as a no then. Check up on it though. Just because he's one of us doesn't mean he can be trusted."

"You figure him for the leak?"

"I'm not the one working the case, Michael. You are. Call me when you've something positive to report."

"Such as what?"

But the line was already dead. Fennick returned the phone to his pocket and went back to looking intently at the three gang leaders again. Two were local. Wilson Merrillies had risen to power on a wave of thuggery, intimidation, and a cold ability to exploit anything and everything which came within his range of influence. Peter Wainwright had gained his criminal power in a much more subtle way. 'Business' mergers, funding start-up capital to budding little 'ventures.' It was an empire built solidly on a foundation of manipulation and control. Whereas Merrillies was an ugly sawn-off shotgun in your face, Wainwright was more the packet of blackmail photographs, delivered in time for breakfast.

Both had serious interests in drugs, prostitution, money laundering and other rackets, but there had always been a truce between them, albeit an uneasy one. Which made Renton Penstone's presence, even via a proxy such as Paul Duffley, all the more difficult to comprehend. Time for a little outsourcing.

Taking out his mobile, he flicked through the contact list, then tapped a name and waited. It rang five times before a Trinidadian accented woman's voice said, "DS Joyce Obletta. How can I help?"

Joyce had been around the Met longer than he had been in the

Force, and although she'd dropped out from time to time as her family increased, she'd been with the Serious Organised Crime Agency, then the National Crime Agency, for some time. If someone was likely to have a good feel for Penstone and his firm then it would be her.

"Hello, Joyce."

There was a silence, then "You still owe me lunch from the last time you were sniffing around me for information, you bastard." Her voice was warm with a hint of laughter bubbling under the surface. "And I heard you got a result off the back of it, too, which makes you a double bastard at the very least."

"What can I say, Joyce? Behind every great man there rests an even greater woman."

"Are you saying I'm fat? You better not be saying I'm fat! Because it sure as hell sounds like you're saying I'm fat!" Finally the laughter broke free and Fennick felt a little happier at being a part of it. "What can I do you for, Mike?"

He looked closely at one of the pictures on the display board. "I need some background on one of your regulars – Renton Penstone."

She sounded curious. "What's your interest with him? He rarely strays north of the water."

"Well, he's certainly seems connected with what I'm working on. At least I think he is. I suppose you heard about Operation Gold Dust?"

"Only what's been buzzing on the news this morning. God, were you involved in that? Oh, Mike, I'm sorry."

Fennick was quiet for a moment. "Yeah, well, shit happens."

"Tell me about it. But I thought you'd gone over to the Cheshires? From what I saw on the TV, Jimmy Raynolds is fronting up the investigation, so when did you defect to the GMP?"

"Never. We're involved because one of our scrotes stitched up one of theirs, and their scrote helped set things up. It's just a shame we lost one of our own."

Joyce's tone became softer. "They didn't say anything about that in the news reports down here. Who was it?"

"An undercover DC. Anthony Cooke. He was stabbed with a knife before AR had a chance to come to the rescue."

"Tony Cooke? Works with a cocky sod called Caradine?"

"Worked with," Fennick immediately felt a touch of guilt for correcting her, but she carried on regardless – the shift of focus merely protection from acknowledging the inherent dangers of their profession.

"Yeah. Whatever." The distraction in her voice was obvious as she tried hard to remember something, but failed. "Look, Mike, I'll get back to you on this, okay? What's the best number to call you on?"

Fennick gave her his mobile number, broke the connection, and went back to looking at the boards for a moment before turning round and finally locating the desks he and Hansen had been assigned.

He started to get himself comfortable when he felt a presence behind him. The dark surface of his computer screen showed the reflection of Ramesh Bashani. As he turned round, Ramesh pulled a vacant seat from a nearby desk and planted himself down in front of Mike.

"It's good to see you again, Mike. How are things? Still with Jan?" Then, "I take it Hertfordshire didn't work out?"

Fennick had known the comments and questions would come, eventually. "No. I put in for a transfer when Jan decided to move her business up this way. There was an opening with the Cheshire force, so I took it. Though Jan hasn't found work as easy to come by as she first thought."

"Is she still doing community support work?"

Fennick smiled and nodded. When the two of them had moved, Jan had also moved her consultancy. Yet, over the last couple of years, what with the recession, government and local council budget cuts, the business opportunities had steadily dried up. It should've been wound down, but Jan felt possessive about it. Shutting it down would be considered a failure on her part.

"She's working with a couple of charities, trying to improve their profile and fund raising strategies. Finding the right branding and market placement, to use her PR-speak."

Ramesh nodded. "At least she still has something. I take it you two still haven't?" He let the question hang, waiting for Fennick to answer.

"No. What with things, we never got around to it. Anyway we seem happy the way we are."

Ramesh patted Mike on the shoulder, then stood up. "Maybe marriage would help stabilise things more? Settle you down. It wouldn't hurt your career either."

Fennick remembered the last official function he and Bashani had both attended five or six years before, when the formidable Mrs. Bashani had been unleashed on the Hertfordshire Police Summer Ball. "We'll certainly take that into consideration when the topic comes up again."

Looking across the incident room, Fennick saw Hansen appear at the door before heading through the maze towards them.

As Bashani watched him approach, he got up and slid the borrowed chair back under the nearby desk. "I'll let you get on. I take it there wasn't anything worth following up in Caradine's statement?"

"Not that we can see at the moment. Still got the fine detail to go through and check out though. See if he really did rent a DVD for the night, that sort of thing."

As Hansen sat down at his desk opposite Fennick's, Bashani smiled. "Well, that's the sort of thing your DS is for, after all."

Fennick could feel the heat of Hansen's glare on the back of his neck and rapidly tried to change the subject. "I take it you've had more success?"

"Nothing at the moment. I'll probably grab some lunch then head on out for the afternoon. Going to see what I can find out from the hospital, and have a word or two with Marcus Swannick – see what he wants to say about it all."

Still oblivious to Hansen's dagger-loaded stare, Bashani headed towards the door, picking his coat up on the way.

Without turning round, Fennick said, "If you don't calm down you're going to say something you'll regret. I know the last couple of months have been rough. But you should've taken the offer of compassionate leave, rather than playing the hard man and refusing."

Hansen just grunted as Fennick turned his chair round.

"You need to do something, Steve. There's still too much anger inside you. You need closure, and you need to start it soon."

*

In the Arkendale Centre the crowds were starting to build as the lunchtime browsers came in for the warmth. Up on the first floor, Gary Tang's head jerked and moved as he tried to spot Scooby's distinctive green parka. With its faded Mod target symbol on the back, it wasn't all that easy to miss amongst the sea of moving bodies. It had become the man's trademark, despite it sticking out on security videos.

Nervously he checked the time. Something was definitely wrong. Wrong because Scooby was late – and the guy was never late. He checked the time again. Scooby always texted him if there was a problem, which was why Gary was always prepared to cut the bloke some slack. A few more minutes. He could be stuck on a bus, or jammed up in traffic, with bugger all reception on his mobile.

A group of curious shoppers started to gather around a fancy silver people carrier, parked on a stand at the far end of the concourse. It was a promotional raffle of some kind, done by a local garage or a dealership. He couldn't see the point to it when you worked out the odds. Anyway, cars were just cars, and he still preferred driving his big old fifth-hand Volvo estate rather than some new, up-market pimp job. If you needed to do a runner on the quick then you'd be fucked if you had a Porsche and you were carrying more than just an overnight bag. Plus no stupid bastard was likely to try and jack his car whenever he stopped at a set of lights.

But like Madonna, he was a materialist at heart. It was one of the reasons he never had much cash to hand, or in the bank. Large transactions always left paper trails. Which was why he'd always put his money into jewellery and stones, and not a collection of dodgy shit from some fence, either. Legal pieces which could be sold openly if ever he needed to in a hurry.

He did another time check. It felt like he'd been waiting an eternity already, and still no sign of the tosser. When things didn't go exactly according to plan it kicked his paranoia into overdrive, no matter how much he tried to reason with it.

He did another quick visual, checking over the crowd by the car raffle, the people coming up the escalators, and anyone else in the vicinity.

The young couple with the kid by the large plate glass windows caught his eye again. Were they checking him out? They had settled there just after he had arrived, sitting on the bench, half hidden behind the plants in the flowerbed. He couldn't swear to it but he thought the three of them had been sharing the same takeaway coffee for the last twenty-five minutes. They didn't look like an undercover team, especially not with the kid and his flat expressionless stare. Mind you, the kid's dad didn't look like much either. Big eyes and skinny, not athletic, just bony and gangly looking. But it was the young woman who jangled him. She kept on moving her head slowly from side to side, checking out everything around them, and even when she made eye contact with Gary it was just for a fraction of a second. Long enough to see, short enough not to stare. No, something was definitely fucked up, and when the going gets tough, the tough fucked off so they could fight another day – or whatever that shit was.

As he made his way to the escalators he saw the woman dump the coffee in the plants, while the bloke got hold of the kid. Stepping onto the crowded down travelling steps, he glanced casually behind and saw the other three heading towards the same bank of escalators, a definite look of concentration on the young woman's face as she weaved them through the crowd like a ship through pack ice.

Thankfully, as he was carried below floor level, he could see the crowd behind him were not about to be pushed and shoved so easily, and several bag-laden shoppers protested angrily. In mute reply, the small kid proceeded to give a group of elderly women the finger, before jumping onto the moving staircase behind the other two.

Then he was on the ground floor, coming off the escalator and breaking into a jogging trot. Gary knew, if he started running, the security teams would immediately zero in on it as highly suspicious activity. If the little fuckers really were serious about trying to mug him, then they were going to have to move faster than he was. Which increased the chances of them getting picked up by security.

From nowhere he remembered the parting words of Father Mitchell, when Gary had been expelled from Sunday school at the age of eight.

"You're an evil child, Gary Tang, and God will send devils, not angels, to collect your soul."

Ten years later Father Mitchell had been arrested for molesting choirboys, and Gary had thanked God for making sure that Gary Tang was tone deaf. Regardless of whether the three were devils, the last thing Gary needed was to be caught while he still had so much gear on him. And he wasn't about to start emptying his pockets on the shopping mall floor.

Keep going, keep going.

He slammed through the automatic doors and nearly tripped down the steps. As he started towards the car park – section C, aisle 27 – he attempted to pick up the pace, fear conquering his body's lack of any real physical fitness.

With a clear section in front of him, he chanced a look behind and saw the three of them coming down the steps and starting to run after him – the little kid managing to keep up with the two adults, arms pumping and legs sprinting. The sight spurred Gary on, but he was starting to get winded. His car had to be around here somewhere – he was already in section C, and the aisle numbers had been painted on the roadway. All he had to do was look down and count them off.

Eighteen, nineteen, twenty. Not much further to run – breathe in through the nose, out through the mouth. Twenty-four, twenty-five, twenty-SHIT!

He dodged awkwardly around a car turning out of the aisle, too quick for the driver to even hit the horn in protest. Then down aisle 27, checking along the right hand side for his filthy Wedgewood blue Volvo estate, and wondering why the fuck he'd parked so far up the bloody aisle in the first place.

Another glance over his shoulder, and – and nothing! He nearly tripped himself up as he suddenly came to a stop, heaving in lungfuls of air and scanning the aisles until he caught sight of the two tallest again. They had gone parallel to him, between the two rows of cars in aisle 24. He checked the row of cars near him, and three down saw the rust trimmed back of his Volvo. Shambling into a nearly breathless trot, he wormed his way between the Volvo and the car parked beside it, one hand in a pocket, fumbling for his keys. Finally unlocking the door he looked over the top of the car, just in time to see the two tallest stop, then start looking around as if trying to locate their own car amongst those already parked up. Ha! No chance! Gary might be carrying some tasty gear, but there was no way either the pair, or that little fucking kid, looked like any kind of threat to him now.

He opened the driver's door, his eye on them, before he got in and slammed the door shut. Leaning forward he pushed the key into the ignition, then for good measure pressed firmly down on the central locking button. Across the rows of cars he could see the young woman and her two companions standing in an empty space, just looking at him – thankfully staying their ground and not moving towards him anymore. They knew it was game over, and he had won.

The engine started first time, and with both hands on the wheel, he pushed himself back into the driver's seat. Leaning his head back against the headrest, he let out a sigh of relief as he tried to calm down before heading back to his flat. It felt like he could actually hear his heart thumping with the excess adrenaline in his system.

Long, slow breaths, like in the Yoga classes. In, hold, then out.

He moved his head from side to side against the headrest and closed his eyes for a moment. Which was why he never saw the attacker.

Hidden down low in the back, gloved hands acted with lightning speed, and in one swift movement slipped a heavy duty circular tiewrap down over Gary's head and the headrest, deliberately pulling it tight under Gary's chin. Without pausing, the attacker's knee came up hard against the back of the drivers' seat, while a black leather gloved hand yanked repeatedly at the free end of the plastic loop. Seconds later, the murmurs of satisfaction coming from his killer were rapidly drowned out by the choking and gurgling noises Gary made, as his throat was crushed by the plastic strap, pulled tight against the back of the headrest. His fingers clawed ineffectually at the ligature biting into his neck, his Adam's apple jamming up against the constriction, knees and thighs smacking repeatedly against the steering wheel as his feet became caught up in the pedals on the floor.

In less than a minute Gary's thrashing around had subsided and the Volvo, no longer rocking on its suspension, stopped its groaning protests. With a wheezing sigh Gary's body finally went limp, his head trying to fall forward onto his chest but stopped by the tiewrap holding him firmly against the headrest.

The attacker gave the tiewrap several more sharp tugs, more for personal gratification than necessity, before cancelling the central locking and stepping out into the cold air of the car park. Opening the driver's door, the attacker reached in and turned the engine off, pocketing the keys as he stood up again. It was only when he turned round did he finally see he'd had an audience.

From the empty parking space several rows up, Mikka, Jason and little Mousey looked at the face of Gary Tang's killer, then immediately scattered in different directions – doing their best to get lost amongst the mass of parked cars and ignorant shoppers.

8

Wednesday Afternoon

In the hospital side room, Marcus Swannick's indignant voice grated loudly as Bashani stood at the foot of Swannick's bed.

"Why you dissin' me like dis, man?"

Sighing in despair, Ramesh shook his head slowly. "You sound worse than the scriptwriters off Eastenders, you know that?" Glancing around he saw a visitor's chair in the corner.

"All I is axing is what's with –"

As he pulled the chair round to face the bed, Ramesh cut him off. "Look, I know exactly who you are. You're Marcus Swannick, twenty-nine, born in Leicester to Afro-Caribbean parents. Your parents sold a successful business and moved to Manchester when you were three. By eleven you were getting a public school education off the sweat of their misguided hard work, and a desire to see their only son do good. So drop all that Jafakian Mockney shit and show them some respect."

Swannick looked away, angry and embarrassed at having his gangsta image shredded in front of the young WPC. She'd been sitting by the door for as long as he'd been awake, and had remained silent even though he'd tried several times to get her to talk.

Ramesh took in the luxury of the single patient side room, and seriously doubted he would be afforded the same kind of medical treatment, even though he still had the remains of some private healthcare insurance.

Swannick deliberately avoided eye contact, but chose to just stare at the far wall in front of his bed. His head, with its close cropped hair, along with his bare arms and hands, stood out in stark contrast to the hospital linen and light blue counterpane.

Ramesh could remember the hospitals of his childhood. They had definitely smelled differently back then. There was still a general medical smell, which partially overcame the attending WPC's perfume, but there was no reassuring whiff of antiseptic, or carbolic come to that. At least they had turned the heat down, either by design or budget cuts, which was something. Still, the sooner he started, the quicker he'd be able to get away.

Ramesh leaned forward a little. "Okay, so tell me what all this crap is about."

Swannick remained silent.

Ramesh softened his voice more. "C'mon Marcus, this isn't you. You do middle-class suburban pimping and titty shows on private internet TV channels. Since when did you start getting heavy and using firearms?"

The angry silence continued.

Ramesh sighed. "We've got you bang to rights for possession of a fully functional firearm, used with intent, and that's just off the CCTV footage. Then we've–"

"I didn't know the fucking thing was loaded!" Swannick's voice was loud and aggressive enough to make the WPC tense and alert.

Ramesh pursed his lips contemplatively, letting the anger work for him. Eventually Swannick calmed down enough to speak again. Looking over at Ramesh, he said, "Vic didn't tell me it was loaded. He said it was a replica, like a starting pistol. He said if I pulled the trigger there would just be a loud noise and some smoke. Scare tactics, was what he called it."

Ramesh shook his head in disbelief. "You're telling me you had no idea the gun was real? Didn't you even check to see what was in the magazine?"

Swannick looked at him sharply. "Are you shitting me, man? I didn't even know where the fucking safety catch was until Vic took me to one side and showed me. You know my form. I don't do that kind of heavy shit. It just leads to killings, vendettas and revenge, and I don't want none of that, believe me. I just thought it was one serious looking prop. Big piece of metal like that, people think twice about dissing you, you know?"

"So what was the deal? What was supposed to happen? I mean, how the hell did you become involved with such a head case as Vic Carlton? And guns?"

Swannick's anger faded away and his voice lost all pretence of a streetwise accent.

"He came to us. Well, he came to me. Said he was looking to put the fear of Vic into someone who'd defaulted on a payment or two, which was bad for his business. I mean, I thought he'd retired, but he said it would be like a personal favour to him. He asked if I knew of anyone who could make up the third. I said maybe Dillon Nichols might, but it could take a while to find him. That was when Vic started getting nasty. He said there wasn't much time, and not to fuck him about. Well, regardless, I was still going to have to pass it back to Dillon anyway, so I said I'd call him the minute I'd heard from Dillon."

"So did Peter Wainwright know anything about you, Dillon and Vic Carlton teaming up?"

Swannick became cautious. "Who? Look, I told you, it was Vic who wanted the two of us as heavies while he talked his wayward client into paying up. Provided we got our cut then Dillon and me were happy to go along with the deal. It was all supposed to be simple –

easy money."

It had been worth a try, but getting Swannick to give up Peter Wainwright had been a bit of an outside chance. "Okay, so that got you teamed up. But why the guns?"

"Vic said he thought we'd need the guns for a bit of a show. That's when he told us we'd be going up against five of them, and the guns would stop things from getting too tasty. I just went along with it. He wasn't bloody wrong though, was he? I saw the knife sticking out of that guy's back, and he wasn't bloody moving, either. Then that psycho wanker goes and blows half my fucking leg off with that sawn-off of his."

Swannick carefully pulled aside the counterpane and sheet covering the metal cage protecting both his legs. Ramesh could clearly see the mess of bandages, tape and dressings wrapped around his legs.

As he yanked the covers back over, Swannick said, "They reckon I'm going to be laid up for six months to a year before they can start me on physio."

Ramesh was quick. "Who said you were staying here?"

Swannick started to protest, but Ramesh broke in. "Unless you're prepared to make a full statement about your involvement, then I'm afraid I'm going to have to push on the violence angle. At the very least it'll put you into a prison hospital facility, for the good of the general public. I mean, you never know who might come visiting if you were out on a general ward."

"You have got to be joking me! What violence? What danger to the public? You're just taking the piss now."

Ramesh leaned back, pleased with the reaction. "For one, you've been involved with weapons. Then there's been all the recent street and gang related shooting incidents of late. Public opinion is on any side which would want to see you strung up by the balls, at the very least."

He paused, letting the reality of the scenario sink in. "Of course, we could always leave you alone, and just drop further down the food chain. Get Nichols to roll over and give you up, along with whatever else he might know about anything else you might have been up to…" He let his voice trail off, leaving the clearly implied threat hanging.

"So what does a full statement give me?"

"It'll show you've been cooperative and helpful from the beginning, especially in regard to Nichols and the Uzi he was carrying. Plus any information you might give up about who supplied the pieces to Vic Carlton would be a bonus. That sort of thing goes down well with judges. Face it Marcus. This isn't like some sixteen year old slapper wiggling her tits in front of a webcam after she's done her homework for the night, is it? This is a nasty, bloody violent crime, and the public don't like it when innocent people and police officers get killed in the process."

"Look, I is axing again. What bliss is in it for me?"

Bashani liked at him directly. "Depending on what you're prepared to put in your statement, and it all checks out as good? I think you're probably looking at maybe eighteen months to two years, which will–"

"Two fucking years? Fuck right off!"

"*Which will,*" Ramesh continued forcefully, "probably be eaten up with remand and hospital time, plus physio. There's bound to be some leniency if you show remorse at the outcome of your actions, regardless of your injuries."

"An' if'n I don't?"

"Then I go out of my way to make you look like a really nasty little *tatti*, who should be flushed back around the u-bend from whence you crawled from, regardless of your privileged background." Ramesh adopted a poor imitation of a street accent. "That is what *I* is talkin' about, reggin, if'n you don't."

*

DCS Raynolds was standing in front of the office window, looking out at the darkening sky. Just past four-thirty, and the landscape was already starting to glow with the lights of the traffic. He glared at his reflection in the window glass.

Fuck Bashani.

The 12:30 in-house brief had been bad enough without the prick being there, but he was sure the bastard had also deliberately held off turning up for the press briefing at 15:00. That had been a shambles. It had even started off confrontational, rapidly turned mutually aggressive, then ended with him being verbally mauled. Having Telford up there with him had not been the advantage he'd first thought it would be. Bashani should have been there to bolster their position, and also help make Raynolds a less obvious target. Without him, the journo's had disregarded Telford, and had focussed solely on Raynolds. And several of the shits had been overly eager in their attempts to goad him on several points.

He thought about the journalist from Northeastern Syndicated News, picturing the bastard trapped in that Sci-Fi film where they made peoples' heads explode just by thinking at them. That was how to deal with stroppy little stringers trying to get noticed and picked up by the nationals. Still, it hadn't been all bad, and no one had really noticed when he'd talked about developments regarding information and witnesses or, at least, the lack of them. The old *'details of which I am not at liberty to divulge to the public at this time,'* seemed to hold them nicely in check.

Trouble was, the red tops were still sniffing around the side-lines, wondering if the carcass was worth picking over some more. Why was there never a right honourable Member of Parliament, getting caught giving someone a blowjob up on Hampstead Heath, when you needed one? That sort of thing was guaranteed front page material for days afterwards, knocking any other news to the middle pages, usually somewhere between Miss 38-Double-D cup and the start of the biased opinion columns.

The slow moving lights came back into focus and Raynolds closed the blinds. Settling himself behind his desk, he picked up the phone and called Jack Telford's Incident Room number.

"DI Telford, sir."

Raynolds' voice sounded tired and worn out. "Jack. I take it DI Fennick and his sergeant are still up there with you?"

There was a rustle as Telford looked around the I.R. "Yes, they're still here. Do you want to talk to them over the phone, or drop down to see you, sir?"

"Tell the pair to come down to my office, Jack. Thanks very much."

He was about to put the phone down when Telford said, "Can I tell them what it's about?"

"Tell them there's been a separate development I want them to head up." Then, as an afterthought, he added, "A couple of Community Support Officers doing a car check at the Arkendale centre this afternoon, turned up Gary Tang's Volvo, with Gary Tang dead inside it." Raynolds sighed heavily. "Can you just tell them to get their arses down to my office ASAP. Once I've briefed them then they can brief you." In a more friendly tone, he added, "I'm not shutting you out of this, Jack. You're one of the best office managers I know when it comes to running and supporting a large inquiry. But it's been a long day, and I really can't brief everyone individually. Anyway, I'm not sure if this isn't just some stupidly odd coincidence, so lumping it together with the main investigation might be doing us more harm than good."

There was a short pause at the other end, and Raynolds closed his eyes, hoping Telford wouldn't feel offended in some way. Good office managers were a strange breed at the best of times. Then Telford said, "Okay, sir, I'll tell them to make their way down to you now."

"Thanks, Jack."

*

In the incident room, Jack Telford looked across the desks. Fennick was mulling over the photos again, jotting down something in his pocket notebook. Hansen was tapping the keyboard of his workstation, head bent forward, looking at the screen as he searched through HOLMES2 and the regional MIRWeb. The new policing. Digging through databases for the most recent scraps of intelligence. Searches often tied times to locations in regard to what were now called Persons of Interest.

Telford came up behind him. "Found anything worthwhile?"

Hansen looked up from the multi-windowed screen. "I've been chasing down our cocaine. From the chemical fingerprint there's about half a dozen hits, most from around the London area. Heathrow managed to apprehend a couple of drug mules with the same batch. They've been able to trace it back, and our cocaine definitely originated from one of the larger South American cartels. Our haul helps to link the distribution to the source."

"Oh." Telford didn't sound all that impressed. "Is the interview with Duffley in the system yet?"

"It's still with the readers for indexing. Not that there's much there. His legal rep kept interrupting every two minutes. We were that close to throwing him out of the interview."

Telford smiled. "He was just feeling you out. Our Mr. Lemon hasn't come across you two before, has he. He was probably just pushing to see how much slack you were prepared to give him."

It was always a good tactic to throw in wild cards now and again, so Raynolds' decision to have Fennick and himself interview Duffley had been a logical one.

Raynolds had come up to the incident room for the 12:30 team brief, and it had been obvious to all that he'd been tense and uncomfortable about it. Then, when he hadn't been able to find The Major, he'd almost lost it. Almost, but not quite. Bashani was going to be in line for a bollocking, that was for sure, but Raynolds had picked up the brief and ran with the planning as if he'd prepared it all himself.

"Okay, I'm going to make this quick. It seems that DC Caradine's statement is holding up. The pizza franchise remembered sending the order out, mainly as the delivery guy had returned with ten pounds as a tip. However, it only proves that someone was there when the delivery turned up, as the driver couldn't make either Caradine or Cooke from a photo gallery. Still, at least it's a start in the right direction."

Then Raynolds had dropped the news that Duffley was looking to do a deal in regard to the surviving Colombian, Alejandro Lucumi.

"It's still early yet – and I've received no confirmation of any agreement from ACC Richardson – but it should hopefully get us somewhere in regard to the Colombian connection for the cocaine. I know most of the gear we pulled in turned out to be rubbish, but there is still a lot of Class A powder to make it worth our while chasing it down. Hopefully we should be able to shut down a supply line, even if it's only for a period of time. There's also a chance Duffley might inadvertently give up other information which could turn out to be useful to others, namely the NCA and SDC7."

Then he had turned to Fennick and Hansen. "I want the two of you to conduct the initial interview."

Fennick had just nodded, covering his surprise that they'd been picked rather than people from the home team. Even Jack Telford, busy writing up the new assignments into the action log, looked at Raynolds for confirmation before carrying on.

From beside Fennick, Hansen had asked, "Is there any specific line we should take, sir?"

"Nothing in particular this time round. It's more a case of shaking the proverbial tree and seeing what falls out. Don't forget, it's not a done deal, and if he admits to other activities outside the scope of this investigation, then there's nothing stopping us from charging him accordingly."

Raynolds glanced around the rest of the personnel. "Anyone anything else to add?"

Near the back, DS Thompson spoke up. "Descriptions of the firearms have been printed off and we're including them in all the Watch briefings, just in case the uniforms can track anything down. Most of the armourers I know would shop each other if pushed, not only to keep themselves out of trouble but also to put the competition out of business."

Fennick had raised his hand to attract Raynolds' attention. "I'm still waiting for a call back from a contact at the Met regarding intel and gossip concerning Penstone."

"Well, make sure the gossip has some solid proof to back it up. I don't want to go to court and find half our case is immediately labelled inadmissible." He took another mental head count. "Does anyone know where DCI Bashani has disappeared to?"

DS Thompson coughed. "He left a message with Dispatch, sir. He's in the process of gathering a statement from Marcus Swannick. Seems he wants to get some kind of a deal regarding tying Dillon Nichols to using the Uzi. There was also something about Swannick being prepared to provide corroborating evidence that linked others to Vic Carlton's role in planning and organising the blag. He said it might even lead to the person who supplied the weapons."

It didn't seem like much, but at this stage they couldn't afford to dismiss any possible source of fresh information.

Raynolds had looked testily at his watch. "Well, when he gets back, tell him I want a full progress report. Anything else from anyone? No? Okay everyone, carry on with your assignments."

Back in the present, Telford said, "Just had a phone call from the DCS. Can you and DI Fennick drop down to see him now? He's got something else for you to chase down." Then a little sheepishly he added, "When he's done briefing you, can you come up here and let me know what's going on? It's for the action log and the continuity files, you understand." It was clear Telford was uncomfortable about being left out of the loop for once, but was too professional to complain about it. Hansen nodded reassuringly.

"Don't worry, sir. DI Fennick and I will keep you updated as to whatever we've got coming next." Locking his workstation, Hansen went across and stood behind Fennick, who was still absorbed with the photographs and notes which now covered most of the boards.

Leaning forward to follow Fennick's line of sight, Hansen said, "They say the oracle at Delphi was so knowledgeable in her answers that they were often totally incomprehensible to the unenlightened petitioners."

Fennick continued to stare at the boards. Unperturbed, Hansen added, "The scholars also say she was probably off her face on home grown for most of the time as well."

Fennick finally cracked a smile. "Sadly, grasshopper, I can't seem to pinpoint what's making us both feel twitchy about all of this."

"I thought you were the one who didn't want to run any parallel investigation?"

"Maybe not parallel, but we could really do with some more pressure on Duffley. Get him on his own and see how he manages without his legal to shield him."

"We can always ask Raynolds for a second crack at him if you want? DI Telford says the DCS wants to talk to us, so we could ask him now? I think it's to do with some new developments."

"Sounds very cryptic. What's it about?"

"No idea. Jack didn't give anything away, except that Raynolds wants to see us now. Oh, and once we've been briefed, Jack said could we come back up and bring him up to speed as well?"

Fennick looked confused. "Curiouser and curiouser, said Alice..."

Then, with Hansen in tow, he headed towards the door. "Best not to keep the DCS, or Jack, waiting then."

9

Wednesday Evening

"Those who are about to die, we salute you."

Beside Hansen, Fennick grumbled, "You could at least wait until we find out what we've been stitched up with."

Hansen pursed his lips sceptically as they stopped outside the door to Raynolds' office and Fennick knocked sharply on the wooden surface.

From the other side came Raynolds' muffled voice. "Come!"

Half under his breath, Hansen said, "Our emperor awaits." Then grabbing the handle he opened the door and stepped aside to allow Fennick to enter first.

DCS Raynolds looked up from his desk then nodded towards several easy chairs by a low table. "Take a seat. I'll just be a minute or two."

As they settled into the chairs, Hansen smiled. It felt like being at the dentist's – unsure what was going to happen, but expecting an unpleasant experience all the same. Even the copies of the *Police Superintendents' Association* journals, placed neatly on the side table, looked well-thumbed and out of date.

Raynolds reassembled and tapped a sheaf of loose transcript pages back into their correct order, then looked up.

"It's the unofficial Duffley interview from this afternoon. You both did pretty well, considering."

Hansen grumbled, "We should've asked for his legal to be pulled as he was being deliberately obstructive."

Raynolds smiled. "Gordon Lemon can be an obnoxious twat when he wants to be, but you managed to shut him down and kept him in check long enough to get some useful information."

Fennick thought back to the interview.

Sitting at the Formica topped table, arrogantly rocking his chair back and forth, Duffley had been smugly confident and cocksure, even though he was still dressed in remand overalls.

His lawyer, Gary Lemon, was impeccably dressed in a dark blue pinstripe and silk tie.

As Fennick and Hansen had entered the interview room, Duffley had stopped rocking and sat up.

"Hello, new faces? You pair up from London?"

Immediately Lemon said, "Remember what I told you about only answering questions?"

Ignoring the two of them, Fennick had checked over the recording equipment, making sure it was functioning correctly, then started off with an official opening.

"Interview with Paul Duffley commenced at fourteen hundred hours. Those also present; DS Hansen, Mr. Duffley's legal advisor Mr. Lemon from Maplethorpe and Gittings, and myself, DI Fennick."

Across the table Lemon had unzipped a thin leather notecase and plucked a silver pen from his inside jacket pocket. Clearing his throat almost theatrically, he said, "I want to reiterate that my client has agreed to cooperate with enquiries regarding his enforced involvement with Mr. Lucumi and the late Mr. Tulio. This help is offered on the understanding he will not, himself, be liable to prosecution for any alleged infringements of the law which he may have inadvertently committed, up to the early termination of your operation."

Totally ignoring him, Hansen looked across at Duffley. "When and where did you first meet the two Colombians?"

"Over in Amsterdam. I was out there on a buying trip." Fennick made eye contact, as Duffley hurriedly continued, "I was after some Jamaican bush." He looked back at Hansen again. "Purely for personal consumption, you understand. I was in one of those nice Dutch coffee shops, sampling some potential purchases, when the tall one, Tulio started getting pally over a bottle of Tuborg."

Duffley sat back, holding his hands up, and Gordon Lemon came into the conversation once more.

"Again, I should point out that my client is cooperating of his own free will and without any caution being issued. It is his intention to help to the best of his ability, on the understanding that he is being viewed as an asset to any prosecutions which may arise from information he has in his possession."

Hansen glared at Lemon. "Rest assured, we are very appreciative of the fact your client is trying to cut a deal to save himself from prosecution. Especially as the end result of his actions – either directly or indirectly – led to the deaths of several people, one of whom was an undercover police officer."

Lemon retaliated sharply, his voice full of indignation.

"Let me also remind you, sergeant, that my client had nothing to do with any of those unfortunate deaths, and he was only at the scene under extreme duress, and fear for the lives of his wife and children!"

"When did you get married, Paul?" Fennick's question caused a momentary break in hostilities.

"What?" Duffley sounded confused.

"Married. When did you get married? There's nothing down here in your record, and no ring on your finger. So what's all this about a wife and kids?"

Duffley shrugged his shoulders. "Common law." Then a little more confidently, "Yeah. She's my common law wife."

Fennick looked across to Lemon. "When we're done here, perhaps you'd like to take your client to one side and explain to him about the common misconception regarding common law spouses." Then, to Duffley, he added. "It's a load of common law bollocks. It just doesn't exist, not even this far north."

Lemon seemed to back down a little. "Well, yes, technically that's true, but we can prove Mr. Duffley believed in its existence, and so he thought and felt about–"

He paused to consult several pages of notes, then carried on.

"About Tina-Marie Patterson as if they had been officially married. Not only from the responsibilities he has gladly taken upon himself, but also from the emotional aspects as well."

This time Hansen spoke up. "And part of this responsible and caring relationship was to go to Holland and set up a narcotics importation business?"

Duffley looked even more confused. He turned to Lemon. "What the fuck is all this about? I thought you said you'd already talked them into doing a deal?"

Before Lemon could answer, Fennick tapped the table to get Duffley's attention.

"There might well be a potential deal on offer, but I want to be sure the goods are real, and not some bullshit fantasy you've concocted in order to save your own sorry arse." Pre-empting Lemon again, he added, "And your legal team isn't helping by opening his mouth every two minutes, either."

Lemon flushed with anger, and jotted something down on his note pad, quickly closing the cover before Fennick or Hansen had time to read it.

"When we're done here I'm going to have words with DCS Raynolds about both of your attitudes. I'll also want a full and complete transcript, not some badly edited, biased highlights."

Fennick looked at him with a slight smile.

"What transcript? I haven't cautioned him, and I'm pretty sure Detective Sergeant Hansen hasn't cautioned him either."

Hansen silently shook his head.

Fennick continued, "All we're having is a nice little follow-up chat. I probably set the recording up out of habit, and I'm sure Mr. Duffley will admit it helps the flow of things not having my sergeant taking notes all the time."

Hansen silently smiled broadly at the two men across from them as Fennick continued.

"Right, you met Tulio in an Amsterdam weed shop. Then what happened?"

Duffley regained some of his composure but still seemed reticent.

"That's where things get a little hazy."

Hansen again. "Hazy? Seriously? This is starting to sound lot like a no-deal, isn't it."

Duffley was quick to try and placate him. "No, it's not like that. The point is, after a couple of the coffee shop's finest, some of my memories are a little bit confused."

"So you admit you were pissed and off your face?"

Lemon immediately jumped in.

"That's not what my client said at all! If you continue to take this obviously hostile line of questioning, then I will direct my client to remain silent until a new interview can be arranged."

Hansen looked calmly at Lemon. "I'm just trying to establish Mr. Duffley's mental state at the time this meeting allegedly took place. I'm pretty sure, as a member of the legal profession, I don't have to remind you that the legal team for the defence will seek to undermine and destroy Mr. Duffley's credibility as a witness. Usually with a spectacular show of cheap and tacky theatrics in front of a pre-arranged gathering of the press and media."

Fennick came in over the top of Lemon's silent indignation.

"Look, Paul, just tell us what you do remember, and we'll see where the problem areas lie, okay?"

The explanation seemed to relax Duffley. "Yeah. Well... After he'd introduced himself we had a couple of lagers, a little more smoke, then felt like a change of venue. So we moved off, found a regular bar, and had a couple more beers in there." He stopped and fumbled in his top pocket for his cigarettes, looked expectantly at Fennick and then at Hansen, before finally realising no one was going to let him smoke one.

Hansen picked up the questioning again. "Then what?"

Duffley looked across at him. "Then nothing. I suspect he slipped something into one of my beers, because that's all I remember about that night. The following morning I woke up with a killer of a headache, and no idea of how I'd managed to get back to my hotel." Again, an overly long pause, then: "The pair of them waited until after I'd got back to the UK before turning up at my place down in London. This time they said they knew all about Tina-Marie and the kids. Even showed me photographs of her dropping them off at school."

Switching again, Fennick said, "So they came to you with the deal. Why you?"

"I don't know. Maybe I'd said something to Tulio. Given him the wrong impression, or something like that."

Fennick persisted. "They must have known something about you before they made their approach." He paused long enough for Duffley to think, before continuing, "Had they done business with Ren Penstone before?"

Lemon sprang to life.

"My client's just told you they contacted him directly. Who these two worked for in the past is irrelevant to this particular investigation, so can we stop all this pointless fishing? Mr. Duffley stated the two Colombian dealers approached him, and under severe duress he agreed to help front their operation. They came to him directly."

Fennick glared angrily at Lemon, his voice icy calm as he held his own anger in check. "I will not tell you again. One more interruption and I will take the greatest of pleasures in having you removed."

Duffley leaned forward, fingernails nervously tapping against the Formica table top. "They came to me with a complete package deal. They'd supply the gear, I'd front the initial deals, and they would pick up the profit. I believe they had connections over in Colombia who are trying to beat the recession by cutting out the middle men and dealing direct."

Hansen picked up the switch again. "So why come up here when you could have worked those filthy rich Southerners, down in the likes of Essex or London?"

Duffley grunted contemptuously. "And go stepping on someone else's business? I don't know what it's like out here in the sticks, but personally I make it a rule not to shit in my own nest. There's some fucking hard bastards down south, in case you lot hadn't noticed. I figured I could set things up for the Colombians, then let the bastards fend for themselves."

"So how was the gear being brought in?"

Duffley folded his arms, the smug smile back in place. "Well, before we go any further, I want my guarantees, in writing, that I'm safe from prosecution in regard to my involvement in the whole business."

In an exasperated whisper Lemon corrected him. "*Forced.* In regard to your *forced* involvement."

Duffley continued, "Yeah, my forced involvement. I want a safe house and protection before, during, and after the trial." Then, as an afterthought, he added, "And also for the wife and kids as well."

"And for all that you give us Lucumi and his dead partner?" Fennick made a derisive sound and Duffley looked at him sharply.

"No. For all of that, I'm prepared to give you not only Lucumi and Tulio, but also the cartel connections and their supply route into the UK. But only after I get the assurances and I'm happy with the security arrangements."

They had terminated the interview there, thankfully before Lemon started to fuss around Duffley like a mother hen protecting her prize chick. Hansen had collected the recordings, sealed them both in front of Lemon, and had made him sign and initial the release paperwork before handing him his copy.

Although officially inadmissible, the other copy of the recording had been passed up to the Op Gold Dust team to be properly logged, transcribed and indexed. As an intel source the rest of the investigation team could access it to gather further evidence if they needed to, rather than using it as evidence itself.

Fennick looked at the clock on the wall behind Raynolds. Nearly twenty four hours since Raynolds had held the first briefing. With Duffley prepared to give evidence once assurances had been issued from those on high – well, higher than Raynolds, anyway – and the still silent Lucumi safely locked down in remand, Fennick had hoped the meeting was going to be Raynolds' way of saying 'thank you for your time and help, gentlemen, but the regulars can take over now.'

There was still the inevitable interview with the beloved IPCC to contend with, but neither he, nor Hansen, had anything sensational to report. Cooke had been killed in the line of duty, albeit whilst undercover, and there was no way anyone could have foreseen his death.

As hardnosed as it might seem, shit happened. You didn't have to like it, but if you dwelt on it for too long then you ended up going insane.

Anyway, he could always talk to the IPCC rep when he was back on his own patch. Maybe he'd even take a couple of days leave before getting back to the joys of Molly Sugden. Maybe an extended long weekend? Go somewhere nice with Jan. that would certainly help take her mind off the way her business had been going of late.

Raynolds finally put the paperwork back down on his desk. In a tired voice he said, "It seems one of our witnesses was murdered this afternoon."

*

Mikka lay on her back, wrapped up in her sleeping bag, looking up at the dim outline of the roofing joists. Her mind was buzzing and sleep wouldn't come until she'd chilled a little. The other two were already asleep. Mousey, with his toy beside him on his pillow. Jason starting to softly snore, until he rolled back onto his side again. Beneath her back, the flooring was cushioned with layers of old blankets and duvets, and there was no denying Jason had done a really good job in fixing up the squat. Not only had he worked things out so they could come and go unnoticed, but he was also good at fixing the electricity and the water. It was one of the reasons they stayed together as a group.

The squat was in the middle of an abandoned row of terraced houses, which had once been part of a council estate during the Seventies. Finally it had been sold to various Housing Associations, who had then rented them back to the council until several of the streets had been earmarked for redevelopment. Then the tenants had been moved out. The proposed demolition and clearance was something Mikka had found out about through reading the notices stuck on the plywood boards covering the downstairs windows.

She switched on the old table lamp beside her, blinking as the energy saving bulb flickered, steadied, then started to glow a little brighter. With a pair of wire cutters, a couple of screwdrivers and some rubber gloves for protection, Jason had been able to get into the electrical supply. Having electricity meant luxuries such as hot water, heating, and carefully shaded light. In her previous squat she'd had to make do with smoky little fires and lifting batteries for the torch she'd used to read by. All in all, the old squat had been pretty shitty. Plus there had been too many junkies using it – leaving needles and other drug crap around. She'd been looking for somewhere cleaner when, by chance, she'd spotted Jason wriggling his way into the house through one of the supposedly boarded up back doors.

She had sussed the trick with the boards, but once inside she'd been unable to find any sign that someone had been living there at all. It was as if he'd simply vanished. So she'd waited, quietly searching the ground floor, then the bedrooms, until she heard a faint creaking of the rafters above her head. Jason was holed up in the attic, not the most obvious place for a squatter to take refuge.

She'd made herself as comfortable as possible and just waited. Early the next morning he'd opened the trap door in the landing ceiling, dropped down a little aluminium ladder, and had been on his way out when she had called after him, scaring him shitless in the process.

He'd tried to bluff it, but had given up once she'd pointed out the advantages of them working together as a team. When Mousey had appeared, it'd been easier to take him into the 'family' than try to drive him away. In some respects, three was always going to be more of a liability than two, but Mousey had proved himself a dab hand at nicking, and quick on his feet as well. And with the three of them safely up in the loft, they had a pretty secure hideaway. Perfect for when the security company thugs came checking for tramps, junkies and squatters. For their own protection they made doubly sure they left nothing outside the attic, and so far they'd remained undiscovered.

That was now the least of her worries. What they'd seen happen in the car park couldn't be pushed aside and forgotten. Not only had they witnessed the drug dealer helplessly gasping and choking his life away, they'd also clearly seen the face of the man who'd killed him in such a sadistic and vicious way. She tried not to think about his face, but it was still so vivid in her memory, she felt she could reach out and touch every feature of it. Anything to distract her from the calculating hatred she had seen in his eyes.

Then, when he'd stepped out of the car, everything around her had seemed to stop – as if some soundproof bubble had dropped from the sky and had trapped them within its transparent walls. It had lasted seconds at best. Then, in an adrenaline fuelled surge, the three of them had scattered in different directions, running around and behind the rows of parked cars, or in Mousey's case, actually rolling under some of the 4 x 4's to try and confuse the killer. But when she had looked back she'd seen the man still standing by the dealer's car, just looking at them running away – though it had seemed he was looking directly at her.

By the time she'd made her way back to the squat, she found the other two had somehow managed to beat her to it. Jason had even stopped off and bought a couple of fish suppers from a nearby chippy. He had left hers still wrapped, sharing his own with Mousey before the kid went to sleep.

She listened to the wind and the rain outside, and wondered if she knew the killer. He hadn't looked familiar, and she was pretty good at recognising faces, but every time she pictured him she felt a cold wave of hatred from his intense gaze. Best thing to do was to get some sleep. It was going to be an early start tomorrow, and they'd need to be ready for anything. She turned out the light and pushed herself further down into her sleeping bag, thinking about what Jason had said earlier.

"If we could find out who the dealer was then we could probably find out where his crib is at. After the Babylon have been over it, we could see if there's anything in it for us, couldn't we?"

He'd said it half as a question, half a statement, looking for her approval that his idea was a good one. He'd figured they'd be the first to know about the murder, so they'd be in with a chance to raid his place. The police would pick up any gear, stolen goods, large amounts of cash – that sort of thing – but the three of them would only be after stuff they could easily sell on, or use themselves. Anything easy to lift, which wouldn't attract attention when it came to selling the stuff on.

There were some people who ran stalls down the local market. They were always good if you needed to sell something on the quiet. Any iPods, mobile phones, PDAs, even netbooks or the odd bit of respectable bling. They were okay for fag money, but they always got a bit sus when it came to bigger stuff.

"How do we find out where his crib is?" Mikka asked.

Jason grinned.

"Easy! DJ DefNin knows everyone. He's the resident at Club De La Paradise, and won't come off the turntables until gone five tomorrow morning. Then he drops by a smoke shop to chill for a while before getting some sleep. If anyone knows the dealer and his car, it'll be DefNin."

"And he'll know where the crib is?"

"If he don't then he'll know a bro' who does."

An element of concern crept into her voice. "How many people need to know we're interested? I don't want every fucker finding out what we're up to and come looking for a piece."

"DefNin's good! Me and him go back a ways."

She looked hard at Jason. He seemed genuine. At least, not like when he was bragging and trying to big it up for the sake of it.

"Okay, but I don't want any of us being left behind if anything goes wrong."

She rolled over onto her side and relaxed a little more. They weren't committed to anything yet, and they didn't have anyone pushing at them for money or stuff. Some of the 'steal-to-order' dickheads got the shit kicked out of them if they turned up with the wrong stuff. Doing it this way, if she didn't like the look of things then she could pull out straight away, which was just the way she liked it. Closing her eyes she pulled the pillow more towards her and started drifting off to sleep. Tomorrow morning was going to come soon enough.

*

Chief Inspector Bashani pushed himself away from his desk and blinked the cramp out of his eyes.

Looking at computer screens for too long is dangerous. Sends you blind, or something. Or is that the Internet?

Whatever, he was thankful he'd finished typing in Swannick's statement. The WPC had taken it down as Bashani guided him away from digressions and lapses into street patois. Even so, he would have words with her regarding the amount of "innits" she'd included, and what looked like a totally spurious "Respect to the righteous, bro." Then again, she had reminded Swannick of his rights before they'd started, which made the interview official and the statement a matter of record – something which he'd forgotten to do himself.

Not that Swannick had revealed anything of Earth shattering importance to the case. He had, at least, successfully put Dillon Nichols in the frame for handling the Uzi, even stating that he'd seen Dillon drop it and kick it as far away from him as he could. There was also some information about Vic Carlton supplying the weapons, but it wasn't a subject Swannick was prepared to be pushed on.

"So, going back to the time Vic turned up with the firearms. You say he just walked into the pub with a couple of old Nike sports bags. He gives one to you and the other to Dillon, before leaving the two of you to sort yourselves out?"

"That's about it, man. It was a real bad nasty, me walking through the streets carrying."

"He didn't happen to say where they came from?"

Swannick looked at him incredulously.

"I think he said they came from parts given away free with some fucking monthly magazines. What the fuck do you think!"

"No need to get sarcastic."

"Look, he told us to meet him in the Brickmaker's Arms, the one halfway down Canterville Road – near the Tricorn estate. Man, I known some no-go areas in my time, but…"

Bashani managed to hold himself in check. The sooner he had something worthwhile, the sooner he could get back to the station and a more familiar comfort zone. Swannick carried on talking.

"So Dillon and me we turn up at the pub, like Vic told us to. He walks in a few minutes later carrying the two green sports bags. He dumps them on us, says we got to take care of them as he's only got them on loan and they got to go back in good condition." Swannick paused and tried to do an imitation of Vic Carlton. "'So no messin' about wiv 'em, you slags.' All very *Life on Mars*. Me and guns, man? I tell you, I know which end to hold, and which end to avoid, and that is it. Even when I got it back to my crib I didn't even take the thing out to look at it."

Ramesh changed his line of questioning. "So who set you up with the cars?"

"Ah, the wheels. We had to supply our own. Vic said we were to go to the hotel separately, so if we needed to get out quick we weren't going to be all jammed into one car. Ha! Dillon turned up in a window cleaner's van, ladder and sign on the side. Vic went nuts, but Dil said it would blend in with traffic and stuff. Pity we didn't get a chance to find out."

"And you didn't think to ask Vic why there would be a need to get away from the hotel quickly?"

Swannick tried to shrug his shoulders, but the movement made him wince. "You know Vic. Once you'd agreed to a job, you just went along with whatever he said. You can take a lot of crap for five grand."

"Is that what Vic offered the pair of you for the job – five thousand?"

Swannick smiled a little. "Are you taking the piss? It was five grand a piece."

The sound of a telephone several desks away broke Bashani's thoughts. He stacked up the handwritten pages, rechecked all had been initialled and dated by both Swannick and the WPC, then looked for Jack Telford. Jack was busy talking to Mike Fennick's sergeant, but Bashani decided he could wait until Jack was free – it helped eat up the time before he clocked off for the day. Back to Mrs. Bashani, and the nest of vipers she seemed to surround herself with these days. Committee group meetings for this and committee group meetings for that. He'd tried his best to be interested, but now, every time he smiled, he thought it felt more and more like some kind of deathly rictus.

Why couldn't he, for once, simply go home and relax? Was it any wonder, of late, he seemed to look forward more and more to the morning commute into work? At least then his time was almost his own. It was supposed to get easier once your children had left for university. Yet even with one at UMIST and the other studying up in Scotland, they never seemed to be out of the house from one bloody week to the next.

Absently he picked up his smartphone, brought up the Internet connection, then logged into a horseracing website. It carried a variety of results and news feeds from around the world, and often streamed video of the races as well. Several pundits blogged what they thought were informed comments on the form and potential of runners and riders. There was also a 'members only' login facility, which also linked him to various bookmakers' sites, for the betting side of the organisation. Not that he could still afford to play. Well, not after the losses he'd managed to rack up last month. Thankfully there was a debt limit on the website. And, after a bit of creative juggling, he'd been able to squeeze the last few drops of blood from a couple of credit card accounts which Mrs Bashani thankfully had no knowledge of. He looked longingly at the screen. Dubai and the Australian tracks would be opening in a short while....

Another glance around the Incident Room and he saw that Jack Telford had finally gone back to his desk. No doubt Mr Efficiency was keying something into the system – probably a memo or an e-mail to everyone, no doubt with the updated Action Log attached.

The following Actions are still outstanding....

Whatever it was, Telford was getting into the emotional swing of it, and it looked like he was trying to hammer the keys through the desk.

There was also Mike Fennick and that sergeant of his – Hansen – muttering away as they headed for the door. Damnit! He'd wanted to get Mike to one side for a bit of a quiet chat. He was still curious as to why Fennick had transferred out of the Hertfordshire force.

As he remembered it, there had been something about a particularly tense and shitty investigation, which had finally topped it for Mike. Vague memories about a child being brutally killed and Mike letting his guard down. To the point here he'd become too emotionally involved. Or something like that. Ramesh had already been on the point of moving up North at the time, so had never followed it up. Still, he was curious to know what the final outcome had been. Obviously the whole business hadn't been too detrimental to Mike's career.

But that would have to wait for another time as Jack Telford had finally finished battering the keyboard and was nose-deep in a thick file of papers. Gathering up Swannick's statement, Bashani called out.

"Jack?"

At the sound of his name Telford hurriedly closed the file and clicked a protective screen saver into action. As he turned around, Jack reminded Bashani of a schoolboy, caught in the act of doing something and desperately trying to cover up his embarrassment.

"Yes?"

"Hope I'm not disturbing you?"

Telford shook his head. With no explanation offered, Bashani continued, "I've put the Marcus Swannick statement into the system. It's still in the draft queue. Could you get someone to proof it and then release it for me? I'll let his nibs know the files are about to be updated. He'll probably want to have a look at it before he does the final team brief this evening." He walked over and tossed the sheaf of handwritten pages into Jack's pending tray.

He was about to walk away when Telford saw a chance to take control of the conversation. "DI Fennick and DS Hansen have just gone down to see him. He's assigning them to another case."

"Another?"

"As far as I know it's another one."

Bashani looked at him questioningly, but Telford wasn't forthcoming with any details. It was the way some of the office managers were. As quirky as a bloody squirrel, forever keeping little nuts of information tentatively out of reach. You had to make an effort to tease it out of them bit by bit, and Ramesh didn't feel like going through the ritual, especially when he was more than likely going to hear all about it tomorrow morning.

Not to be outdone, Telford said, "Are you going to be at this evening's briefing? The DCS was more than a little pissed off when he found out you'd gone off to interview Swannick."

Bashani felt his jaw compress tightly. *One day, you smug little bastard.* But he kept the thought to himself.

"I don't think so, Jack. What with the Gold Dust hours already well into the red, overtime-wise, and the need to show restraint in regard to expenses and personal claims, I'm officially going off the clock as of now. We all have to be responsible people, Jack, and that includes taking time to de-stress. Please pass on my apologies, with my reasons, and you can give me a quick five minute update in the morning. Goodnight, Jack."

He turned and started to walk towards the door. Mrs. Bashani would be at her book reading club before he got home, and that also helped to put a spring in his step. There was also the little ultrabook he'd bought himself the day after Mrs. Bashani had come back from one of her many night classes. She had proudly shown him how she could now go to the family computer and see where the children had been surfing on the internet....

Jack Telford managed to wait until Bashani had closed the Incident Room door behind him before he started to vocalise an uncharacteristic stream of expletives.

10

"You're not telling us someone's already got to Paul Duffley, are you, Sir?" In the confines of DCS Raynolds' office, Fennick's voice sounded a little surprised.

Raynolds shook his head. "Jack didn't hint at anything like that, did he?"

"No, he said once we're done here we should go back up and brief him as to what this is all about."

"Well, he got that bit right at least." Raynolds picked up a buff coloured folder, then came round and handed the file to Fennick.

"These are the Community Support Police notes and preliminary reports on the murder of Gary Tang. It happened this afternoon." He sat down behind his desk again, visibly more comfortable once his familiar barrier back in place.

"It was a couple of CSP officers, out on a general foot patrol, who found Tang around three this afternoon. He was in the Arkendale shopping centre car park, still sitting in his car. Someone had put a large tiewrap around his neck and the headrest support poles, then pulled it extra tight, as you'll see from the initial crime scene photographs." He nodded at the folder in Fennick's hands.

Fennick left the folder closed. "I'll study them later, sir, if you don't mind?"

"Suit yourself. But it was a deliberately fatal attack, rather than a prolonged torture session."

Fennick felt Hansen nudge his arm, then take the folder. Raynolds waited while Hansen examined the top photograph. It had been taken from outside Gary Tang's Volvo, the driver's door open to give the photographer better access to the body. Hansen looked a little annoyed.

"Either someone doesn't know about Vic Carlton, or someone's paying homage to the bastard."

Raynolds slid himself deeper into his office chair. "Forensics were not impressed to hear that the CSP bods had touched the body, searching for some kind of ID. They found his wallet and driving licence, but they also found that Tang was carrying enough Class A and B narcotics to put half a dozen people into orbit. Judging by the amount they found, the general consensus is none of it was touched after the killing. Still, with everything else going on, I don't want anything discarded without proper consideration, which is why I want the pair of you to pick this up and sort it out as fast as you can."

Fennick looked confused but Raynolds continued.

"Primarily I want you to find out who killed the little bastard, but I also want to know if his death has anything to do with the Gold Dust investigation. For all we know it could just be some sort of screwed up revenge killing we can put down to coincidence." Looking over to Hansen, he added, "I'm like you, sergeant. There's something about the choice of murder weapon which makes me wonder. Plus, Tang was the informer who helped set up Duffley and the Colombians. Before I divert any more time and manpower to it, I want to be sure where his death fits in with the grand scheme of things. Is it a revenge killing for being part of an undercover operation? Or is it just one of his deals gone totally wrong? I just hope this doesn't turn out to be the start of some kind of turf war."

Fennick took the case file back from Hansen.

"What's immediately available? It's a big shopping centre, with an equally large car park. I take it uniform have done the rounds and already collected any CCTV?"

Raynolds shook his head. "What little they brought back looks to be a waste of time. The contractors skimped on the external coverage, and when they did put some in, they placed the cameras too high up on poles. Add to that the wind and poor weather, and the result is that the picture quality is utter crap. The best we've got is an indistinct figure who moves in from behind the camera, and leave in the opposite direction, keeping their back towards the lens all the time. We don't even get a clear shot when the killer pops the locks on the car. What we do get, however, are some obvious witnesses, or very good potential witnesses at least. After the killer gets into the back of Tang's car, the next people in shot are Gary Tang, who looks like he's being chased by a further two, or possibly three, people. Again, the quality of the material is disgusting and wouldn't stand up as evidence. The only reason we know it's Tang is because he gets into the car and doesn't come out again. There's a possibility some of the cameras inside the centre managed to get something worthwhile, but it's going to take time."

Fennick looked up. "And we can call on the Gold Dust resources to help?"

Raynolds shook his head slightly. "Sadly no, not unless there are obvious overlaps. You should be able to pull an updated copy of Tang's file from the system, and you'll be kept in the briefing loop, but apart from that, you're on your own." As an afterthought he added "I'll tell CI Bashani and DCI Sugden the two of you have been re-tasked for the time being."

Fennick went through the mental check list he used whenever he was duty officer and found himself being called out. Background he could get from the Gold Dust files and the forensics team would be busy with the materials. Scene of crime management would still be in the process of bagging and indexing evidence and certainly wouldn't welcome any intrusions this early on. No requirement for any house to house or statement gathering just yet – maybe talk to the Gold Dust PR team and see if there was a chance of a thirty second appeal on the local TV and radio, on the grounds that it might just be connected after all.

Nodding to himself Fennick said, "Provided I'm not missing anything, then I'm pretty sure there's nothing for us to do at present, except let the others finish off. We can pick it all up in the morning. It'll give the pair of us a chance to view the scene of crime footage with a fresh mind." Looking over at Raynolds, he added, "When do you want to be briefed on our progress, sir?"

"If it's anything important let me know as soon as it happens, otherwise it would probably be best to update me prior to the Gold Dust briefings. If you do find a connection, even if it seems tenuous, then I want to be able to follow it through into the other investigation without too much hassle."

At that, Hansen and Fennick stood up. Fennick said, "If there's nothing else, sir, then we'll make a start into it tomorrow morning."

"Fine," and Raynolds was already reaching for another folder off his pile before the two of them had finally left his office.

*

Eddie made a conscious effort to stop grinding his teeth. He knew he'd be the first to admit it – the way things had been set up wasn't perfect.

But needs must when the Devil drives.

That was something his dad always used to say a lot, before he finally pissed off and left them for good.

As it was, Eddie was already regretting using the Mondeo. During the afternoon he'd had one white van wanker cut him up on a roundabout, and another had nearly rear ended him when he'd stopped at some lights, instead of shooting through on amber.

Cookie had signed out the unmarked vehicle as their unofficial safety net. It wasn't anything special, just a nondescript Mondeo with a tasty two-point-five litre engine under the bonnet. They'd taken the precaution of renting a garage in a block near to the Tricorn and Jervis estates; both had rough reputation, but nothing radically drastic. The pair of them had made sure they'd only used the car when they were out on surveillance. If anyone had any reason to check the plates then they would see it was registered to the Greater Manchester force for covert operations, and would leave it alone.

After he'd left the Cat & Fiddle he'd caught a bus heading back towards his flat, but halfway there he'd changed his mind, and decided to go for the unmarked. They were going to be calling him about it soon, anyway, so why not make the most of it? Except, when the second bus had been held up in traffic, the wiz had made him more than a bit sparky – to the point where he finally realised he was starting to freak some of the other passengers. Luckily the Tricorn estate was only a couple more stops away, so Eddie got off the bus and, despite the drizzling rain, jogged the remaining distance. It was also the quickest way he knew for him to pick up a little Jamaican Bush, and after a few good puffs it had taken the edge off just enough to keep him buzzed up, but more chilled with it, so he could focus himself more.

He'd stayed on the Tricorn estate for an hour or so, chatting to some of the local scrotes he knew, then phoning around some more, all the time knowing he had to go cautiously and not sound too eager. The trouble was, nobody seemed prepared to talk. Word was that supplies of quality gear were going to be drying up and dealers were telling their users to start stocking up, else they'd end up having to go sick. No one seemed to know who had recent dealings with Vic Carlton, and even the offers of money didn't get him any nearer to finding out. He figured he could probably get a name eventually, but despite another good blunt of Bush, there seemed to be way too much uncontrollable stress building up inside him. Not just from the meth, either.

He'd driven around several more old haunts, leaving messages and getting no results, but come the evening he felt he had to go somewhere to cool down otherwise he'd totally lose it. Parking up a side street, he backtracked on foot until he'd found the Cat & Fiddle.

The evening bar staff were standing around waiting – the lull before the night started to pick up. He got a pint of lager, then did a quick check of the ground floor, trying not to attract suspicion from people who were habitually suspicious of everyone.

Seeing a free table near the fruit machines, he picked up his pint and headed over to it, collecting an abandoned newspaper off a nearby table as he went. Settling down, he kicked his chair back a little and flicked open the local rag. On one page was a photo of a middle-aged yokel from the sticks, standing in front of some lake, smiling inanely and cradling a fucking ugly looking fish in his arms. The other page was taken up with some advert for a supermarket, offering the two-for-one deals on stacked up cases of beer and lager. Eddie brought his free hand up to his mouth and absently licked the top of his index finger, making it look like he was about to turn a page. Instead he discretely slid his hand into the side pocket of his jacket. The little Ziploc bag of wiz was easy enough to locate and open one-handed. Then all he had to do was carefully dab his wet fingertip into a little of the powder.

Just a booster. Something to keep him going until he'd sorted things out proper. Anyway, he always thought better whenever he had a little bit of a buzz on.

The powder felt gritty as he licked it off and pushed as much of it as he could down between his cheek and gum. Slow release. Like those anti-smoking nicotine lozenges. Automatically he picked up his pint and gave it a quick swirl to bring the head back to life, swallowed a mouthful then realised he'd washed the crystal meth down his throat as well. Ah, what the hell. Wait a moment to feel it kick in, then do what he had to. Today was turning out to be one for making life-changing decisions.

Folding the paper, he tossed it onto another table, then took out his phone and popped the back off it. From another pocket he took the small plastic box he kept his collection of SIM cards in. He'd made a point of going by the Sealy Street shopping arcade and picking up a fresh one. New account. New number. Simone wouldn't have it blocked and would probably answer when Eddie called her. He still had some unfinished business to deal with, but once those few problems were sorted then he would be free of it all. Whether Simone wanted to come along with him, or not, was another matter. If she did then fine. If not, then he'd be off and away, regardless.

Eddie snapped the phone back together again, then caught the barman looking at him from behind the bar.

Oh God no. Don't let the bastard finally sus me out. Not now. Not when things are getting close.

Staring back at him, it was the barman who finally broke eye contact and went back to serving the slow but steady stream of customers.

Maybe it was time for Sean to be killed off? Find a new local, and a new persona?

He picked up his glass and moved to one of the deserted tables at the back of the pub, where it was more quiet. Time to phone Simone, then get the fuck out of the place for good. It rang several times before she picked up.

"Hello?"

God it was good to hear her voice! Trying to calm down, he said, "Hi. It's me." He desperately wanted to add *Don't hang up, please!* but was afraid he might break down and embarrass himself. In the Cat & Fiddle you never showed any sign of weakness.

In his ear Simone sighed. "Eddie. Should have guessed it was you."

"Hi Babe." He paused to make sure she was still on the line. "Look, I know you're really pissed off with me at the moment."

"At the moment?! Christ, Eddie, what bloody planet are you on?"

Shutting his eyes for a second he tried to calm down as much as the meth would let him. "Look, I'm calling to tell you I'm finally quitting."

"What?"

"Quitting. I'm finally jacking it in. I'm going to ask about a transfer over to another section. You were right, Babe. It's got nothing for me anymore." Absently he took out his plastic cigarette lighter and started to rhythmically tap it on the table top.

"You really mean that, Eddie?"

"Sure I do, Babe." *Well, at this moment in time. Later on, when I've been able to sort some things out...* "Look, I've had a real chance to think about what I want to do, you know? Tony getting killed made me realise –"

Simone broke in over the top of him. "Tony's dead?" Her voice was a mixture of shock, surprise and disbelief. "When?"

"Yesterday afternoon. Wasn't it on the news?"

"I've not seen any for days. Last time I looked it was all job losses, government scandals and somebody's troops getting killed. After a while I realised I was just sitting there, watching the pictures go by."

Eddie could feel his pulse pick up as he mentally relived the incident in the car park, caught up in a wave of frustration at the way he'd lost control of his life of late. Tony being killed felt to Eddie like the ultimate bad luck scenario had started to come true. Before then, each operation had been wild. A real, serious buzz and rush. They knew the chances they took, but you didn't get big results from just pulling in the bottom feeders. You had to get further up the food chain where the smarter boys were. Simone didn't seem to realise that was the way the job worked. When they'd first met, she thought it had just been bravado and show – bigging it up for the ladies. Even though she'd loved the excitement of it, at first, she still thought it was something that would disappear in time.

As he wiped his sweaty palm on his jeans, he heard Simone say, "Eddie? You still there?"

His reply sounded distant and distracted.

"We were in the process of finishing off an assignment. We had to show them we were the real deal, otherwise they wouldn't have been taken in and our cover would have been blown."

"Eddie? You okay?"

"They hijacked us in the car park, Babe. We were crossed up before we started. Three got killed." Eddie smiled a little wistfully. "Two of them to one of us."

He was silent for a moment, listening to Simone's breathing in his ear and thinking about the Colombian pushing Tony's body to the tarmac. In slow motion, Eddie saw him falling face down onto the roadway, the black handle of the knife clearly sticking out of his back.

"Tony was unavoidable collateral, Babe."

"What are you talking about, Eddie?" Her voice sounded worried. Maybe a little scared. "Are you saying Tony's death wasn't an accident?"

Eddie looked across the pub and stared hard at the back of the landlord's head, intently watching as the landlord gave one of the bar staff a bollocking for something.

"Well, if we'd played it a little different, Babe, perhaps Tony wouldn't have been knifed. Maybe, if he had offered to stay with the bastard Colombian in the hotel room. Or if we'd put the cash in one of the hotel night safes, rather than going down to collect it from the car..." His voice trailed off into silence again.

Over the phone he heard Simone hand stifle an emotional sob.

"Listen to yourself, Eddie. You're starting to do it again." There was a distinct tone of accusation. "You're talking as if this kind of thing happened all the time."

He was about to say *'It's all part of the undercover life'* but held it back. That'd been one of his automatic comments that'd always really pissed her off. That was the last thing he wanted. But, before he could defend himself, Simone asked:

"Has anyone told his parents yet? He said they were moving to Southern Ireland – last week, or the week before."

"I don't know." Eddie knew nothing about Tony's parents – moving or otherwise. "Who told you they were moving, anyway?"

A short hesitation, then, "Tony did. A while back."

The meth was really starting to buzz in his system. Unconsciously he began to nod his head slightly and tap his foot to the fast music coming from the CD jukebox. A steady stream of street talking gangsta rap vocals were now underscoring their conversation.

"When did you see Tony? He didn't tell me he'd been around to see you?"

"What? Look, what's it got to do with you whether or not I see –" She corrected herself "Whether I saw Tony or not? We're not married Eddie. We lived together for a time, that's all. Only you just couldn't leave your bloody fantasies, could you? You prefer them to being with me in the real world, don't you?"

She stopped for a moment, her outburst angrier than she'd intended, and it made her realise that not all her anger was actually caused by Eddie. In the background she heard the rap song finish, then the sound of glasses clinking and the fruit machine sing-song mixed in with general pub talk.

Then the jukebox started up again – one of those rock anthem things. What was it Eddie called them? Power ballads? So typical.

In a slightly trembling voice, Eddie said, "Babe?"

Even though she'd known it was coming, the nickname had always made her cringe inside. It was all so Posh'n'Becks. All so media celebrity unreal. All so bloody Eddie Caradine.

"Eddie, if you're really serious; if you really are going to transfer to something with better promotional prospects, then maybe I'll consider us getting together again. You've got to grow up. Stop all this running around and take some responsibility, Eddie. You've got to show me you're prepared to work on our relationship. I don't want someone who just turns up for sex and a cup of tea before going off to play cops and robbers again."

Eddie's turn to be silent. Then, "I mean it about transferring, Babe." When had Tony told her about his parents moving? "You mean the world to me, you know that?" No, not when. Why? Why her and not him?

"Then treat me with a little respect, Eddie. Remember the last time? You ended up hitting me, Eddie."

"I know. I've been sorry ever since." *But you provoked me into doing it, though.* "Look, I want to make a proper apology. Can we meet up somewhere? I'll buy you dinner – some place nice. You pick the restaurant. On me. Price no object." He could hear himself starting to sound a little pleading – like a puppy, eager to please, but not entirely sure what to do – and immediately hated himself for being that way.

But Simone held off.

"I don't know. I'll need some time to think about it. I'm not a kid any more, Eddie. I want security, a place of our own somewhere, and a proper life. I don't want to be always watching the news and wondering if you're coming home, or lying dead somewhere."

Eddie chewed at his bottom lip.

"Okay. Tomorrow would be fine, if you like? Or any evening this week would, if that's any good?"

"Like I said, Eddie. Give me time to think things over first, then I'll call you. But I mean it, Eddie. I still need some space to be on my own. I don't want you pestering me with calls and asking me if I've come to a decision yet."

"Okay, Babe. Whatever you want is fine by me." He broke the connection, his mind still focussing on Tony and Simone. Perhaps it'd been the other way round? Had she gone to him? That must be it. Tony was his partner. They did everything together. Their lives even depended on each other. There was no way Tony would have gone to Simone without asking Eddie first.

As he sneaked another fingertip lick, the song on the jukebox changed to an American police siren, overlaid with someone saying:

"Before I pass sentence, have you anything to say in your defence?"

Then the guitars broke loose and the lead singer screamed from the speakers:

"She calls herself Madonna!

Ya Honour!

An' she's the sexiest whore in L.A!"

*

The dashboard clock glowed 20:35 as Fennick parked up into their residents designated parking bay. The brick exterior of the converted warehouse still managed to maintain an austere Victorian industrial appearance, regardless of the season. The harsh sodium lighting didn't help soften the image either. He sat for a moment watching the windscreen become smothered in rain. According to the forecaster on the radio, the wet weather had settled in for the night. Relentlessly steady, at least the drains were coping with it all. He breathed slowly several times, trying to unwind a little before heading up to the flat.

When Hansen and Fennick had finished their meeting with Raynolds, both had gone back up to the incident room to be greeted by an obviously annoyed Jack Telford.

"I saw the new links in the Gold Dust database suddenly appear out of nowhere. As if I haven't got enough to fucking keep track at the moment. I take it you two have now been moved over to this Tang investigation?"

Hansen took the folder over to Telford's desk. "Certainly looks that way. Here's the preliminary reports, plus some pictures from the scene."

Telford looked expectantly across at Fennick settling himself at his desk. When he saw Fennick start typing, Telford made a tutting sound in the back of his throat, then looked up at Hansen.

"Perhaps you'd like to give me a bloody verbal brief then."

"Don't worry. When he gets involved with something new he's not always so good at vocalising."

Telford sniffed.

"So I've heard." Then, in a slightly more appeased tone, "What's all this Tang business about then?"

Hansen recounted what they'd been told by Raynolds, which didn't actually amount to much.

"The initial informant, Gary Tang, was found dead behind the wheel of his car by a couple of CPS. It was parked in the Arkendale shopping centre, and someone had choked him to death with a white plastic tie wrap."

"You're kidding me." Telford sounded surprised.

"Wish I was. Trouble is, the CPS handled the body trying to find a wallet or something to identify the guy, so they may well have screwed up a load of trace evidence. Forensics have taken samples in order to rule out as much of the CPS as they can, but it's still going to hamper things."

"I'll bet. Well, it obviously wasn't Tiewrap Teddy. Have they got any clue as to who might've actually done it?"

"They're still going through video from the scene, but most of it's crap quality, even after the techies have messed around with it. The only thing anyone's sure is that Gary Tang had been running from two, maybe three people. It may all be connected, or it may not. The killer had already jacked the locks on his car and had been waiting for him."

"Sounds like another dealer to me. Those bastards are forever trying to get rid of the competition."

Hansen frowned. "Don't think it's that simple. Tang was still carrying all his merchandise when the CPS found him. Another dealer would've cleaned him out after killing him. Anyway, it could turn out that the chasers are unconnected. Hopefully the SOCO should have put together a more detailed report by tomorrow morning. You never know, they might actually come up with something that'll be worth following up on."

Telford seemed to be a little more placated. "Okay, I'll set up a sub-set under the Gold Dust header in HOLMES2, link it up to Medusa via the Airwaves firewall, so you can access everything externally as well."

Cautiously, Hansen said, "The DCS isn't sure if this is actually connected to Gold Dust or not. As we've been tasked to see if we can prove something either way. We caught it because he thinks it might distract the main investigation if the whole team were involved."

Telford smiled conspiratorially. "I wouldn't worry about that. I'll create a secondary entry under the header, and if it proves to be something totally different then I'll just delete the original. Far easier to do it that way than to try and merge an independent investigation into one that's already logged and indexed. Anyway, it'll give me a link in if I want to do some work on the case from home."

Telford's fingers started to dance across his keyboard, and various different coloured folders and icons started to appear on his screen. With a side nod of his head, he said, "You can leave that folder if you want. I'm going to be here for a while longer, so it's no trouble for me to type the thing and index it up. You can have it back tomorrow morning, first thing."

Hansen was uneasy. Telford had been curt with him from the start of the investigation. And now he was offering to work late in support of what might amount to nothing.

Still wondering what Telford's angle was, he said, "Are you sure? I can easily stack this into the system myself tomorrow."

Telford plucked the founder from out of Hansen's grasp. "It'll give me something to do while I'm waiting for the database to sort itself out."

Hansen took a slow walk back to his desk and started to check through his emails. That done, he stuck his hands in his trouser pockets and slumped down in his office chair.

It had been something of a long day, but there was no way he fancied spending another night in the Grafton. It had been almost six weeks since he'd walked out of the Ellesmere Port flat, systematically putting off the inevitable by staying for short periods with an assortment of friends. They had been understanding and supportive in their own ways, but he had migrated from one to another in a depressingly regular fashion, unwilling within himself to settle and mourn his loss. It was as if he feared openly acknowledging Felix's death would, somehow, make the memories of their time together fade away into nothing. It was all irrational and unfounded, and a part of him knew it was probably rooted in some variation of Survivor Guilt Syndrome.

Yet the thought of spending another bloody awful night in the Grafton hotel had finally pushed things to a head. Mike's advice came back to him, and he had to admit the DI had been talking a lot of sense. Time to start getting it back together again.

Sitting up, he peered over the top of his screen, seeing if Mike had started to clear his desk down for the night. Sensing the change, Fennick looked up.

Hansen took a deep breath.

"Would you mind dropping me off at my flat? It seems a little senseless to be staying away from it any longer. I need some things," He raised his arms a little and shrugged his shoulders. "A change of clothing for one. And if I don't start using the place, then there's no point in paying the mortgage for it, is there?"

Fennick managed to mask his own irritation with a weak smile. He'd originally wanted to get an action plan together before heading off home. Then he'd found his e-mail box held one from the IPCC. An appointment with a Mrs. Jenny Halls at 2:30pm, tomorrow. He'd known it was coming, but it still put a down on his emotions all the same. He'd automatically sent an acceptance reply. Anything to get the bloody ordeal over and done with as fast as possible.

But he'd also worked with Steve Hansen for some time, and although Fennick didn't really understand all that Steve was going through, he still had some compassion for the guy.

Fennick nodded and started to log out of the system. "Who am I kidding? We'll know more about the whole fucked up mess tomorrow, anyway. I can drive you over to your place, but you'd better ring and cancel the booking while I finish up. Then we'll be off."

Hansen had grabbed his smartphone, thumbed through the contact list, and jabbed at the entry for the Grafton Hotel.

Five minutes later the pair of them had headed towards the lifts.

Back in his Lexus, Fennick unclipping the safety belt, got out of the car, then pulled his collar up in a futile defence against the rain. Not that it did much. Neither did jogging to the protection of the alcove sheltering the front entrance.

He'd pushed the key card in his wallet up against the door sensor, then tapped in his PIN. It was almost the same as going to work.

Inside the foyer he paused, eyes adjusting to the warm glow of the wall lights, then went over to the corner, away from the stairs leading up. It wasn't much in the way of privacy, but it was either that, or intentionally break one of their agreed house rules. Unless unavoidable, all unsavoury police work stopped at the front door.

Taking out his phone, he flicked through the address book, until he found Sugden's home number. Before Sugden could speak, Fennick took a quick breath and started in on what he wanted to say.

"Hello, sir. Just to let you know Raynolds has put Steve and myself onto what might be fallout from Operation Gold Dust. On the other hand it might not – still too early to tell just yet."

Sugden sounded a touch pissed off.

"Just tell me what you've actually got, not what you think you might have, Michael."

Fennick deliberately glowered at the handset, safely protected by the silence of his action, then put it back to his ear.

"As of close of play this evening then. Paul Duffley has managed to cut a deal and is going to turn on the Colombian, Lucumi. Personally I suspect there's not much to be gained from it. However, Duffley's legal seems to be able to influence several of the Gods and has been able to swing a better than average deal. I still believe his potential worth is in another direction, and we should make some kind of try for Ren Penstone. If we can find something that's going to stick to the pair of them then it'll be more profitable in the long run."

"Let Jimmy Raynolds play with that idea, Mike. Penstone isn't going to be easily caught doing anything obvious. Or stupid, come to that. He pays a bunch of people to take the rap for him, which is why he's rarely been touched. Not only that, but Jimmy is more fireproof than you are – especially where the likes of Gordon Lemon and Area Commanders are concerned."

Yet more internal politics. *Almost every fucking time it came down to 'you stroke mine, and I'll tickle yours.'* Without thinking, Fennick said, "Would it help if I were to join the Masons?"

Sugden laughed. "I doubt it. Jimmy Raynolds is probably one of the Grand High Hoochie-Coochies, or whatever the hell they are."

"Warlocks, sir."

"No, it's the truth."

Fennick chuckled a little. Still relatively a new boy, there'd been times when he'd failed to engage with Sugden's dry and often black humour. But he seemed to be getting the hang of it. Humour was one of the best cures for the depression of reality, especially when you often ended up catching the shitty end of the job.

Then Sugden became serious again. "What's this I hear about Tiewrap Teddy coming back from the dead?"

Inwardly Fennick sighed to himself. He just wanted to get into the flat, grab a meal, settle down for the night. Recharge his batteries ready for the following morning.

"Not entirely sure at the moment, sir. Gary Tang, one of the Gold Dust small fry, was strangled with an industrial tiewrap. Either someone doesn't know Vic Carlton's dead, or else one of his fan club has decided to pick up where he left off."

"Well, I've told Jimmy Raynolds I want you back double quick. Things to see, people to do, and the pair of you still have cases here."

"I'll know more tomorrow when some of the initial reports are in."

In his ear Fennick heard three long, steady beeps, and Sugden had just enough time to say "Shit, the batteries are flat," before his connection died. Fennick looked at his phone, then up at the ceiling. So maybe there was a God after all? As a devout atheist he sincerely doubted it, certainly going by some of the villains he'd been up against in his time. Yet sometimes an open mind was the best way of hedging your bets.

Fennick could feel his mood lifting as he climbed the three flights of stairs. At the top he unlocked the front door and stepped into the small hallway. It felt good to let the comforting atmosphere wrap him up like a warm blanket. In the background he could faintly hear music, overlaid by the sound of Jan in the kitchen area. It was either pasta or rice. With both of them putting in odd hours on a regular basis, they had steadfastly refused to go for the 'meal for one' supermarket options. The cooking was down to whoever was in at the time.

Hearing the front door shut, Jan called out from the kitchen area.

"You've got enough time for a quick shower. I'm doing chicken korma, with okra and brown rice for a change. The rice'll take about twenty-five minutes."

"Sounds good to me."

Fennick slipped his coat off and hung it up by the door. As he crossed the living room, Jan came around the freestanding kitchen cupboards, one hand holding a wooden spoon – the other cupped underneath it to catch any drips. She was wearing one of her massively oversized t-shirts, bought from a local market stall. This one had the words 'Pure Old Panther Piss' encircling a simple line drawing of a panther, which actually looked more like Fritz the Cat. It was standing up on its hind legs, sending an arc of urine high into the air to land successfully in a nearby liquor bottle. The baggy white cotton came down almost to her knees and was cinched at the waist with a plain manila rope belt, the sort monks were supposed to have used. She was older than him, by five years, but it seemed she had been blessed with a wrinkle resistant skin. With no make-up on, and her soft brown hair pulled back and held in place with a scrunchie, she managed to lift his spirits with just a smile.

She raised the wooden spoon and tasted the korma, then said, "Don't hang around. You can make yourself useful and open a bottle of wine when you come back."

"Wine? Are we celebrating?"

She cocked her head to one side. "No, we're not celebrating. I just thought it would be nice if we could have a civilized evening together for a change."

He thought for a moment. "Line dancing got cancelled at the last minute, didn't it."

"Yeah." She pouted, her tongue playfully poking out at him for a second or two before she smiled again. "But, although I shall miss it terribly, it does mean we get to spend a whole glorious evening together." She headed back around the storage unit and into the kitchen again. "So get your arse in gear and hurry up with that shower. The rice is already cooking, and I don't think I can slow it down just for you."

Twenty minutes later, as he finished towelling himself off in the bedroom, he had looked at himself in the wardrobe mirror. There was thankfully still more love than handle, but with their new flat requiring DIY time, and money, previous luxuries such as Sunday league football, gym membership and the station squash ladder had all been put on hold. He hung the damp towel over the heated towel rail then, as he walked back into the bedroom, he made a resolution. No matter what, he was going to find more time from somewhere, and use the facilities at work. Rather than slipping out for an illicit bacon buttie now and then.

He changed into a plain t-shirt and what Jan insisted were 'lounge trousers.' From the baggy look and loose feel they always reminded him of up-market pyjama bottoms. He adjusted the waist tie, then headed back into the living area – though paused by the wine rack to take an Argentine merlot from the collection of bottles. By the time Jan had brought two large serving bowls to the table, the bottle had been uncorked and he'd poured out two generous glasses of the dark red wine.

There was no doubt about it, life still felt good.

They'd eaten in a comfortable, familiar silence for a while – appreciating the quiet atmosphere – then conversation slowly started up. Jan had been able to successfully hold onto a client, despite the opposition somehow undercutting her quote. She'd ended up being forced to tell the clients they would have to choose between either the cheap and untried new company, or let Jan's reputation, customer trust and satisfaction speak for itself.

Mike told her about the sideways move to a new investigation which meant more time with the Manchester force, though hopefully not for very much longer. When he'd deliberately left the conversation hanging, Jan had glared at him, wanting to know more, but not wanting to break house rules.

Finally, when things had been cleared away, they had both settled down on the sofa, spending an hour or so together – listening to a low volume cocktail of jazz and just relaxing in each other's company.

Later still, as she lay on her side, she felt the comforting warmth of his chest pressing against her back. She gently pushed against him, fitting her body into the contours of his, parting her legs a little to allow his erection to slip between her thighs. In response, she felt his hand slowly slide up her inner thigh, his palm cupping her hip, then around to lie flat against her stomach. Then his head lifting from the pillow, breath warm against the nape of her neck, his lips brushing against her shoulder, then upwards – teeth gently pulling and teasing at her ear lobe. The wonderful sensation of the tip of his tongue running down her neck, to kiss her shoulder. Turning her head towards him, as she opened her mouth to his kiss, further down her body she felt his fingers spread wide, their tips performing erotic little circles. Then the flat palm of his hand travelling down over her stomach as she started to relax into the beginnings of their foreplay.

Let's face the music,
  And dance....

11

Thursday Morning

Down in Interview Room 3, Paul Duffley was starting to get agitated, which was a state that suited Hansen. Keep the suspect stressed, and you never knew what might turn up.

Gordon Lemon had been due in at 09:15, but had called to say he would be delayed. The call had been transferred to Hansen's desk, and he'd been treated to an irate Lemon, ranting about being stuck in traffic. Three lanes closed due to an overturned lorry and a six mile tailback. At least that's what he thought Lemon had said. Then Lemon's car had been forced to stop under a flyover, successfully dropping the signal. He'd waited for Lemon to call back, then took pleasure in letting the solicitor know that both he, and DI Fennick, were no longer on the Gold Dust team.

"Well put me on to someone who fucking well is then!"

"May I suggest, sir, that the use of expletives will do little to help relieve the obvious amount of stress you appear to be under. Also driving a motor vehicle, whilst in a stressed and agitated condition, is known to have an adverse effect on the driver's judgement and abilities."

He savoured the sounds of Lemon's anger and frustration reaching near critical mass, then added: "Chief Inspector Bashani is not at his desk right now, sir, otherwise I would've passed you over to him. I can only assume he's with your client, awaiting your arrival, so I shall endeavour to locate him and pass your message on." The click and hiss of Lemon's mobile phone losing its signal again had been loud in his ear. Closely followed by the purring of the dial tone once more.

Fennick looked up from his screen. "How many times have I told you – don't tease the animals. What did Lemon want, anyway?"

"He wanted to let the Major know he's snarled up in traffic. He's down for a nine-fifteen session with Duffley, and the CI." Hansen looked across to Bashani's desk. "And as you can see, the Major is out on manoeuvres. He's probably already down chaperoning Duffley." He stood up and rolled the stiffness out of his shoulders. "I'll drop down to the interview rooms, see if I can find him. I could do with the break"

Fennick picked up the Tang file and started heading for the door. "I'll come with you. The Major could probably do with a cup of tea and a break, and I'm pretty sure we wouldn't mind babysitting Duffley for ten minutes or so."

They rode the lift down in silence, Fennick still engrossed in the case file. Hansen was grateful he didn't have to make polite conversation about spending the previous night back in the empty flat.

It hadn't been as bad as he'd originally thought. Cold, but not totally uninviting – the creaks and clanks of the heating and the boiler helped keep the ghosts at bay. He would have to confront them soon, and the familiar ground of the flat gave him an element of safety. And the emotional privacy he sometimes needed for when the memories caught him off guard.

The lift doors opened, bringing him back to reality again.

The glass panel in the door of Room 3 provided a view of a complacent Duffley, rocking his chair on its back legs. He'd been allowed to use the station's facilities, and Lemon had sent in some fresh clothing. Clean shaven, and in what looked like designer labels, it was clear Duffley felt in control of the situation. On the other side of the table sat a very bored Ramesh Bashani, in an equally tired and creased, off the peg suit.

Fennick checked the booking list pinned to a clipboard by the side of the door. Duffley wasn't due out until 11:00. Given that Lemon was still stuck in traffic, he felt confident they could give Ramesh a fifteen minute break. Time enough before Lemon would crash in on them and cut them off from Duffley. A quick tap on the door revived Bashani from his boredom.

"Michael? But I thought...."

"Sadly Mr Lemon has been caught in a tailback of some kind. There's been a nasty motorway accident and they're filtering lanes until it's cleared. He doesn't know how long he's going to be, so we thought we'd come down, pass the message on, and let you take a tea break. Or something."

Behind him, Hansen entered the room. Deliberately ignoring Duffley, he'd nodded politely to Bashani before quietly telling the uniformed PC he could also take a break.

Bashani headed towards the door. "Cup of tea sounds good. If Lemon turns up in the meantime, you can give me a call on the mobile." Without even looking at Duffley, he followed the grateful PC out, both clearly happy to be heading towards the canteen.

Fennick pulled the door to, nodding when he heard it click shut behind him. Duffley, unsure of what was happening, looked up as Fennick put the Tang folder on the table as he sat down. Then Duffley turned to look at Hansen standing behind him, near the far corner of the room.

"I've been advised to say nothing without my solicitor being present."

Fennick remained silent. From behind Duffley, Hansen asked, "You've not been cautioned again, have you?"

Duffley frowned, pressing his lips shut.

Hansen continued, "If you had been cautioned then the recording equipment would be up and running, wouldn't it?" He moved from the corner and sat down next to Fennick. Looking directly at Duffley, he contorted his face into an exaggerated smile. "Elementary, my dear Watson."

Duffley's anger flared. "I told you, I'm not saying anything to anyone until Mr. Lemon is here! I'm not going to get set up for any other stuff."

Hansen flashed Duffley his watch. "He's got ten minutes. Then we throw you back into the holding cells until he turns up."

"I thought I was getting transferred to a safe house? I'm sure that was part of the deal?" Duffley didn't sound too concerned, just a little whiney. "They have threatened to get me, after all."

"With one dead and the other locked up? I doubt the tax payer would stand for that kind of budget frivolity." Hansen gave him another exaggerated smile. Beside him, Fennick flipped open the case folder, allowing a crime scene photograph to be clearly visible. It was a close-up profile showing head, neck and shoulders of Gary Tang. Also plainly visible was the plastic tiewrap holding Gary tightly to the headrest.

Still reading the file, Fennick asked, "What made you pick Gary Tang?"

"What?"

Fennick looked up at Duffley. "Gary Tang. You must have had some reason to single him out?"

Duffley petulantly folded his arms across his chest. "Look, I've already told you, I'm not saying anything about anything until Lemon is here." But his eyes were drawn to the photograph as if hypnotised by it. "Looks like someone wanted to make sure he was dead, doesn't it."

Hansen put his forearms on the table and leaned forward.

"You picked Gary out. Things went wrong. Now Gary's dead. However, Gary wasn't important after he introduced you to the undercover officers, so the powers that be feel his death should be treated as a separate murder case. So you see, your deal is a no deal when it comes to this."

Duffley started to protest, but Fennick cut him off unceremoniously. "We're not going to talk to you about it just now. One charge – sorry – one case, at a time. But once Chief Inspector Bashani has finished with you, then we're going to interview you about this killing, and next time it will be official and on the record. Still, if you want to tell us who put you onto Gary as a potential buyer?" He let the question hang, hoping it might act as an incentive for Duffley to start talking.

Duffley leaned forward aggressively. "I've told you bastards enough times already. I'm not going to tell you anything until Mr. Lemon's in here with me."

Fennick turned the crime scene photograph around, giving Duffley a chance to study it more closely. "It's Tiewrap Teddy's signature. Only by the time this was done they were stitching him back up after the autopsy. So for once we know for sure that he didn't do it."

Hansen took over again. "And we know you and Lucumi are out of the picture, as are the two hijackers. So we've either got some new players who've come in from somewhere," Hansen paused for a moment, "Or else we're left with persons – or Penstones – unknown, who seem to be rapidly tying off the loose ends."

Fennick quickly picked up the thread, encouraged by Duffley's slightly confused expression.

"Maybe that safe house might not be such a bad idea after all." Fennick let a second or two slip by before continuing. "Or we could drop you into Risley for, say, a month or so. I mean, they do that in Africa, don't they. Tie a goat to a stake when they want to attract some lions to entertain the tourists. Or hyenas. Just to long as it's got teeth and claws, and puts on a show."

Obviously uncomfortable, Duffley fidgeted in his chair. "Look, it's your job to protect me. You know I've got nothing to do with Gary Tang. We only picked him –"

Hansen came back at him fast. "Who's this 'we' Paul? I thought you said it was all set up by the Colombians?"

There was panic in Duffley's voice. "No, look, what I said was –"

The door suddenly burst open and Gordon Lemon exploded into the room.

"What the Hell is going on here?! Get out! Get out, now!" Lemon noticed Fennick pick the folder off the table as he stood up.

"What's that? Have you been interviewing my client without me being present?"

Fennick remained silent as he, then Hansen, slipped around the apoplectic Lemon and headed out the door. Lemon, his anger cranked up several more notches, called out, "Answer my question! What have you got there?!"

Fennick continued walking down the corridor in silence. In frustration, Gary Lemon turned to Hansen as he started to walk out. "I want to know what DI Fennick has under his arm?!"

"Hair, I suppose, like the rest of us." Without giving Lemon any chance of a reply he reached around the doorframe, took hold of the door knob, and pulled the interview room door shut. Through the glass observation panel he gave Lemon a little wave of goodbye, then walked down the corridor, catching up with Fennick.

*

Sitting in the driver's seat of the unmarked Mondeo, Eddie's teeth were chattering. Rapid little clicks and clacks sounded inside his head. It had been a rough night, dropping in and out of sleep, his body clammy with a sweat that several showers had been unable to defeat. Breakfast had been black coffee with four sugars, followed by three roll-ups – which he'd chain-smoked, one after the other – in an attempt to kill his craving for anything sweet.

Not only that, but the IPCC had been calling his police registered mobile. He'd deliberately let it ring, watching the compact phone buzz in circles on the coffee table like a dying bluebottle, until it had finally gone to voicemail. The message was from some plummy-voiced woman saying she'd booked him in for an interview at 16:30 that afternoon. She had left her number and instructions to contact her if he couldn't make it. The arrogance of the bitch!

His initial reaction had been to disregard the summons, and just simply not turn up. The thought had made him feel good for a short while. Then reason finally took over. Much better not to piss them off. Turn up to the interview and tell them what they wanted to hear. In their eyes he was clean. He must be, otherwise a whole load of uniform plods would've been round before now. Reading him the riot act before stuffing him into the back of a patrol van, then driving him down to the station for further questioning. Better not to give them any reason to think otherwise, especially while he was trying to sort things out himself. Top of the list was straightening his life out, along with Simone, and finding out what the fuck had been going on with Tony. His best mate in the whole bloody world. Or so he'd thought. How much of the Gold Dust failure was down to him?

The mid-morning sun finally came up above the opposite row of shops, glaring in through the windscreen and making him squint against the light. Opening the glove box, he scrabbled out a pair of designer knockoff sunglasses in a desperate attempt to stop his eyes from watering too much. The one time he could have done with it being overcast and raining, and what happens? Just one more reason against staying in the GMP. It was clear now, from the way they had been treating him, they were just looking out for themselves. No sense of team effort. No words of appreciation for Cookie and him, always sticking it on the line, while the likes of the ACC and DCS took the credit in the newspapers and on TV. But the hierarchy had always been happy to let the two of them get results, so the lazy bastards could increase their percentages and clean up figures for the end of the quarter. Bollocks. Come the end of the month, it sometimes felt as if those who were supposed to be in support of the undercover ops were nothing more than frigging sales personnel. They were all trying to make their monthly target for their bonus. Well, fuck 'em. Every last one of them. He just needed time to put things in place, confirm a few suspicions, then he was going to be out and away from all this crap.

From behind the protection of the dark glasses he looked over at the half dozen shops, and the flats above them. With his thumb he scratched at the stubble on his face. The beard was beginning to thicken up and cover the remaining pellet scabs. Before he'd parked up he'd managed to find an all-night pharmacy. The girl behind the counter had sold him a tube of medicated skin cream, along with a couple of packets of dextrose tablets to help keep his energy going. Yet despite rubbing the pink gunge into his face it still itched like hell.

Ten past nine. Jules came out the side door between the hair salon and nail bar. Short skirt, slim, medium height – her long straw-blonde hair a mixture of streaks and highlights, which picked up the sunlight and framed her face attractively. From this distance she reminded him of the more classier Romanian and Russian women he'd often seen arrested by Vice. Only Jules wasn't on the game. Well, as far as he knew, she wasn't. Cookie had said she had a part time job, working three days a week at a building material reclamation yard further down the road. Tits and teeth always helped with the sales. He watched her stop for a moment, put her keys back in her shoulder bag, then move off again. She rented one of the flats above the large bookies, and lived opposite Cookie's place. Well, Cookie's other place. He tried hard, but he couldn't remember Tony ever mentioning another place somewhere else. Just the flat he used for work purposes.

Now, with Jules out of the way, he could make his move.

He reached around the driver's seat and picked up an age-worn black canvas roll, about eight inches long and three thick. It was a neat little toolkit he'd blagged off an old B & E pro who he'd put away several years back. Undoing the tie straps, he checked the tools over one last time, before tying the roll back up again. All set and good to go.

Out of the car, Eddie cut through a gap in the traffic, heading for the side door as he pulled out a set of keys on a cheap Union Jack key ring. Tony had given him the spare set so long ago he couldn't remember which one it was that fitted. He swore under his breath as the first one he tried slid in, but failed to turn. In frustration he violently yanked it out, then felt his anxiety rising at the possibility of attracting attention to himself.

The second key fitted, and this time it turned in the lock. It let him into a narrow passageway, with a flight of stairs leading up a floor to a landing running along the front of the building. It was all 1980s painted concrete and ageing aluminium. The varnish on the wooden front doors had gone from a translucent brown to something waxy and opaque over time, flaking like dried fish scales and slightly powdery to the touch.

Two doors down was another front door set at right angles to the others. The smaller end flat, running front to back of the building, had been Tony's. The accommodation had been signed up for their undercover work. A rolling monthly lease at an over-inflated price.

Eddie opened the door and walked in, shutting it firmly behind him and feeling himself relax a little. Not only had he made it into the place without being seen, but he knew there was no one next door to hear him as he searched the place.

The layout was simple enough, similar to his own place. The small hallway had one door leading off to the kitchen and, to his right, was the door leading off to the rest of the one bedroom flat. Through that was the living room, then the bedroom, and then at the far end, overlooking the buildings at the back, was the bathroom. That was the ideal place to start. Look in there, then work his way back to the front door. Do the kitchen last then leave, hopefully with what he was looking for – provided Tony had left something for him to find in the first place.

As he opened the living room door and walked through, the smell of stale takeaway and cigarette smoke hung heavy in the air. The coffee table was littered with rubbish and ash trays, and on the sofa was a pair of remote controls. The movies had been crap, but they'd decided not to get on the games machine, because they always lost track of time whenever they played.

He carried on, through the bedroom and into the bathroom, closing the door behind him. It was barely big enough for the three-quarter size bath, wash basin and toilet. Dropping the toilet lid, he put the canvas toolkit on top, rolling it out flat to expose an assortment of screwdrivers, pliers, and a tiny nail bar. Time to start hunting.

*

Ten forty-five, and as she walked along the street, Mikka was feeling uneasy, though she couldn't exactly say why. It was probably down to the fact that Shelbourne Hills wasn't an area she was familiar with. In the event of any trouble she didn't know which turns might lead her into a blind alley. Even with the sun out, there was little to endear the area to her. It was one of those turn-around places. Three tower blocks had been turned into luxury flats. No, what did they call them? Apartments. All very posh and American. Except, the Shelbourne Hills development hadn't taken off as expected.

That much had been obvious when the bus had stopped in the square. Getting off, she'd seen where the up-market outlet shops had slowly faded away, leaving in their wake a plethora of cheap and tacky burger bars, betting shops, convenience stores and unisex hairdressing salons.

She turned left into Collingdale Road, and carried on walking towards the bus stop where Jason and Mousey were waiting. She kept checking and re-checking the area as she worked her way up the street one more time. There were very few people out, and those who were seemed more intent on going about their own business than nosing into someone else's.

Another casual check confirmed no obvious signs of danger, and that the police had finally left as well. Two had driven off in a van marked Forensic Science Team, then two uniforms had come out and taken off in a patrol car about five minutes later. There didn't seem to be any more hanging around, but it always paid to be careful. She'd never been caught, and the longer she went without a police record the better.

As she got closer to Jason she could smell the skunk smoke still on him, even in the open air. It would be days before the stink of it finally disappeared. That was saying Jason would let her wash his stuff, rather than just dump it in a bin or a skip somewhere. That had been one of the reasons she hadn't gone into the smoke shop with him when he went to talk with his DJ friend – DefNin, or whatever his name was. Before he'd gone in she'd reminded him about not taking a hit or two off any spliffs, because there was no way they were going to turn over the dealers' crib if he was even half way buzzed up, or hash happy.

But Jason had come back with the goods – not only a name, but an address as well – and it hadn't taken long on a couple of early morning buses to get the three of them out to Collingdale Road. During the ride, Mikka had gone over the initial plan several times. It was simple enough; find the flat, then see if they could get in. If they could, then it was going to be a quick run through to pick up anything which they could stuff in their pockets. That was always the secret to a successful home invasion. Keep things small, portable, and easy to move. Anyway, what the fuck would they do with a big screen TV, or the latest iPod docking station?

As she walked past the bus stop she just nodded to the other two without stopping, knowing they would catch up with her as she approached the main door.

*

The picture wire snapped as the photograph was yanked off the living room wall, and the screwdriver handle shattered the glass – pushing the picture out through the back. The photo was of a younger Tony and Eddie in the Man Fu Kung Chinese restaurant. One of the waiters had taken it. They looked back up at him from the carpet, still celebrating after their first successful operation together. Frustration sent the frame spinning across the room to dig into the surface of the large flat screen TV. Anger, frustration and meth had finally turned a logical search into something like a squatters wrecking party. Furniture overturned, drawers pulled out and contents scattered. In the bathroom he had originally started putting things back, but by the time he was half way through searching the bedroom he had been slowly losing it. It had been the living room which had finally done his head in completely, and a blind destructive rage had taken over.

Standing in the middle of the carnage, he fought against the anger and adrenaline until he felt himself back in control, and thinking clearly again.

The only things he'd found so far had been bills, a few more photographs of what he assumed were family, or friends Eddie didn't know, and a stash of fake IDs – passports, drivers licences – the sort of thing you needed for basic undercover work. That was all. Nothing in the bathroom, or the bedroom, and now the living room seemed to be a complete and utter bust. The only place left was the kitchen, but he couldn't remember Tony ever using it. It had always been takeaways or something he could bung in the microwave.

As he pulled open the living room door and started into the tiny hallway, something made him stop dead in his tracks. The sound of someone on the landing outside; whistling an out of tune version of

My Way, underscored by the jangle of a large bunch of keys. He tensed up, waiting for the rasp of a key in the lock, frantically looking for something he could use as a weapon – adrenaline and paranoia sending his heart rate sky high, fuelled by the knowledge he was well and truly trapped. There was no back door, and escape through the windows meant dropping down onto the pavement out front as the bathroom window was way too small for him to get through.

The whistling grew louder and he could hear the distinct sound of boots on the tiled passageway. He hurriedly looked around him again, still coming up with nothing suitable to defend himself with. There was no time to go into the lounge or the bedroom to find something to use as a weapon. It was going to be a case of standing his ground and using his fists. He stared at the door. What he desperately needed was a snap plan. He'd wait until the door was half open, then throw himself against it, slamming it shut against the bastard. Only he'd still be trapped in the flat. Okay, when it was half open he'd grab hold of the bastard and drag him off his feet into the small hallway. Then it would be a case of punching the fucker senseless.

Yeah, that was it. That was about the only feasible plan he could come up with at such short notice. He concentrated hard, listening for the sound of the key in the lock while the sound of his own rapidly thumping pulse became almost deafening.

Come on you bastard, come on. Let's fucking do this!

But it never came. Instead, the whistling continued, and the sound of something being opened, but the front door remained solidly shut. Gingerly Eddie's fingers grasped the knob of the Yale and slowly turned it back, gently easing the catch until the door was free enough to open. He paused and listened hard for any movement outside, wondering what the hell was going on. It didn't sound like there was anyone immediately in front of the door, but the whistling continued, echoing slightly in the corridor, and still badly off key.

Nothing to do but chance it.

Laying belly down on the carpet he used his fingertips to open the door a fraction further. It was a move which had saved his life before. Brief memories of the McKinnery brothers trying to kill him by firing both barrels of a shotgun through a similar front door bounced through his mind. He'd just shoved the remains of the door shut with the heel of his hand and let the Armed Response team sort the wankers out.

Looking down the passageway, at floor level he could clearly see the work boots and worn blue jeans of someone standing between the other two front doors. But the rest of the person was obscured by the large wooden cupboard door which protected the electricity and gas meters for the flats. My Way had been replaced by something he didn't recognise. Not that it mattered – it still sounded out of tune. Pushing the door back up against the catch, he stood up, softly eased the catch back and silently closed the door.

He turned around and rested his shoulders against it, feeling the relief go through him almost like some kind of sexual release, and at the same time he realised he was sweating like a pig from the tension. As he moved off into the kitchen he started to giggle, and try as he might, he found it difficult to stop the giggling from becoming full-blown laughter.

His hand dipped into his pocket, and came back out holding the small Ziploc bag. It was getting close to empty again, but there was enough to sort him out for a while.

Grinding the coarse powder up between his front teeth, he felt the remains of the adrenaline rush meld with the amphetamine, and the renewed thumping of blood in his ears. He would have to pace himself and he'd need to do something to bring himself down before the IPCC meeting later on, that was for sure. For the moment, though, it felt like he was fucking invincible.

*

"Stevie, love, lend us your lighter a sec." Georgina-May smiled at Hansen as he handed it over. Several clicks then a satisfied sigh, and the pre-lunch smokers club had increased its number by one. Not quite noon, and already there was half dozen people in and around the shed. The earlier arrivals had already formed into in small groups. Outsiders and visitors were huddled off to the side. Separate from the regulars, their position marked them out as interlopers to the various office department tribes.

He returned the lighter to his pocket. There was probably a couple more pulls left in his small cigar at best. Then it was going to be back up to the incident room and the Arkendale CCTV material. Bowing his head against the weather he surreptitiously watched his temporary companion. She wasn't really a stranger to him as such. He'd talked to her frequently in the past, over the phone, regarding some newly implemented procedure or form. But she was part of the Administration Section – something that'd been contracted out to civilians. Thus, according to some, she was depriving old coppers of cushy positions and postings they would, at one time, have dreamt of filling. By comparison, were she back in her grandfather's native India, she might've been considered less of an untouchable. But probably only just.

There was an insistent buzzing in his inside pocket, and stubbing the cigar butt out with the heel of his shoe he answered his mobile.

"DS Hansen."

From the receiver, Jack Telford said, "Are you doing anything, sergeant? If not, then I need a favour." Without giving him a chance to reply, Telford carried on. "A woman called Jean Turner has come forward to identify the body of Vic Carlton. She's been his next of kin for years. Trouble is I need to go out to re-interview someone – Peter Wainwright. The PC who did the prelim made a right pig's ear of it. Anyway, can you get over there? Just make sure she identifies the body and gets the release paperwork signed and stamped."

It was either sorting out Vic Carlton's ID, or going back up to the office. There was also a chance the favour would help break the ice between the two of them. And you never knew when you might need to call in a favour.

"Okay, sir, I can make some time for that. When's she due in?"

"She's already at the morgue, waiting for you now."

Oh fucking great! "Okay, give me two minutes to let DI Fennick know, and then I'll be onto it."

"Thanks"

As he called Fennick's mobile, he wondered what could've been so important that Jack Telford felt he had to interview Peter Wainwright himself. The fact that he'd turned the job of seeing to Jean Turner over to Hansen meant something had to be pretty screwed up in order to get Telford out of the Gold Dust Incident Room.

The mobile phone made the connection and Fennick answered on the third ring.

"Jack wants you to do it? Hold on a minute." There was a rustling sound in Hansen's ear as Fennick looked around the incident room for Telford. "No. Can't see the bugger up here at the moment. Okay, well, you deal with that. I'm going to grab some lunch and then head on over to Inquisition Towers for the IPCC interview. Mistress of the red hot pokers will be one Jennifer Halls. Know her?"

Hansen thought for a moment. "Doesn't ring any bells. Anyway, I'm too far down the food chain to attract IPCC attention."

Fennick snorted. "Ha! Your turn will come. Catch you tomorrow."

*

It had taken a while before someone had finally let the three of them into the block of flats. The time of day had been all wrong. Too late for returning school mums, and too early for any of the home-to-lunchers. Without them there'd been no one they could tailgate through the main door with. It had been down to just poking the call buttons and hoping someone would finally answer. After the seventh press they got lucky.

"Hello?" The youngish voice of a woman, TV on in the background. On cue Mousey started to grizzle and cry, putting his hand half over his mouth to help add to the effect. Mikka got closer to the speaker.

"Hi! Sorry to disturb you, I've locked myself out. I only popped out to get some Calpol for little Julius, and…."

Mousey let out some more anguished baby sounds, and a second later the door buzzed open. Mikka bent close to the speaker as Jason grabbed the handle and pulled the door open. "Thanks very much!"

Inside, the foyer smelt of spray polish and citrus air freshener. Across the tiled floor were muddy boot prints from where the coppers had been tramping in and out. At the back of the foyer was the lift. For a moment Mikka thought about taking the stairs which ran up and to the left. On stairs you had the freedom to escape should anything happen. In a lift you were stuck with no alternative route, and that always made her feel uneasy and on edge. Then Mousey went ahead and pressed the call button, and the doors opened immediately. He looked back over his shoulder at Mikka, his face bright with a genuine smile for once. She smiled back, nodded her silent agreement, and the three of them rode up to the eighth floor in silence.

They stepped out onto a landing and hallway almost identical to the ground floor. Only this time there was carpet instead of tiles, with tropical looking plants in troughs, stalks pointing towards the windows to capture the sunlight. To their right the crime scene tape hung loosely across the doorway to Gary Tang's flat. The door seemed to be firmly shut, smooth against the frame, and no padlock. A good sign the lock was still intact, rather than broken when the forensic team went in.

Jason slipped a hand inside his jacket, unhooked the collection of keys he had pinned to the lining, and stepped up close to examine the lock. Smiling, he unclipped one of the bump keys and started to slip it into the mechanism. He'd bought the keys from an old guy in one of the local pubs. The old guy had been about to go away for a five stretch and didn't want to be caught with even more incriminating evidence. They always came in useful for his rare adventures into B&E.

Twist, tap, tap, jiggle, tap, turn, and in moments the catch turned easily.

Inside, Mikka held the bolt in and pushed the locking stud, stopping the catch from locking the door. As always, leave the escape route as clear as possible. Closing the door behind her, she took a swift look at her watch.

"Fifteen minutes, then we're off. No more than fifteen minutes. Nothing you can't carry in a pocket or under your arm, casual like, and nothing we can't get rid of. This is purely for funds, not for ourselves. Understood?"

Mousey nodded rapidly half a dozen times, smiling broadly. As usual, it seemed the whole thing was still an adventure to him. Jason just nodded once, then moved off towards the back of the flat.

Still feeling uneasy, Mikka opened a side door and found herself in the bedroom. Apart from the bedside cabinets there was only the built-in wardrobes and a large, floor standing mirror. It was obvious the place had been searched by the police, but they weren't interested in the same things the three of them were. Around the side of the bed Mikka checked through the drawers, but found nothing more than a strip of supermarket aspirin, half a dozen condoms, several cheap ballpoint pens and a couple of half used note pads. When she opened the bottom drawer she wrinkled her nose in disgust. Staring up at her from the cover of a magazine was a woman with her hands on her hips. She was wearing a dark purple and black lace bustier, pushing her breasts out towards the camera. Mikka kicked the drawer shut with the toe of her trainer. That was almost as gross as going on the game, something she'd never done even when money had been short.

With Jason in the kitchen, Mousey went into the lounge. The window blinds had been left half closed, cutting the sunlight and making the room dim. Catalogue furniture sat uncomfortably with the up-market pottery and small bronze animals, several of which fitted nicely into his pockets.

Casually he opened the top drawer of the sideboard and found a jumble of odd looking papers, while at the back were four old mobile phones. Even he knew they were old – one had a stubby aerial poking out the top of it. He picked one up. He'd never had one of his own before. Turning it over in his hands he found the 'on' button half way down the side of the case. But when he pressed it, nothing happened. He pressed it several times, but the screen didn't light up at all. It even rattled when he shook it.

Still, it looked nice, and he could add it to his collection of things back at the house. He slipped it into a pocket and took another quick look around the room. No iPod, no laptop computer, but a couple of silver photo frames looked worthwhile. Mikka had shown him what hallmarks looked like, so he knew the frames were genuine, not cheap plate.

Jason stuck his head around the door. "Got anything?"

Mousey nodded and held up the frames, then patted his coat pockets, heavy with the brass animals and his new phone.

Jason gave him a quick smile. "I'll grab Mikka and we'll be off."

He disappeared back into the passageway, then walked over to the bedroom. Standing in the doorway, he said, "Grab us a pillowcase. I've got a few bits from the passage and Mousey's found a couple of things as well. We can wrap them up in one of those, stop 'em from rattling. You got anything?"

She shook her head. "No. There's some cheap bling from the dressing table, but a couple of the gold chains might be worth some fag money. Got a bit of loose change from the stuff in the wardrobe, though no notes. Either he had sod all, or the coppers have blagged all the easy stuff. You find anything?"

"Nah. The kitchen's got nothing worthwhile that's small enough for us. Looks like someone's going to get a bollocking though. There's one of those Forensic suitcases down by the side of the fridge."

"What?" She stared at him in horror for a second. "Shit! Why didn't you fucking say something when you found it? They're bound to be back for it once they find out its missing."

She pulled a pillow off the bed, tugged the cover off and handed it to Jason. "Use that, and we get out of here, now!" She stuffed the pillow into the wardrobe. That way, when forensics came back, they might not get suspicious when they did their search for their missing kit. She certainly hoped so, because there was no way they were going to have the time to wipe down everything they'd touched. Hurriedly she scooped up the money and jewellery from off the bed and stuck it in her pockets. At least they'd got more than just the return bus fare out of it all.

In the passageway Jason held the pillowcase open for Mikka to check over what they'd collected, in case she wanted to throw anything back. Tying it closed, she handed the makeshift bag to Mousey.

"You can carry it over your shoulder for a while. Pretend you're one of the seven–"

She stopped talking at the sound of someone trying to unlock the front door then, finding it open, pushing the door inwards. To Mikka it felt like a scene out of her worst nightmare. Framed in the now open doorway stood the man from the Arkendale car park.

Immediately Mousey dropped the pillowcase and charged at the door, almost closing it with the force of his impact. But the stranger had already put a foot against the door frame and had a hand grasping the door edge, holding it in place while Mousey pushed ineffectually from the other side. Mikka shook her head in frustration. They needed to be out and away, not only to get clear of Gary Tang's killer, but also because the coppers could be back at any minute to collect their forgotten equipment. Without thinking, she pushed Mousey to one side, grabbed hold of the stranger's hand and pulled open the door, yanking the stranger into the passageway. A swift turn and a solid push in the small of his back as he passed by sent him stumbling through, while an outstretched foot from Jason knocked his feet out from under him. With his hands flailing, the stranger dropped to his knees, but the momentum kept him going forward until he smacked his forehead on the frame of the bedroom doorway.

In the confusion Mousey came out from behind the front door and scooted back down the passageway. He successfully retrieved the pillowcase but got tangled up with Jason as they both tried to get out of the flat. Wide eyed, Mikka glared at him.

"What the fuck are you doing?!"

She could feel her fear kicking her system into overdrive, and behind the pair of them she could see the stranger already starting to get back on his feet again. There was an ugly cut close to his hairline, which had started to bleed heavily, and his anger turned his words into nothing more than grunts and snorts, like a furious bull.

As Jason and Mousey tumbled over each other, then staggered out into the foyer space, Mikka reached in and pulled the door shut as the stranger came charging back up, his face red with anger and the blood mingling with his sweat.

She was halfway across the landing when the sound of their attacker exploding out of the flat came to her from behind. Ahead the stairwell wasn't particularly narrow but Mousey, still in the lead, froze at the top, his hand part way to the handrail. Jason, dodged nimbly around the small boy, then started on down, taking the steps two and three at a time before he quickly vanished down below the next floor.

Then, as she came to the head of the stairs, she was torn between swerving around the child as Jason had done, or try to make a stand and defend the child against the bastard coming up behind her. Distracted by a moment's indecision, Mikka felt a sudden massive force hit her between the shoulder blades, propelling her uncontrollably forwards.

There was no way she could stop herself. As she barrelled into Mousey she could feel his feet collide with her shins as the rest of his body slowly dived out into empty space. As she grabbed hold of the handrail to stop herself from going over the top step, she saw him falling as if in slow motion, still clutching hold of the pillowcase. Then he was landing almost head first onto the lower steps, tumbling and bouncing down until he hit the next landing, his head smacking hard against the wall with a sickening crack.

12

Thursday Afternoon

Hansen rolled his shoulders as he felt the coldness of the corridor touch him, and he doubted he would ever be able to forget the smell. No matter what they set the heating to, the viewing area used to identify the dead never seemed to lose its chill.

At the end of the corridor he paused by the door. Through the small reinforced glass window he could see there was only one person, sitting in the middle of the row of plastic chairs that were pushed up against the back wall. She was a tall, well dressed woman in her early sixties, her light green raincoat open but still loosely belted. She'd aged since he'd last seen her. There were wrinkles and creases in amongst the lines of her face which hadn't been hidden by her makeup. Classic old school Rubenstein champagne silk in a gold Italian compact. Carmine lipstick in a slight cupid bow, and just a touch of eyebrow pencil. Her hair had been dyed a glossy chestnut brown – a professional job, rather than something done at home.

It was rare to see her with her guard down, and Hansen made the most of it, watching as she looked down at her hands clasped together in her lap, then up to the non-descript beige curtain which hid the viewing area. Unguarded, Jean Turner didn't, at first, appear to be one of life's natural victims. Conscious decision or not, she seemed destined to remain loyal to those who deliberately pushed her loyalty to the limit – apparently accepting it all with a smile.

The sound of Hansen opening the door broke into her thoughts, and immediately the trademark cheerful demeanour slid protectively back in place. Standing up, she picked up her handbag from the chair beside her.

"Hello, Mr. Hansen, I've not seen you for a while. I'm here to collect the paperwork and sign for Victor's release. The funeral parlour is eager to make a start." Her voice sounded a little like some stereotypical aunt enthusiastically greeting a nephew.

"Good to see you as well, Jean. I'm sure you're the only thing Vic had left other than his work associates. Has Wilson Merrillies paid his respects yet? Or is he waiting for the funeral?" He knew it was worthless to go fishing, but he tried it all the same.

Jean Turner just pursed her lips a little, accentuating the cupid bow like some 1930s Hollywood actress.

"Now Mr Hansen, you know Victor never discussed his business, or his associates, with me. Still, I expect the funeral will be a quiet one. Immediate family and close friends."

Hansen resisted the temptation to say 'So, just you then.' Whatever she'd done in the past – always ready with an alibi for whenever Vic needed one – she didn't deserve that kind of backhand comment. 'Aunty Jean' had never shopped Vic to the police, and he knew she never would.

He gestured towards the closed curtain and the two of them stood in front of it. "Are you sure you're ready to make the identification, Miss Turner?"

She nodded and Hansen pressed a small button on the wall. From somewhere beyond came the muted ringing of a bell, then the curtain slowly drew back revealing the featureless anteroom. Victor Carlton's body rested on a gurney, green cover drawn back to reveal his head and neck – but still high enough to cover the large 'Y' incision and Frankenstein stitching left by the post mortem.

Careful, so as not to break the moment, Hansen observed Jean

Turner from the corner of his eye. Her shoulders seemed to sag a little under her raincoat, her expression a mixture of sadness and resignation now that a large part of her life had finally come to a decisive close.

He was about to break the silence when she suddenly said:

"Chalk stripe."

"Sorry?"

Hansen didn't turn his head but looked at the ghostly image of her being reflected back at him off the surface of the glass.

"I've found a lovely navy blue wool suit of Victor's. Hardly seems worn at all. It's got this nice, pearl grey strip running through it. There's a Peter London shirt without too large a collar, and there's a grey silk tie he was always fond of whenever he got dressed up to go out."

She sniffed, then reached for her handbag, taking out a paper tissue to wipe her nose before putting it back and closing the bag again.

Gently, Hansen said, "I'm sorry about this, but for the record, could you please identify the person in front of you."

She took a quick, ragged breath. "It's the person I've always known as Victor Carlton." She went on to give his address and date of birth. It was unnecessary, but he let her ride the emotional wave, trapped for a moment in his own emotional empathy. They stood in silence for another minute before Hansen finally reached out and pressed the button again – waiting for the curtain to be drawn across completely before stepping aside to let Jean Turner leave.

She was almost to the door when she stopped, opened her handbag again, and took out a long, plain manila envelope. Turning around, she looked Hansen directly in the eye and, for the very first time, Hansen saw 'Aunty Jean' slip into the background, and a much colder and emotionless Jean Turner come to the fore.

"I don't know what you think of me, Mr. Hansen, and to be totally frank with you, I don't really care. I know that the law considered Victor a bad man, but I will say here and now that he never, ever, did me any harm in all the years I knew him."

She paused to give Hansen the envelope and to consider what she was going to say next.

"Inside that envelope is as much as I can remember about the last person who came to see Vic with a business proposition. I always made sure I knew nothing about what Vic did, but this is different. He visited Victor several times and, apart from the initial meeting, every time after that they always went into the back room to discuss things. So what I'm able to give you isn't much. However, I just hope it's enough to catch the person who put him up to this. Because, as far as I'm concerned, if that man hadn't turned up and offered Victor the job the way he did, then Victor would still be alive."

With that, she turned on her heel, opened the waiting room door, and left.

*

Eddie sat at the small kitchen table amid the results of his efforts. Every container had been up-ended on the counter top and the contents scattered and searched. The fridge had been pulled out to see if anything had been taped behind it, and if there had been any other kitchen appliances then they would have been opened and checked as well.

The meter reader had finally disappeared a while back, and as Eddie sat on the kitchen chair with his back against the wall, he was wracking his brains to think of anywhere else Tony might have hidden something important. Maybe there was a loft? Something up in the roof space? He didn't remember seeing a trap door anywhere.

Maybe it was outside in the corridor? C'mon, think.

In his frustration he started banging the back of his head against the wall behind him, as if the effort would jar loose some important piece of the puzzle. It didn't. All it gave him was a pain in the head and a hollow sound in his ears.

He turned around to look at the wall behind him. It had been painted over the same colour as the rest of the kitchen, which was why he'd missed it before. It was the original fuse box and meter cupboard, set into a stud and plasterboard wall. Yet, despite running his hands over the surface several times, he couldn't feel any easy way of getting the door open. Shifting the table and chair away, he checked the rest of the wall.

And there it was.

A simple steel screw, flush with the door surface, below table height. From the counter he snatched a screwdriver from the tool roll, and set to work.

With the screw removed, the door had swung stiffly open, and inside – apart from the old electrical fittings – was a black and white box file, which felt heavy when he picked it up. Closing the door, he pushed the table back up against it and sat down.

He didn't open the box immediately. He just sat there with it in front of him, his hands trembling and inside his head a thin constant whining noise, like one of those high speed dentist's drills.

Okay. Just need to calm it down, relax and chill.

Digging around in his tobacco pouch he located the remaining crumbs of some Moroccan Red, and despite the jitters he managed to roll a makeshift spliff. A couple of good puffs and he felt himself start to mellow. Not too much, got to keep his wits about him, but enough to take the tension down a level or two.

Time for the box file.

Inside, on top of a mass of papers and file folders, was an iPhone. For as long as Eddie could remember working with him, Cookie had never used an iPhone. He put it to one side, then lifted out the loose papers and laid them on the table. Underneath were four or five files, several full of what looked like old police report forms – the packs held together with old fashioned Treasury tags.

Before he could start to read any of the material, the knock on the door startled him.

Another three or four knocks, then a woman's muffled voice. "Hello? Is anyone in there?"

Eddie held his breath, his tension and heart rate spiralling up, making him feel light-headed and feint.

Another woman's voice, "I told you Lisha, there's nobody up here. You're hearing things."

"No. I definitely heard something, and the back storeroom is right under this flat. Hello?"

Shit, shit, shit, shit, shit! Okay, breathe in through the nose and out through the mouth. Calm down. They haven't got a key, otherwise they would've used it.

"C'mon, Lisha, we need to get back in case we miss some customers. You're just hearing things. Pipes or something. Maybe a bird's got in somewhere."

"Then it's a fucking big bird."

"Look, I'm going back down. You coming?"

Eddie silently stood up and moved close to the front door, listening so hard he thought he could hear the noise of the high street traffic despite the double glazing. There was silence from the other side of the door for what seemed like an eon, then:

"Lisha?"

"Yeah, okay, I'm right behind you."

Eddie pressed his ear carefully to the front door. The click-clack-click-clack of two pairs of heels got fainter until they disappeared down the stairs to ground level again.

Fuck! That was close!

He went back into the kitchen, dumped the papers and iPhone back into the box file, tied up the tool roll, and twenty seconds later he was out the door and headed back down to the Mondeo as fast as he could. Throwing the box and the tool kit in the back, he half stalled, half barged his way into the flow of traffic. He didn't care what direction he was heading in, he just wanted to put as much space as he could between himself and Tony Cooke's old flat.

*

"Jack, its Mark Sadler from Greensborough Remand." The background noise of a lorry revving up and changing gear sounded deafening. "Bloody hell, are you on a mobile? I called your landline but seem to have been diverted."

Another lorry rumbled by Telford as he stood outside several offices. It didn't seem to matter what time of day it was, traffic was always heavy. When he got back to the station he would have to sort the phone out.

"Mark, I'm just about to interview someone. Can it wait?"

"Not sure. It's about one of your collars – an Alejandro Lucumi? He was booked in on Wednesday."

How many bloody Colombians do you think I deal with, for Christ's sake?

"Yes, he's one of ours, Mark. What's up?"

"Well, you'll be delighted to know he's stopped doing Terminator impressions. I don't have to tell you, all that silent shit was starting to psych some of the other nutters we've got in here. Still is, in fact. We're already thinking about keeping him in his present solitary routine for his own good. But there's all sorts of diplomatic shit and procedures we're having to go through courtesy of some arsehole of a legal he's called in from somewhere."

"That would be Frank Amberly from Maplethorpe and Gittings?"

"Couldn't tell you without looking it up. All I know is there's a mountain and a half of bloody paperwork, all being shuffled backwards and forwards. Some of it even on fancy Embassy headed paper. Not the sort of thing we're used to dealing with, I can tell you."

Telford could feel his frustration rising. "So why are you calling me, Mark?"

"Well, the bugger's just lodged a verbal request to speak to you."

Telford was silent for several seconds.

"Jack? Hello? Are you still there, Jack?"

"What? Er, yeah. Yeah, I'm still on the line. Did he…. Did he say what it might be about?"

"No, he just upped and told one of the warders he wanted to speak with you, personally. I'm assuming it's about the drugs deal you lot are wrapped up with at the moment. He said he knew you were one of the people in charge, so you were going to be the one he was prepared to speak to."

"Ah, fuck!"

"Say again, Jack? Couldn't hear you over the traffic."

"Look, I can't make it today, Mark. I've got an interview already running late as it is. Peter Wainwright – and I don't want the bastard scarpering off somewhere else. Plus I've got other evidence backed up that needs processing otherwise the prosecution could do us for a potential break in the chain. Tell him I'll be there tomorrow morning, around nine if that's okay with you?"

"No problem, Jack. I'll get the paperwork started this end."

"Might be best to hold off doing that until I can confirm it with you."

"You sure? Okay, no problem. I'll let the gate staff know you might be up to see us, just in case. See you tomorrow."

"Right, see you tomorrow."

Telford stuffed his mobile back in his coat. The day was turning into one fucking enormous ball of crap.

*

Raynolds looked up at Hansen, then back down at the sheets of paper spread out on his desk in front of him. The handwriting was neat and flowing, confident rather than hesitating, and written with what looked like fountain pen. However, it was the fact it was there at all which most impressed him.

After the meeting with Jean Turner, Hansen had waited until he was back in the incident room before opening the letter. Six sheets of Queen's Velvet notepaper recounted the one and only meeting Jean had been accidentally privy to, late one evening, about four weeks previous. Jean and Vic had been to an evening cabaret and afterwards a meal, and were on the verge of ordering coffee when a gentleman had approached out of nowhere and started to talk to Vic as if they had been old friends.

Vic had initially seemed wary of the stranger and had asked what 'Ren' was doing this far North. He told Vic he was in the process of putting together a one-off crew and was scouting for a foreman to help with a solo project, adding that he'd been surprised to hear Vic had retired. The gentleman had gone on to say he really wanted Victor involved, mainly as he was a stranger to the area, so needed Vic's local knowledge and reputation. Vic would be paid a set fee, half now and half once the job had been completed, success or fail, regardless of the outcome.

Vic had mentioned the fact his retirement had not gone down too well with his previous management, and that it might be better if Ren looked elsewhere. Ren had dismissed his comments, saying the result would be more than enough for Victor to disappear on, regardless. If Victor were to use people from a different management company, then there would be less likelihood of his previous employer knowing he'd even had a hand in it. The fine details would all be left up to Victor, naturally, and there would be initial funding provided, with the balance extracted from the profits once the job had been completed.

Ren and Victor had then agreed to a further meeting the following day, and the gentleman had handed Victor a piece of paper with a phone number on it, something which Jean Turner had gone out of her way not to see.

They'd shaken hands, and that had been when Jean had noticed the small outlines of scars, made more obvious by the nightclub lighting, where a tattoo or something had been removed from the back of the stranger's hand.

Raynolds rearranged the sheets back into a neat pile.

"So Carlton went to Wainwright because he'd fallen out with Merrillies?"

Hansen nodded as Raynolds sat back in his chair.

"You realise, sergeant, someone's going to have to talk her into making an official ID? We can't just trot down to London and see if we can pull Penstone on the grounds that Victor Carlton met up with someone called Ren, regardless of whether or not Penstone has any incriminating scars. After that, there's the joyful problem of trying to get Penstone to stand in a line-up. Anyway, I thought both you and DI Fennick were working on the Tang murder?"

"DI Telford asked if I would see to Jean Turner when she came to ID Carlton's body. The DI said he was tied up with something else – out on an interview, according to his calendar."

"The only thing he's got at the moment is Gold Dust. He could have interviewed her himself. Or at least found out more while she was here. Talk about opportunities missed."

"She's not been noted for her cooperation in the past, sir, and she didn't seem to want to talk to me about it either."

"But she was emotional enough to want to pass on these details, in writing, to someone. You've been out of the loop, whereas Jack is still working with the statements and the finer details."

Hansen tried not to look disgruntled. Jack Telford hadn't been in the incident room when he'd returned. With no note on the

Whereabouts Board, he'd asked a couple of the statement readers if they knew where Jack might be.

"He's out at the moment, Steve. Gone to check on some details in one of the interviews. Didn't say when he was going to be back."

A quick check on the GMP intranet had only shown that DI Telford was Out Of Office until further notice. With no one to pass Jean Turner's letter over to, he'd made several photocopies of the sheets, put one set on Telford's desk with a hastily scribbled cover note, and slipped another copy into Fennick's private folder. Then, after entering the details into the evidence log, he'd called Raynolds and taken them down to the DCS himself.

Hansen tried to be optimistic. "At least it helps connect Carlton and Penstone, sir. The only other alternative would be to hand this part over to the Met or the City down in London. And you know what glory grabbing bastards they are."

Raynolds shifted awkwardly in his chair. So far he'd taken a lot of public flak over the case, and had been made to look like some kind of bumbling wanker by the press. Much better if he were to let the media know there had been 'developments'. A new source of information. The press always loved that. A new source equalled a new line of inquiry. And that meant the bastards could squeeze some more mileage out of the copy they'd already printed, in the form of recaps and the like. On the other hand, he'd let other cases go in the past without any ill effects.

Raynolds nodded to himself. "Okay, sergeant, let DI Telford know about this as soon as you can." Then, almost as an afterthought, "How's your own investigation going?"

"Still running through the Arkendale CCTV material. We're pretty sure one of the door cameras must have picked up the four going in and coming out. That should give us something to print off and pass around. They searched Tang's Volvo, but the state of it means it's basically screwed for reliable forensic evidence – though there's a possibility of DNA from a fresh trace of saliva off the back of the headrest. It'll help build a case, but I don't think it will be strong enough to stand up on its own. The samples are likely to take a week or more to come back once we submit them."

And no doubt that'll cost a bloody fortune, all out of my budget, thought Raynolds. "You've not sent them to the lab yet have you? It might be easier to hold off doing so for a day or two. See if good old fashioned police work turns something up first."

"Right, sir, I'll let DI Fennick know, as soon as he comes back from his interview with the IPCC."

"Okay, let me know ASAP if you get a break with the CCTV."

Hansen left and made his way back up to the incident room. Still no sign of Jack Telford. Rather than leave the document in Telford's in-tray, Hansen found one of the Statement Readers and told them to enter it into the system as fast as they could.

Back down in Raynolds' office, the DCS picked up his phone and tapped out a number. It rang several times before the far end picked up. Raynolds smiled resignedly.

"Hello Suneel? It's Jimmy Raynolds. How are you these days? … Yes, don't I know it, and it's turned into a bit of a shit storm as well. Look, there's been some fresh developments you might be interested in hearing about."

*

With the anaemic sunlight coming through the far windows, the IPCC reception area had all the appeal of an NHS A&E department. Ivory coloured ceiling tiles, strip lighting, pale cream wash on the walls. To one side of the waiting area was a desk with an efficient looking receptionist. Further down the wide corridor were the interview rooms. Every so often the receptionist would answer her phone, make a note of the time, then inform whoever was waiting which interview room to go to. Cold, impersonal – the official process of gathering of information on incidents, then passing judgement down from on high.

Fennick sat on one of the chairs placed up against the wall. Down the line sat someone else. Fennick didn't recognise the man, but both of them consciously resisted making any kind of eye contact. Such was the nature of the place. The interviewees made to feel as if they were outcasts or social lepers. Even he still felt uneasy, despite knowing he had nothing to worry about. Every time he'd rehearsed the interview in his head he'd found nothing untoward in his actions. Or those of Steve, come to that.

After Willie Symonds had set up Gary Tang, both Steve and he had left the rest up to the GMP and the undercover team. They'd only been brought back in as a courtesy, to see the final result and to close the case off.

Fennick started to poke at his back teeth with his tongue. *Maybe this Halls woman doesn't know about Gary Tang being killed?* As far as he could see, that aspect was of no concern to the IPCC at all.

There was the squeak of a castor as the receptionist move her chair, then: "Sergeant Devlin?"

Devlin looked up as she continued.

"Room number six." Then she sat down behind her desk again. No emotional engagement. The sergeant was just another tick in a long list of boxes. Just tick off and move on.

Devlin stood up, then walked down the line of doors until he found the one with 6 on it. Check tie, jacket, flies, then with a sharp knock on the door, he opened it and disappeared inside.

Fennick thought of knights, dragons, and Jan as his damsel in distress. It didn't help ease the tension. He still felt defensive and on edge. This time he didn't have anything to worry about. Last time, though, he'd been damn lucky. Thankfully it hadn't gone as far as an official report or complaint.

That particular case would've been stressful for anyone, regardless of what his superiors down in Hertfordshire had said. Mason Walker had been an important part of a dog breeding and fighting syndicate, making incredible money from illegal betting and organised dog fights around the UK. He'd shown no remorse towards Cameron Daley, the five year old boy one of his dogs had killed while its supposed owner had been parading it in a local park.

The dog had been successfully captured and put down. And for once there had been enough eye witnesses prepared to come forward and ID the dog handler. From there the investigation had led back to Mason Walker. Slow work, but the investigation team had started to build up a more extensive picture of Walker's organisation.

The final coup came as part of a raid on a suburban backwater pub that had a massive 90-inch TV wired up to a DVD player. Usually the TV was for major sporting events, but once a month, after midnight, the dog fight syndicate supplied the disks and for four or more hours punters would bet on the results of the recorded dog fights. Local fights were mixed in with those from the West Country, the Midlands, Scotland, and even as far as Ireland. All of it designed to generate further revenue from the illegal activity.

The raid had successfully netted three incriminating DVDs before the organisers were able to drop them into a shredder, and on one had been clear footage of Mason Walker, patting and stroking the distinctively marked dog.

But it had been his attitude in the interview that really started to niggle at Mike. The anger soon built up inside him until the point where Mason had been shown a picture of the child's dead body. Mason had studied it for a minute or so, then with a smile on his face he'd looked Mike directly in the eyes and just said: "Sweet."

His memory of his own reactions bore out what offenders had tried to explain to him in the past. A red haziness as everything shifted and slipped into a detached reality. He'd grabbed hold of Walker's head and slammed it down onto the table top two or three times in rapid succession before the other officers had pulled him off and hustled him out of the interview room. Later, after Walker's legal team realised just how damaging their client's comments would sound to a jury, it was mutually agreed the whole interview would be left off the relevant official records

An unofficial reprimand had been issued behind closed doors. It wasn't immediately evident from his annual performance write ups, but he was sure something had probably been annotated in a handwritten sidebar in his HR files. The incident turned out to be the spur for his decision to move away from Hertfordshire, heading north in the hope that the great North-South divide would also help serve as a barrier for any adverse reputation he might have acquired.

During that time he'd also tried to analyse himself, but he still didn't really know why he'd acted like that against Walker. Prior to the incident he'd dealt with other cases involving children. Some involving both physical and even sexual abuse. The first had been a series of child murders, back when he'd been a humble DC starting out on the Fast Track Programme towards becoming a DI. That had been a real baptism of fire. In Walker's case it was the fact he didn't seem to care about the death of a child which he'd randomly and indiscriminately caused. Fennick had wanted to make him care, and the only way Walker could be made to care about anything was if it was made to hurt.

"Detective Inspector Fennick?" The receptionist's voice cut through his contemplation.

"Yes?" Time to focus on the present, and let the past rest in peace.

"Room two." Then, almost as an afterthought, she added, "Second from the far end."

Fennick stood, then walked down the corridor until he found the right door. Another quick check of tie, flies and jacket, then a sharp knock before entering the IPCC office of Mrs. Jenny Halls.

*

Still watching the screen, Hansen reached out and picked up the ringing phone.

"DS Hansen, how can I help?"

"Good. At least one of you buggers is still working." Molly Sugden's voice boomed in his ear. "I've been trying to get hold of Mike but his mobile's turned off."

"He's seeing someone from the IPCC this afternoon, sir."

"Then it's your turn to have the pleasure of bringing me up to speed. What's happening with the Tang murder?"

"Still ploughing through material, but I think we're starting to build up a reliable timeline now."

"What about the car? Anything worthwhile to be had from that?"

"Too much human traffic for any of it to be reliable, sir. Next move is going to be tracking down any potential witnesses from the video material."

"Got your work cut out for you there then. Any new developments on the other one?"

Hansen automatically checked around to see if anyone might overhear. "Looks like we have a new player on the pitch. I met Jean Turner when she was here to ID Vic Carlton's body. It's early days, but I'm pretty sure from what she's written in a letter that she can actually put Renton Penstone in the frame for organising the hijacking crew."

In his ear he heard Sugden hurriedly swallowing his mouthful of tea. "Aunty Jean giving up a villain? My God, what is the world coming to these days?"

Hansen felt a little smug. "In the letter she talks about a meeting with Carlton and a bloke he called Ren. She also mentioned the tattoos Penstone had removed from his hands a while back. Says the scars stood out under the nightclub lights. It also sort of confirms bad blood between Merrillies and Carlton, which was why Carlton recruited two of Wainwright's for the hijacking."

"And you've turned all this over to?" Sugden sounded more than a little curious.

"DCS Raynolds, plus a copy to one of the statement readers. I've also left a copy for DI Telford as well, as he's the office manager. It's still early days, after all, and unless she can make a positive ID, and also come across as a credible witness, it might still all fall apart."

"Fax me a copy."

"What? At the moment we don't know how key this thing is, sir. Couldn't you just pull it off the system yourself?"

"Because if I did that, sergeant, then people will know I've got it."

Hansen tried not to sound exasperated. "Would you like to tell me what's going on, sir?"

"That's for me to know, and for you to find out when the time is right. Just fax me a copy, pronto."

Hansen shook his head in silent exasperation. "Okay, sir, it'll be with you in about five or ten minutes."

"Don't forget to pass a copy on to the Major as well. He's the one heading this up, along with the DCS. It wouldn't do to keep him out of the loop, now would it. Right, I'm off to stand by the machine, so don't keep me waiting."

"No, sir."

Five minutes later a photocopy of the letter had been faxed over to Westwitch, for the immediate attention of DCI Sugden.

*

Mikka couldn't remember running down the stairs, or even leaving the building. All she could remember was the feeling of hands pushing at her back, then the collision that had sent Mousey flying off the top step. She could also remember him falling and smacking his head on the stone landing below. In anger, she'd used her momentum to swing herself round and face their attacker. He'd taken a step back so that when she'd lashed out with her foot, aiming for his balls, she'd only been able to kick him in the stomach instead. It'd still been enough to wind the bastard, and gave her time to run down the steps, jump over Mousey's body, then carry on down to the ground floor. Even now she could still see Mousey's staring eyes, his neck at a funny angle, and the blood pooling from the back of his head somewhere.

She'd run to the shopping area, then kept jogging until she found a bus, all the time checking behind to make sure she wasn't being followed. At the station she'd changed routes, and finally made it back to the squat as the afternoon light was fading.

Jason hadn't beaten her back, which made the attic retreat seem all the more desolate, and the last thing she wanted was to be alone with her thoughts. She could see Mousey's sleeping bag and the backpack he kept all his possessions in. They were going to have to do something about that. Poor little Mousey didn't have much, but there was no way she'd let Jason try and sell any of it. She moved closer and picked up the battered Paddington Bear backpack, it's big black eyes looking back at her from a mass of worn out nylon fur.

There was the photo page from a passport which had his proper name on it. Paul Spencer. Mikka wondered about his family. Mousey had never really said anything other than the occasional please or thank you. She didn't even know if he was a runaway, or if he had somehow been abandoned. He'd just trusted them from the time they'd found him. And now look where it'd got him.

She picked the bag up, hearing the movement of his ballpoint pen collection. Everywhere they'd been, Mousey had collected free ballpoint pens – from banks, bookies, supermarkets – anything with a promotion on it. He took them so he could always have something to draw with. He always loved to draw animals. And he was good at it, too. She had kept one of his sketchbooks clean and tidy, and he'd filled it with drawings he copied from pictures he saw in old issues of National Geographic. She'd found them thrown out of a local library and brought them back for him to look at. Next thing she knew, he'd filled the blank A4 pad he'd lifted from one of the pound shops in the high street.

She could feel her emotions starting to get the better of her, and for the first time in years she felt herself start to cry – all the hurt and frustration boiling up – yet thankful Jason wasn't around to see the state she was in. It just wasn't fair! Life wasn't fucking fair! Mousey hadn't done anything to deserve this kind of shit, and now the bastard who'd killed him was going to get away with it. Her tears were coming more freely now, and as she looked down she could see little dark wet patches in Paddington Bear's dirty fur. She closed her eyes and slowly started to regain control again. This wasn't the Mikka she had created to protect herself. This was someone totally different. Someone she hadn't seen in a long time.

Slowly she moved back to her own little space and wrapped herself up in her sleeping bag. The only thing to do was to keep remembering the good times. Keep thinking of the things they did together. She looked at the trapdoor leading down into the house. Jason was going to turn up soon, and then things would sort of be all right again.

*

I wonder if they ever said 'Jenny Halls breaks your balls'? Fennick mused, tapping his fingers impatiently on the steering wheel. The local radio station kept breaking between a talk show and early evening traffic reports. Only the reports were more than a little redundant when you were stuck in the bloody jam they were reporting.

His mind went back to the interview with the pencil-thin Mrs. Halls. At least he assumed she was a Mrs. She had looked to him as if she were in her late forties, with fashionable glasses in metallic burgundy perched on the bridge of her sharp nose, and she reminded Fennick of one of his old school teachers conducting an oral language exam. She'd deliberately centred her questions around what he thought were the contributing factors in regard to the failure of Gold Dust, and whether or not the deaths could have been avoided.

"Would you say – in your opinion that is, Detective Inspector – mainly as I understand you were not attached to the operation directly yourself – that the decision to go down to the hotel car park had been a bad one to make?"

As he talked she had seemed fairly detached about the whole thing, listening to him, making notes on a pad, always keeping her questions open ended as much as possible. What had irked him had been her lack of body language or verbal feedback to his comments, which had made him feel self-conscious, and mentally question his own answers and judgements. All in all, it had been a bit of a depressing experience and, instead of heading back to the station, he'd squeezed his way into the evening traffic, deciding to head on home. Far better to start afresh in the morning and see what statements the knock-knock team had brought back. Sometimes it was a waste of time, but there was always the possibility of a genuine piece of information coming to light.

Anyway, there was a moratorium on "unnecessary" overtime, and somehow the death of Gary Tang didn't seem to figure that highly in many peoples' books.

To take his mind off work and the sluggish traffic, he started to think about the enjoyable way things had progressed the night before.

Just being on the sofa together had reminded him of how much he'd been neglecting their own relationship of late.

Maybe neglecting was too strong a word? Maybe too accepting?

Not that he took Jan for granted. Far from it in fact, even though it wasn't often that they got to spend close personal time together. As one of their friends had put it, they were at the point in their relationship where they were comfortable with each other's silences.

Then afterwards, together in bed, had been mutually enjoyable as well. Jan always seemed to be able to bring him to the edge, then let him gently sink back, teasing him into – well, into more adventurous things than he might normally have thought of. In the past she'd also hinted he could be less cautious as well.

The last time she'd brought the subject up had been over coffee, one lazy Sunday morning while they were still reading the newspapers. They'd been down to the magazine supplements and inane exclusive offers.

"It's just that you're sometimes too polite when it comes to sex."

He'd looked up from his reading. "You mean I say please before, and thank you afterwards?"

"No, nothing like that." She was annoyed at his attempt at humour. "What I mean is, sometimes it seems you're too concerned about me, rather than just getting down and dirty now and again."

The comment had initially stung. "But what if it's something you don't like to do?"

"Then I'll tell you." She put a softer edge to her voice. "We're not that fragile, Mike. I'm not going to leave you just because you might want to paint me all over with honey and chocolate, then spend an hour licking it all off."

"Would you like that?"

"I don't know – but it might be nice if you surprised me with something like that now and again."

"Seriously? Honey and chocolate?"

"Yes. And before you ask, I don't care if it's Fair Trade or eighty percent cocoa, because you'll be doing the licking, not me."

"But what about the sheets?"

Jan had just grinned mischievously at him. "Bugger the sheets. That's what John Lewis is for."

He smiled at the memory. Perhaps he would stop off at a supermarket on the way home? He'd never had peanut butter as a child, so maybe that would be an ideal place to start for both of them. Plus he also needed to pick up a packet or two of condoms.

The flash of red light from the car in front brought him rapidly out of his pleasant reverie, forcing him to jab at the brakes and causing the car to jerk as it stopped. Maybe he would drop by the supermarket, if he ever got out of the bloody traffic in time.

Just then the radio cut out, replaced by the ringing tone of his mobile phone, and his thumb tapped a button on the steering wheel, triggering the hands-free.

"DI Fennick."

"Sir, it's DS Hansen." His voice sounded a little weary in the confines of the car. "I've got some news regarding the Gary Tang investigation, and I don't think you're going to like it."

Inwardly Fennick swore. "Are you sure it can't wait? I'm stuck in traffic, and it'll take me a while to get out of this bloody mess."

"It could probably wait until tomorrow, but I just wanted to give you the heads up in case someone – our mutual friend, for example – starts asking questions you don't have any answers to. We've had a call from the Esterleigh division, and this is where it gets a bit complex."

Fennick sighed heavily. "Go on, how complex?"

"Okay, here goes. Our Forensics had been over to Gary Tang's flat this morning. They had done a cursory dusting, video and stills. No sign of anything untoward, though the remains of Tang's merchandise was impounded and taken back to the evidence warehouse."

"And?"

"Well, one of the dickheads left one of their SOC cases in the flat. Didn't even realise it was missing until after they had logged and locked down the drugs in the warehouse. They then decide not to report it, but do a quick detour back to the station via Tang's flat."

"And that's the problem?" Fennick sounded a little confused. "As long as nothing's missing then they'll just get a bollocking."

"No, this is where it gets more complex. When they returned they found the body of a young boy, dead in the stairwell, and Tang's flat wide open with a makeshift jemmy key stuck in the lock."

"Oh. Fuck."

"Oh fuck indeed, sir. Mainly because one Miss Janine Mickleroy, the neighbour from across the hallway, had already found the body and had called the local division in. She pops into her flat for a glass of gin to calm her nerves, then sticks her head out to see our two arguing about what not to do next. So when the local force arrives, they're in time to find a distraught and confused Miss Mickleroy, and also Snitch and Snatch using what little kit they had left in the SOC case to secure the scene and call through for reinforcements. To put it bluntly, it's apparently been fucking chaos, as the Esterleigh division have rightfully claimed it as being on their patch."

"But when they left the scene the first time, Forensics had secured the flat, and there was no dead body?" Hurriedly Fennick said, "No, forget I said that. Okay, what's to connect the boy to the flat?"

"Well, they found his prints, plus three others, all fresh and new, in the flat itself. And this is where it starts getting really messy. Of the other three, one set is unidentified, and one set belongs to a scrote called Jason Stubbs. But there's also a fair set of prints from someone we both know only too well: Wilson Merrillies."

13

Friday Morning

Alejandro Lucumi hung his towel on one of the hooks by the entrance to the shower room. It wasn't busy this early in the morning, which was why it had been reserved for those in Solitary. The kitchen work detail had already been through – washed and shaved prior to breakfast duties – followed by the two long term sex offenders, Collingdale and the diminutive Beckett. Once they'd finished and been escorted out it left things free for him to shower in peace. At least the facilities were better than in any Colombian prison. No stalls, but there were a dozen shower heads in a row, and the floor was properly tiled and drained. Over the other side of the main room, around a dividing wall, were four lines of utilitarian stainless steel wash basins and a set of twelve toilet cubicles. Back in Cartagena, his parents would have called the facilities a luxury.

Turning on one of the jets he soaped himself down, enjoying the luxury of the hot water; something he would have to come to terms with if the Embassy failed to work its magic. Renton Penstone's legal expert, someone-Amberly, said there were several other possibilities he was also looking into, on the off chance that the diplomatic angle didn't happen. It was just bad luck he'd been forced into using the knife to finish off the hit. Self-defence would be tricky – a case of misguided self-preservation and little understanding of English. Amberly had successfully defended much worse, so for the moment the situation was still pretty good. He closed his eyes and let the water run through his hair and over his face, then set about rinsing the soap off the rest of his body.

When he heard the boots on the tiled floor, he was immediately alert.

Looking up, he saw that a tall, heavy set inmate had walked into the shower room and was standing at the far end, blocking the exit. He was wearing washed out denim dungarees and a stained kitchen apron. Lucumi immediately recognised him by his shaven head and tattooed neck – Nelson Blackwood, a professional white supremacist gang thug and one of D-Wing's enforcers. He watched as the heavy set inmate moved further into the showers, both men keeping silent. There was no point saying anything because they both knew Blackwood wasn't there to chat. Even if Lucumi were to call out, he doubted anyone would come to his aid. Certainly no prisoner would, because Blackwood was under the control of 'Mad' Frank Moffatt – and to go up against Blackwood was the same as going up against Mad Frank. He also knew the prison staff would also turn a deaf ear, as the man wouldn't have been able to get into the showers without help from at least one, maybe even two of the prison staff.

Blackwood brought his hands out of his pockets. One held a shiv made from two razorblades pushed into a length of wooden dowelling stolen from the prison workshop. The other held a wicked looking eight inch metal spike. It reminded Lucumi of the marlin spikes he'd seen the fishermen use back home.

Then Blackwood was moving in, grinning inanely as he slashed out with the shiv. Lucumi took a quick step backwards, out from under the water, legs slightly apart, mind focussed on the fighter not the weapon. That way he could see weaknesses rather than being hypnotised by the razorblades or the spike.

Rapidly he brought his hand up and through the running jets, throwing water into Blackwood's face, blinding him and gaining a second to attack.

Forward onto one foot, turn and lash out with the heel of the other – protect the toes, use the heel – and felt it connect with Blackwood's leg, but missed the original target of his kneecap.

Blackwood grunted and stabbed down with the spike, nearly sinking it into Lucumi's exposed calf, still shaking his head to clear his vision while backing off and away from the shower.

Coming in low, Lucumi shoulder charged and came up between Blackwood's outstretched arms, feeling the top of his head make contact with Blackwood's chin, snapping Blackwood's jaw shut and pushing his head back. He tried to follow it up with several rapid jabs to Blackwood's stomach. But when the first one landed it sent pain through his knuckles and wrist, and Lucumi realised the apron was covering a protective metal tray Blackwood had managed to take from the kitchens.

Nursing his hand, Lucumi stepped away to his right, but even with his attacker no longer blocking the exit, Lucumi looked around for anything he could use as a potential weapon. Nothing immediately to hand, except what Blackwood had brought himself.

Then he saw the towel still hanging from its hook. Snatching at it, he felt it catch for a moment, then it was free, and he wrapped it around his bare arm for protection while he reassessed the situation. It didn't look good. Even if he were to turn around and try to escape, Blackwood would be on him immediately. Lucumi had no choice. He had to finish it, one way or the other.

Panting heavily, Blackwood brought the back of a hand up to his mouth and wiped at the blood coming from his bitten bottom lip. His jaw moved from side to side as if he were trying to set it back in its sockets. Then with a jerk of his head he spat a large gob of bloody spittle towards Lucumi, rapidly followed by a lunge forward. Favouring the shiv over the spike, he slashed low towards Lucumi's stomach.

Lucumi tried to step backwards, but felt his feet lose their grip on the tile floor, his towel-covered forearm only just managing to deflect Blackwood's attack before he regained his balance and put some distance between the two of them.

As Blackwood advanced, Lucumi backed out of the shower room, into the deserted ablutions area. It gave him less freedom to move, but Blackwood was much larger, so would be even more restricted.

Keeping his eyes on Blackwood, Lucumi unwrapped the towel from his arm, glanced at the long slash the shiv had left, then ran the towel through his other hand until he was holding it out by its two farthest corners. He'd only have one chance for his idea to work. If it didn't, then there was no alternative he could think of that offered any better chance of survival.

Moving between two rows of stainless steel wash basins, he slowed his retreat down until he felt Blackwood was within optimum range, then with a vicious flick of his wrist, he released one end of the towel. The audible snap as the flying corner gouged into Blackwood's eye was smothered by the man's howl of pain. Automatically the hand holding the spike flew up to protect his face, sending the weapon clattering loudly down between two of the metal washbasins.

Pressing home his attack, Lucumi stepped in close and lashed out sideways with his foot, his heel landing firmly into Blackwood's groin and balls, his toes pushing hard up against the bottom edge of the kitchen tray. Without waiting to see Blackwood's face hit the tiled floor, he moved quickly around the row of basins, coming up behind the prostrate body. Kneeling down hard into his lower back, Lucumi twisted the towel before wrapping it around Blackwood's neck. Bending forward to make sure he had a firm grip, he used Blackwood's body for leverage, pushing himself up and back at the same time.

There was a sharp noise as the thug's neck snapped, several violent spasms, then the body was limp and still beneath him.

Breathing heavily, Lucumi stood up, freeing the towel from around Blackwood's neck, and shook it out. One end was torn from the coat hook, and there was a gash in it from Blackwood's shiv. Still, it was all he had to cover himself with, and a little bit of modesty would help when he walked back to his cell.

Wrapping the towel around his waist he bent forward and looked down at the dead body, then spat on it as a mark of his disrespect.

As he straightened up again he felt the searing pain of a blade, made from a length of sharpened sprung steel, being thrust into his back half a dozen times. Falling back on top of Blackwood's dead body, his last regret was not having realised that however dumb and stupid Blackwood appeared to be, he would've always made sure he had a wingman in place for protection.

*

Eddie looked down at the chaos scattered across the coffee table. In the centre of it all sat the box file, plus the iPhone he'd taken from Cookie's flat, all untouched since returning home. On top of the box was a rainbow collection of pills and capsules. Beside it sat several half empty bottles of water. He'd needed to down three of them just to rehydrate himself and help stop his head from aching so much.

He'd driven away from Cookie's place in a blind panic – emotionally fucked up, not knowing what to think. To help clear his head he'd spent some time driving around the Tricorn Estate, tapping a couple of dealers for a little more meth, some blunt, and whatever else they had to help him come down and relax. He'd been so preoccupied he'd completely forgotten about the meeting with the IPCC. It wasn't until he got back to his flat and turned his force issue mobile back on, had the thing squawked into life, letting him know he had voicemail.

He'd listened numbly to several messages from the snotty sounding secretary asking if he was going to be delayed, and if so, could he let her know immediately. The next was to tell him he was overdue for his appointment. He poked the erase key, angry that she'd sounded particularly smug. The last one was from her again, telling him to contact the office as soon as possible, so she could re-book the interview immediately. She'd finished by adding that the IPCC interview was part of an on-going high level investigation, and took priority over other engagements wherever possible.

Well, fuck you, too.

He took another bottle of out of the fridge, sat down on the sofa, and knocked back a couple of yellow and pink caps. He wasn't sure what the hell they were but they'd taken him down and zoned him out until around 6.30 a.m.

Crawling off the sofa, he stumbled into the bathroom and climbed into the bath, pulling the shower curtain across just in time to stop the spray off the showerhead from soaking the floor.

Back in jeans and a cleanish sweatshirt, he'd looked over the collection of gear he'd bought, resisting the temptation for a quick lick of the meth. He'd picked out a couple of the lighter stimulants, then rolled himself a couple of smokes, just in case he started getting jittery again. It was a crazy see-saw, but when this was all over he would get back with Simone, then go put himself through rehab. Not that he had a problem, but it would give him time to rest, recharge and get himself sorted. When he came out he would find another branch he could happily transfer to. Or go private. There was still a lot of money to be made doing security consultancy work. As an ex copper, that was bound to be more than ample when it came to suitable qualifications.

Feeling the buzz coming from the pills, he started checking through the contents of the box, putting the folders to one side while he picked through the loose papers. Part way through he found a batch of phone records for several mobile phones and landlines. Every so often there were blocks of bright orange highlighter, with cryptic scribbles in the margins – initials, rather than names, all followed by question marks. PW? JT? CC? There were also dots and asterisks penned beside them in biro or felt tip.

Moving them to one side Eddie turned to the first folder containing surveillance photos stapled to a report. The pictures showed a close group of three people, all in conversation. Eddie thought for a moment but didn't recognise any of them, then read the paperwork underneath.

It had been a London case from the previous year – a combined operation between the Met and the City, involving a new cocaine and heroin route into the UK. The stuff was coming in via Europe, concealed in building construction parts such as prefabricated walls. The report mentioned Customs finding around 25 kilos of heroin concealed in a consignment of hollow roofing beams. The picture of the group had been marked up with felt tip pen, giving a name to a Spanish port authority manager, along with a Moroccan. The third man in the group was identified as Renton Penstone himself. There wasn't much else in the file, and even the report stressed that the content was purely down to an intelligence gathering exercise. No official surveillance had been authorised, due to Penstone's lawyers getting court injunctions on the grounds of repeated Police harassment.

Eddie felt himself getting angry again. Tony had said nothing about this to him at any time, let alone a year or more ago. He closed the folder and tossed it on top of the phone records. Opening up the thicker second folder produced cargo manifests, the most recent being only two months old. Figures were scribbled in the margins and Eddie took an educated guess that they referred to consignments which had either been smuggled in, or discovered in original shipments.

He closed it up and put it on top of the Penstone file. A quick finger down the rest of the folders and he counted five remaining. He rubbed at his neck and shoulders to try and ease the mounting stress.

This wasn't something Cookie had put together overnight, and Eddie was starting to wonder. He picked up one of the makeshift spliffs, lit up, and took down several long hits to help calm himself a little more.

When he opened the next file, he was greeted with a full on photograph of someone he immediately recognised. It was the arsehole who'd contacted them through Gary Tang. Only, in the photograph, he wasn't dressed in an up-market three-piece, and there was no moustache on his upper lip, either. The detailed report beneath the photograph called him Paul Duffley, a well-known close associate of Renton Penstone.

*

Fennick checked the incident room clock. 07:55 was still damn early, regardless of what he needed to catch up on. Another swig of coffee left an oily taste in his mouth, and as he opened up his Action folder, the photocopy of half a dozen handwritten sheets caught his attention.

He read them through several times, looked for a signature, found none, and wondered why Hansen had put a copy in with his other stuff. He didn't see what connection Vic Carlton had with the death of Gary Tang, the death of the child found at Tang's flat, or even Wilson Merrillies come to that. Everyone knew Tang had bought his products from Merrillies to sell on, so maybe he'd found out Tang had been involved with another supplier? Even so, killing Tang was certainly unusual. At best it would usually only warrant a punishment beating of some kind. Using Carlton's preferred M.O. was curious, albeit in the extreme, but it would at least ensure the rest of the dealers maintained their loyalty to Wilson's brand of Class A shit.

However, there was the fact that Vic Carlton had been known to work with Merrillies in the past. But it was also common knowledge that Vic had supposedly retired, in order to spend his ill-gotten gains from his loan sharking and protection rackets.

The call had gone out for Merrillies the previous evening, and later he'd been bumped up the list by adding he was also wanted in regard to two suspicious deaths. Nothing had come back from the trace they'd found at the scene of the young boy, but Fennick was all for ruling Merrillies in, rather than out.

He logged onto the system and was about to pull up the Esterleigh division's input when he felt his mobile vibrating; Joyce Obletta calling back.

Putting the phone to his ear, he said, "And the sexiest woman on the planet says 'what?'"

"What?" Joyce sounded slightly distracted, then, "Oh. Now I get it."

Obviously this early in the morning wasn't the best time for humour. "Sorry, Joyce. Old habits and all that. You've some info on Ren Penstone?"

"There's a whole load of background and history at your fingertips – nothing you couldn't pick out of the regular filing system – but I guess it takes a woman to sort it all out for you Neanderthal DI types."

"Ah, Joyce, admit it. It's not our minds you like us macho types for."

"You know your ego's writing cheques your body is *never* going to cash, don't you?"

"So many miles between us, and so little time." Fennick sighed theatrically. "Make my day, Joyce. Bring me up to speed with Mr Penstone."

There was a throaty chuckle, then she was down to business.

"Renton Penstone, professional thug and all-round villain of this parish, is a second generation hard core professional. His father came up from the Southeast coast and spread like a rash below the river during the Sixties and Seventies. This was going on while Renton received an education at several quality schools. From there he joined the family firm, and rather than take a directorship alongside his father, he started off towards the bottom, running an assortment of little rackets. He was adept at money laundering, tentatively linked to three or four long firm scams, and from there he worked his way up to the shit he is today. Sadly, he's one of those lucky bastards who proves that sometimes crime actually does pay. Provided you get enough idiots who're prepared to take an occasional fall for the right amount of money and family support."

She paused to turn over some papers, then continued. "His visibility is usually where he's been implicated in various other activities. When cases aren't dropped or dismissed due to lack of, and they progress to trial, we've had witnesses who suddenly can't remember details, or fail to turn up on time, or even fail to turn up at all."

"Okay, so no one's been able to put him away yet. Is there anything pending you can talk about?"

"No. Nothing I've heard about from our side…."

"But? C'mon, Joyce, there's always some informer skulking around in the shadows, just like a Sunday tabloid journalist."

"Well, I understand from several Major Crimes people that our Ren is not flavour of the week with some South American narcotics suppliers. One of our midnight raids paid off quite nicely a few months ago. I don't have details, but something happened just before our team went in, by which time most of the bad guys had already disappeared. Penstone's firm was rumoured to have fronted the money for what was an impressively large buy. When the raid went down it nailed a very large stack of cash, bonds and certificates, plus the cocaine as well. Everything in fact, except the main players. In fact, the only people hauled in were several freelance protection men, along with half a dozen heavy duty weapons. One even had a sniper rifle."

"So you're saying Ren lost a lot of money in the deal?"

"No, Mike. I'm saying that *rumour* has it he lost a shed-load of money. It's just an assumption that he had been the one who fronted the buy – they didn't manage to get a direct connection to him. At least not yet. They're still working on it, but it's been more than a couple of months since that successful raid."

"Do you happen to have the narcotics profile to hand? I'd appreciate you sending us a copy." Fennick gave her his secure email details. "It may come in handy, or I may just be chasing my own tail."

"You don't want to do that too often. Makes you go blind."

His turn to laugh, but the humour was short lived. "So, if Penstone was hurting, that might help explain the scam with the consignment they were looking to sell up here. Especially if he was out of pocket to the tune of, what? Seven figures?" Then another thought struck him. "Is one of his lieutenants still working for him – goes by the name of Paul Duffley, but I'm sure he's got a couple more aliases up his sleeve somewhere."

"Duffley is still on his books as far as I know. Why?"

"Well, it was Duffley plus a couple of freelance Colombians who started brokering the deal up here. If I can confirm it was Penstone behind it all, then we'll have some serious leverage to use on Duffley. At the moment all we've got is the bastard doing a deal. He wants to hand us the surviving Colombian, along with details of a new supply route."

"Not sure you'll ever get him to roll over on Penstone. Ren doesn't need to rely on violence any more in order to keep his people in line. He has people queuing up to do that for him."

"Yeah, but what if?"

"There's no 'what if' about it, Mike. If he hasn't already, then Penstone will get Duffley a very classy and expensive legal who will tie you up in so much red tape you won't even know which bow to try and untie first."

Fennick was quiet for a moment, considering some of his

immediate options, until over the phone Joyce said, "When did Gold Dust come up with the ID for Duffley?" The cautious undertone of her voice made Fennick wonder what she might be holding back on.

"It only came to light after the operation had blown up in our faces. Once he'd been arrested and processed. What makes you ask?"

"I sort of used to know Tony Cooke from way back – maybe six or seven years ago, around the time I was about to have our youngest, Adrian. Nice guy, always seemed keen and eager, but he was still relatively new. He was down here on various courses, procedurals and technicals, that sort of thing. I remember him being seconded to the Met for what should have been six months, but turned into eight or nine because he became involved with an investigation. A team had been doing a bit of lucrative bag snatching, taking the ready money and selling the plastic and paper on to an identity theft crew. We couldn't prove Ren Penstone was financing the operation and come the bust we also pulled in Paul Duffley on a couple of weak partials, and the old catch of known association. Usually that sort of thing doesn't stand up too well, but at five in the morning with a bunch of uniforms shouting and stomping around, it's far easier to just come quietly and sort it out down the station."

She paused for a soft chuckle. "Duffley alibied himself quite nicely by saying he was down one of the local markets, selling knock-off handbags, and some pirate DVDs. Eventually the team passed his case on to FACT – the Federation Against Copyright Theft. They got themselves well and truly lost in the paper maze and finally ended up having to let Duffley off on a technicality. The thing is, given his involvement with the original investigation team, I'm sure Tony would've recognised Duffley, even after all this time."

Fennick shifted uneasily in his seat. "What are you saying, Joyce? That DC Cooke knew what was going on?" He scrabbled around his desk, picking up a pen and a pad of post-it notes.

Down the line, Joyce seemed slightly reticent. "I don't know, Mike.

It just seems odd, that's all. Especially when it was someone who was as keen as Tony was. Has his partner said anything? Maybe they both knew the guy was Duffley, and were looking for enough solid evidence to lock down a prestige collar for themselves. I just don't know. But something seems screwy with it all, and that's the only fact I've got."

"Caradine hasn't said much, and he's on sick leave at the moment. He took some shotgun pellets in the face, but nothing too serious. I'll pass this on up and see what the big boys say about it all. Perhaps it would be best to pull Caradine in and make it something more official."

"Whatever, Mike. But I'd appreciate it if you could try and keep me out of it if you can? If you have any idea of the paperwork even a simple expenses claim generates down here, you'll understand why."

"I'll do my best, Joyce."

"By the way, did the couple of surveillance photos I posted help at all?"

Fennick paused his note taking. "You've lost me, Joyce."

"Yesterday morning. Two photos – long range shots of Ren Penstone talking to someone we couldn't immediately identify. I put them up in the HOLMES2 section for Gold Dust. We've been able to identify the other person as someone from your neck of the woods. Peter Wainwright?"

"Yeah, he's one of ours." With the phone pressed to his ear Fennick tapped at the keyboard. A couple of mouse clicks, and he'd finally found the two photographs. One was a shot of the two of them talking in the street, with the time and the location added in a text box. The other was of the same two men. Both of them going in through a side door to what looked like some high street offices above a row of shops. Beside the photos were links to the surveillance authorisation, other relevant Action logs, and one to a Gold Dust update.

Still with an uneasy feeling about the photographs, he said, "Look, Joyce, I'll not keep you. I'm going to follow this and see what results. Bye for now." He half-heard Joyce Obletta say "Be lucky," before he broke the connection.

Still concentrating on the screen, when he clicked on the update, the link produced a report from Jack Telford. It had been posted the previous evening, but didn't seem to be on any priority distribution list. Okay, so it was Jack's call as to where he thought it fitted in with the other Gold Dust leads, but it struck Fennick as odd that it hadn't been given a much wider distribution. He opened the report and started reading.

As part of his role, Telford had set the system to automatically notify himself of any new updates – which was standard practice for anyone in the role of office manager. Only, after Joyce had posted up the photographs, Jack had decided to go see Wainwright himself, hence not being available to take care of Jean Turner. Yet despite the photographic connection, according to Jack's report, there wasn't anything solid enough to warrant pulling Wainwright in. Both Swannick and Nichols hadn't given him up and, according to Telford's report, the alibi Wainwright gave for the time of the hijacking had been easily checked out. He'd been attending a trade lunch on the Tuesday, with a guest list of several 'right honourables' and a good half dozen or so of the 'upstanding members' fraternity, all of whom could vouch for his amusing after luncheon speech.

As to the meeting with Renton Penstone? According to Wainwright, Penstone had approached him with some business proposals, all of which Wainwright didn't like the look of, said so, and that was the end of it. Had he known that Penstone was under police surveillance then he would have cancelled his meeting immediately.

Based on that interview, Jack had simply input the details of the alibi, included Wainwright's comments about meeting Ren Penstone, then he'd marked it all as low priority. Doing that effectively put it to the bottom of the electronic pile, to be tidied away at a later date.

*

Mikka felt herself desperately trying to hold onto the dream for as long as she could. To have it fade away meant she'd have to wake up and face the fear of reality again. At least, in the dreams, her parents loved her, and didn't get off their faces on cans of cheap supermarket booze and fuck knows what else.

They took her to some unknown place called the seaside, and she had a dog – a nice one, not one of those bull terrier things the wankers paraded around with. She threw a stick and watched the black and white Collie go happily running after it. She started to follow, watching Boots running ahead of her, up and over the grassy hill, but she felt her feet get tangled up with something. She started falling and tried to put her hands out to stop herself, but they didn't seem to work either, and she was rapidly diving over the edge, and Mikka woke with a violent start.

Only half awake, she didn't realise her sleeping bag was wrapped around her, so struggled to control the blind panic she felt when trapped in small spaces. It had made her throw up once before, and that was the last thing she wanted to happen in the confines of their attic.

She rolled onto her side, pushed with her arms, and felt the zip start to slide open. Free of the constricting material, she looked over to where Jason usually slept. The bedding was still in a mess from the day before. She looked around at the rest of the attic, straining hard to hear anything – movement, snoring, anything to say he'd come back safely. But nothing. Only the occasional car or lorry rumbling past the squat, and the sound of magpies squawking in the abandoned back garden.

Suddenly it all felt cold and alien, as if there was nothing beyond the attic except loneliness and a depressing pointlessness.

The next thing she knew she was crying uncontrollably and the more she tried to knuckle the tears away, the more they came. Finally she just pushed her head into the pillow, finally letting herself go as the pent up tension and stress broke in an emotional release.

*

Chief Inspector Bashani took another sip of takeaway coffee, then a bite from some muffin concoction the young girl behind the counter had sold him as part of a 'special' breakfast deal. It tasted gluey and sweet. It also stuck to the roof of his mouth so much, Bashani had been forced to wash it away with several large mouthfuls of coffee. A mocha-wocka-choca, or some such twaddle.

The day before had been one of two halves. Duffley and a screaming Gordon Lemon in the morning, then wrapping up Swannick and Nichols in the afternoon.

There was nothing they could do about Lucumi. The Colombian had remained silent, so he'd been put to one side until an initial trial date had been arranged. That, in itself, was proving to be more a diplomatic pain than a legal one, even though there was no question of his guilt. Apart from the forensic evidence, there was video footage from half a dozen Armed Response helmet cams as well. And with Duffley sticking to his story that they had threatened him and his family, Bashani was sure Lucumi would be banged up in recess for some time to come. Mind you, the bugger had Frank Amberly from Maplethorpe and Gittings as his legal, so for M&G it was going to be a win-win, regardless of the outcome.

Lemon was also happy with the way things were proceeding with Duffley, judging by the wide smile he'd left with – and Ramesh wasn't going to bet on whether it was due to the easiness of the case, or the massive fee he was obviously charging Duffley's sponsor.

Swannick, on the other hand, was still proving loyal to Peter Wainwright and going out of his way not to implicate him in any of Marcus' activities. Nichols was just as bad, but only because he didn't have the sense to see what was going to hit him when the prosecution had finished presenting their case. Marcus had happily turned on him as a way of not turning on Wainwright, and with Victor Carlton dead, there were no obvious nasty loose ends to hang himself with.

Some more of the muffin clagged itself to the roof of his mouth as he pushed open the door to the Incident Room. Thankfully there was enough coffee left to dislodge the gunk, before he tossed both the remains of the muffin and the dregs of the coffee into the bin beside his desk.

As he sat down he glanced over at his In tray and saw no green folder from Jack Telford. What he did see were several photocopied sheets, face down, on top of the regular files. He stabbed the power button on his workstation as he picked them up.

He glanced through the material once, then immediately read it through again. On their own the pages meant little or nothing. Put them in association with the rest of Gold Dust and things got pretty interesting. Especially if Jean Turner was prepared to connect Penstone to Carlton. Officially the handwritten material might be classified as hearsay, rather than hard evidence – but it would certainly put it in the 'probable cause for further investigation' category. Once that was initiated, there was always the chance something else would be unearthed that they could use to nail Penstone's organisation with.

Bashani put the copies to one side and checked the on-line evidence log, surprised to see it had been tagged in by DS Hansen. Looking across the room he could see Mike Fennick at his desk, but not Hansen. How come the DS had handled the evidence rather than one of the Gold Dust team? There were no follow-up notes, and no new assignments in the Action Log either – but he was sure that Hansen must have shown Jean Turner's letter to someone. Had Raynolds included it in last night's press brief? He would have to brief Raynolds about yesterday's results, and the fact the team had not been able to immediately pinpoint any internal leaks prior to the operation's collapse. It all seemed to boil down to external forces conspiring against them, by the feel of it. Originally Bashani hadn't given any consideration to the idea that the undercover team had been set up by Duffley and Penstone. But, with the new evidence, it had started to make lateral logical sense. He still had no idea why Penstone would want to lay his hands on that amount of money, but it seemed to be a more believable proposition than someone from inside the operation setting things up.

His workstation bleeped and a desktop icon flashed, indicating that he had a priority email. It was from Raynolds. Speak of the Devil, as they say. It was a call for a meeting with his lordship, as soon as – if not sooner. It didn't say much, only that:

Some fresh information came to light yesterday evening and, coupled with events earlier this morning regarding Alejandro Lucumi, I'm calling a meeting to discuss a new course of action prior to the 10:30 press briefing.

Bashani had yet to log into the HOLMES2 system, so he wondered when the Colombian Embassy had been successful in getting the bastard freed. But that wasn't his problem. A quick check showed the message had also been sent to Mike Fennick as well. Better if they went down together, that way Ramesh wouldn't be stuck making small talk with Raynolds while they waited for Mike to show up. He got up and wandered over to Fennick's desk.

"You get an email from the DCS?"

"Yep. I just need to finish typing up some fresh info into the database, then I'll be heading down. It's a bit of background from a contact down in London. With a touch of luck, it should help move the Gold Dust case along."

"Really? Well, I've just read an account of a meeting between Penstone and Victor Carlton. Written in the fair hand of none other than Jean Turner, no less. It was brought in by your sergeant, yesterday afternoon."

Fennick remembered the unsigned photocopied sheets. "Sorry, who's Jean Turner?"

"She used to be Carlton's get out of jail free card." He looked over Fennick's shoulder at his screen. "So what have you got from down south?"

"I've been talking to an old contact in the NCA. It seems DC Cooke probably knew Martinez was Duffley, and also knew Duffley was a major player in Ren Penstone's organisation."

"When the hell did that come in?!"

"Literally just now. I started typing it up as soon as I got it. I'm going to be a couple of minutes then I'm going down to show it to the DCS."

"And this puts Cooke in the picture as an informant?"

"Not sure. All it shows is prior contact, back when he was a trainee."

Bashani wasn't happy. "We're going to have to tread very carefully with this, Mike. Apart from the fact DC Cooke was killed in the line of duty, I don't want to create the impression we're using a dead man, who obviously can't defend himself, to sort out our own in-house clean-up."

Fennick looked a little irritated. "Look, all I have so far is a connection. We need to bring Eddie Caradine in, get him to answer some questions regarding his relationship with Cooke. How they did business, who they deferred to, and what else the two of them might've known beforehand."

"But I thought you and that DS of yours had been taken off Gold Dust and put on the Gary Tang murder." There was a tone of guarded suspicion in his voice.

"I set this going before we were moved over, and she's only just come back to me this morning."

"You haven't got anything else on the go that I might need to know about, have you? Mainly as I don't like being made to look a fool in public, especially when the audience consists of promotion board members."

Fennick was taken by surprise. "You think I'm doing this for myself?"

"I think you better print that off and we both go and see DCS Raynolds now."

Bashani collected the photocopied sheets off his desk, then went over to stand by the door waiting for Fennick.

Clicking the icon, Fennick crossed to the printer, took the sheet from the tray and in stony silence walked past Bashani, heading straight for the lift.

*

Mikka sat uncomfortably in the reference section of the Pelman Square Public Library. In front of her was a well-thumbed copy of the local A to Z. The cover was badly creased, with some of the pages missing where people had surreptitiously ripped them out. She looked back down and absently poked at it with a finger. Jason still hadn't come back by the time she'd got herself ready. She'd even gone down into the back kitchen and made enough hot water to give herself a proper wash. If you didn't keep yourself clean and tidy then people tended to notice you all the more, especially on public transport. Also the longer she took getting ready, the more chance there was of Jason coming back. Yet she knew if she didn't do something, Mousey would probably just be written off as an unknown runaway.

Down by her chair leg was his Paddington Bear bag with all his belongings in it. If she handed that in as well, then maybe they could find out where his parents were. Even if they didn't care about him, they would at least want to know that he was dead. She didn't know what the police did with dead bodies if they weren't collected after a period of time. Well, whatever it was, she was sure little Mousey deserved something better.

With her mind made up, she took a notepad and a Biro from the backpack, laid them on the table, and flicked through the street maps until she got to the index. Right at the start were half a dozen or so pages of "useful lists of important places and organisations" such as hospitals, bus stations, libraries, and 24-hour police stations. In a slow, neat hand, she copied the list of police stations with their map references, then copied the reference for the library in Pelman Square. Then she went back to the start of the book, where there was a rough map of the area with numbered squares on it. The numbers were the page numbers for the area underneath it.

Carefully she put lines through the police stations she felt were too far away. Without any real bus money, she had to rely on something being within walking distance.

Twenty minutes later she'd got the list down to two. She tore the sheet off the pad – the sound of ripping paper in the silence had immediately attracted the unwanted attention of several people studying nearby. She looked up and glared at a couple of students across from her as she put the pad back into Mousey's little bag, then she flipped the A to Z open at the Pelham Square page. From there she traced her way across the pages until she found the Morningfield Cross police station. It seemed to be a mass of streets and back roads, crossing and re-crossing several of the motorways. She couldn't remember all the twists and turns, not the way her head was at the moment, nor did she fancy trying to draw the thing on another sheet of paper. Photocopies were expensive, and she didn't have the money on her anyway. She thought about pulling the pages out, like others had done before. But the thought of attracting yet more attention to herself put her off the idea.

Turning back to Pelham Square again, she traced the route over to the other police station. It seemed easier. Just a case of remembering the lefts and rights, but at least they occurred at the ends of roads, and there was only a couple of roundabouts and some traffic lights to get over. Thankfully there was no motorway to cross.

Folding the sheet of plain paper in half, she started to write down the directions in simple instructions, tracing the route from the Pelham Square library, over to the police station in Elizabeth Slinger Road.

*

Bashani knocked aggressively on Raynolds' office door and stormed in before the DCS had even looked up from his desk. Fennick, close behind in Bashani's wake, carefully shut the door behind him in an effort to control his anger, then took the other seat in front of Raynolds' desk. Bashani had already started before Fennick had sat down.

"I want to register a complaint in regard to the working practices of DI Fennick. I am not going to be undermined by someone who seems to be withholding information pertinent to a case he has already been removed from."

Fennick glared at the CI next to him. "As he already knows, I had previously started several lines of information and intelligence gathering. One of those has now come up with something this morning, and it seems the information pisses all over one of the assumptions made by the Gold Dust investigation."

Raynolds held his hands up for silence. "Okay, let's stop all this fucking about right now. DI Fennick, what's come up that's so important?"

Fennick handed Raynolds the printed report, leaving his superior to scan through the text. When he'd finished he looked up.

"Okay, it's something we're going to have to deal with, sooner rather than later." He looked over to Bashani. "Now, what have you got?"

Bashani handed over the photocopy and was about to start in on his snap report when Raynolds again held up his hand.

"I've already seen this. DS Hansen brought it to me yesterday afternoon."

Bashani let his anger get the better of him. "Fucking typical! They're both at it!"

Raynolds glared him into silence. "As I was going to say, DS Hansen brought this to me yesterday afternoon while you were out with Nichols and Swannick, and he couldn't find Jack Telford. That is why he handed it over to me. It was this, plus the death of Alejandro Lucumi, in Hollowell wing this morning, which has prompted me to re-evaluate the whole situation."

Raynolds paused to let the implications sink in before announcing the rest of his news. He hoped that by springing it on the pair of them without any preamble, it would defuse their aggression towards each other.

"After some deliberation I've decided it's time to hand this over to the National Crime Agency and their organisation. They have a better knowledge of Penstone's activities, and can hopefully turn this into a solid conviction encompassing more than we ever could. They also have far better resources and budgets than we have. More importantly, it takes the whole shitty heap away from us, regardless of what the press might think about it being handed over to someone else. After a couple of weeks it will have completely died down, and in a couple of months they'll be tearing some other poor bastard apart in public."

With that, he stood up and walked to the door, calling over his shoulder, "If you two would care to follow me, I'm about to do something I think I'm actually going to enjoy for a change."

The three of them headed down to the ground floor in silence – both Bashani and Fennick privately fuming in anger, Raynolds for once with a genuine smile on his face. He led them to Interview

Room 2, and without pausing to knock, he entered and indicated to the uniform WPC that she should leave. Pulling the chair from under the table he sat down while Bashani and Fennick were forced to stand together behind him. On the other side of the table sat Paul Duffley and Gordon Lemon.

With a contented grin on his face, Lemon said, "At last, people who are going to take us seriously! Though, to be honest, Jimmy, I don't know why you called for a meeting with my client at this time."

Ignoring him, Raynolds said, "Mr. Duffley, I have some good news or bad news, depending on how you interpret it. This morning, at around seven o'clock, Alejandro Lucumi was killed while defending himself from an attack by other inmates. He was being held in the Greensborough Remand Centre – not the highest of security, I'll admit – though I doubt his death could've been prevented one way or another, regardless of where he was being held. Still, whoever ordered it certainly wanted him dead and out of the way. Which brings us to our first problem.

"Without him, I suspect you have nothing much left to bargain with in regard to any deal the Assistant Chief and Gordon here may have struck. So that killing could, in fact, be viewed as probably being detrimental to your case."

Lemon broke into Raynolds' flow. "Jimmy, I'm sure ACC Richardson will keep to his end of the bargain. My client can still be of use in regard to the supply line."

Unperturbed, Raynolds continued as if Lemon wasn't there.

"Another way of looking at the murder of Mr Lucumi, might be that someone has it in mind to do some damage limitation and tidy up loose ends. I suspect the death of an undercover police officer wasn't part of your original plan. Which puts this whole business in a totally different light, for all concerned. So the easiest way would be to try and ensure this whole business doesn't make it to trial. Dead men, as they say, tell no tales – and we certainly seem to be stacking them up on this one, don't we?"

Without breaking his eye contact with Duffley, Raynolds held up a hand towards Lemon. "You'll have a chance in a minute, Gordon. I mean, it's not you, but Mr Duffley here, who might end up in Greensborough over a weekend while he's on trial for other, more minor offences." To Duffley, Raynolds said, "Also, I have here a photocopy of a document which has recently come into our possession. In it is a description of a meeting between Victor Carlton and Renton Penstone, one of several meetings I might add, in which the hijacking of your deal was openly discussed."

Lemon immediately stepped in, the strain of trying to control himself evident in his face.

"I'm sorry, but my client has not admitted it was his deal. Also, I've not been advised of this document before now. To be honest, Jimmy, I thought we were working together on this. I'll need time to examine its authenticity at the very least. Who's it from?"

Raynolds moved his head slightly to look at Lemon. "For once, Gordon, shut the fuck up." Looking back to Duffley, he said, "There also seems to be an indication that one of the undercover teams may have been involved in providing Penstone with intelligence information. That information may well have been used in disrupting Operation Gold Dust, and it may have been instrumental in getting a police officer killed. And believe me when I say it, I have complete and utter faith in this source."

Duffley looked a little confused. "Are you saying the bastards who came at us in the hotel car park were actually working for Ren?"

"It's an avenue of investigation we'll probably be pursuing, and obviously I can't say more than that. Another possibility is that you knew Renton Penstone intended to rip the buyers off by bringing in Victor Carlton and his team. In other words it was a sting to gain Penstone a large amount of fairly clean money. That way, he could start paying off the cartel and other backers who lost their consignment in a raid down in London."

Duffley looked hard at Raynolds, then at Lemon. Raynolds picked up on the uncertainly.

"I wouldn't ask Mr. Lemon here for advice. He's represented Mr. Penstone in the past, on many occasions, as you know. So, if anything, he has a vested interest in protecting the more profitable of the two of you." Raynolds smiled. "I'm pretty sure even you can work out who Mr Lemon will want to side with."

Lemon glared at Raynolds. "That's bloody close to slander, Jimmy." His voice was cold and emotionless.

"At the moment, Gordon, I really don't give a toss, because another reading of the scenario is that Mr. Penstone set up Mr. Duffley."

"What?" Duffley sounded surprised.

"Exactly what I said. If you're as innocent of the situation as you say you are, then why would Renton Penstone set up an armed hijacking without your knowledge? Or are you going to say you knew all about it?"

Duffley immediately took the bait. "I didn't know a fucking thing about it! Seriously! When that psycho came at us with that bloody sawn off, do you think I pissed myself for the fun of it? I had no idea what the hell was going on, and that, for once, is the fucking truth."

Raynolds pursed his lips a little. "So what was the original plan, Paul? We know Penstone was in deep shit with the South American suppliers. It couldn't have looked good for him around the manor, could it? Losing all their gear, *and* his money as well. Or were there other backers besides Penstone? Now that would be nasty, wouldn't it."

Gordon Lemon immediately jumped in. "Don't answer that! As far as we've been told this isn't an official interview, nor is it being conducted under caution. But that doesn't mean you're not liable to incriminate yourself, regardless of what deals have already been made."

It was enough to throw Duffley into confusion again, which was exactly what Raynolds wanted. Taking his chance, he said, "You know, Paul, you're probably within your rights to ask for a new counsel on the grounds of a lack of confidence in the one you have now. Personally I wouldn't blame you if you did."

Lemon stood up sharply. "I'm going to put in an official complaint to the IPCC directly." Angrily he looked up at Fennick and Bashani. "You two are going down as witnesses," he emphasised it with an accusing finger. "So don't think you can deny this ever happened. Believe me, by the time I've finished you'll be out patrolling the bloody streets, so fucking help me!"

Without even flinching, Raynolds said, "If you two officers would kindly escort Mr. Lemon off the station premises, Mr. Duffley and I are going to discuss what he thought was supposed to happen out at the hotel. Then I'm going to see about putting Mr. Duffley somewhere safe, at least until the Metropolitan NCA unit can arrange to transport Mr. Duffley, along with our other witness, down to London. No doubt the pair will be spending some time in the company of a particularly eager section of the Met's Organised Crime team."

*

Fennick had barely made it back to the incident room when he felt his mobile vibrating. It was DCI Sugden. For a moment he considered letting it go over to voicemail, but decided it would be better to take it, regardless of how surprised he was feeling.

"Hello, sir. I was just about to call you. There's been a few new developments in regard to Gold Dust. The Colombian, Lucumi, is dead. I've only just heard he was attacked in Greensborough Remand early this morning. They still haven't put together any preliminary reports, or even started an internal investigation, but general feeling is it's somehow connected to the whole Gold Dust business. Maybe it's just as well, because other breaking news is that the DCS has cut a deal with the NCA, and they're going to be picking it all up when Duffley is handed over to a team from SDC7."

"So I heard. Sunny Peterson hasn't stopped crowing about it. Well, it's not every day you get handed a willing witness and the chance to bring a heap of glory on yourself, is it?"

"No, I suppose it isn't." Fennick sounded a little crestfallen. "I suppose you've also heard about Jean Turner as well then? I can send you a copy of her letter if you want?"

"Got a copy of it yesterday, courtesy of Hansen. You've got a really efficient sergeant there. Should make a damn good DI, but don't tell the bugger I told you that."

"Bloody hell. Is there anything you know that I don't?"

"Not at the moment. Look, don't feel you've been left out, Mike. I need you to print some documents off for me out of HOLMES2. I need a full copy of Jack Telford's recent input. I'm looking for literally anything since Thursday morning."

"Anything?"

"Aye, that's what I said. If I start poking around myself then people such as Jimmy Raynolds will start asking why. The last thing Jimmy needs at the moment is something else he might think he has to worry about. I just want to see what Peter Wainwright had to say for himself. Word has it he's been doing a bit of work for the community, namely investing in a carjacking gang out Wemton Green way. Nice area, that, very countrified and genteel, wouldn't mind moving out that way when I retire. Also lots of nice nick-to-order vehicles, too. Now, I don't mind villains trading up and moving onto our patch now and again. Means they've got bugger all sense and are easy to catch. But nicking by proxy? That's more than a little upsetting."

"Well, there's not much of anything in Jack's report. Apart from the fact Wainwright's covered his arse for last Tuesday by speaking at some lunch. And he doesn't strike me as a particularly hands-on kind of criminal."

"He's not. Which is why any intelligence is always worth having. Once I've Jack's report I'll go nosing around the guest list. See if there are any dots that might be worth joining up."

"Okay, sir, I'll get onto it."

"Thanks. I'll be expecting a fax in five minutes."

"What?"

But Sugden had already broken the connection. With an uncomfortable feeling the request was not as innocent as it seemed, Fennick started pulling up and printing off the relevant files, before faxing the results to Sugden over at Westwitch.

14

Friday Afternoon

It had been easy for Eddie to figure out once he'd aimlessly driven the Mondeo around for a while.

Reading through all the material, he'd come to finally realise that the box contained all of Cookie's research and notes on Renton Penstone's organisation. In with that had been intelligence and reports on a pair of local villains – Wilson Merrillies and Peter Wainwright – the two biggest known suppliers of narcotics in the area. There had been an uneasy truce between the two of them for years. But with the arrival of Duffley as a new supplier, it looked as if Penstone had plans to exploit their rivalry as he expanded his operations up from the South. Cookie had filled a notebook with theories, and the margins of various photocopied reports with dozens of question marks, scribbled and scratched all over the place. You didn't need brain cells to realise a new player on the scene would upset the balance, which was exactly why Penstone and Duffley had targeted Gary Tang. He was a known buyer from Wilson Merrillies. Tempt him away, and others would've been more willing to follow his lead.

And despite Wilson's ferocious reputation for violence against those he felt had wronged him, the promise of serious protection would certainly have helped sway things. Hence the use of the

Colombian muscle.

He parked a little way from Jarrold Street, and another quick lick from the Ziploc bag brought on a rush of guilt for a moment or two. He'd promised himself he wasn't going to do it so often, but he knew it would give him the edge. He had plans, and needed to be more than just on top of his game. Then the buzz came up and he felt invincible again. Rock steady, any time Eddie. He'd even caught himself whistling as he walked through several side alleys and into the Cat & Fiddle.

The lunchtime office crowd were in, most of them around the top end of the bar, or chancing their luck on the fruit machines. Just counting off the minutes before going back to their desks and their quotas. In his regular back corner, The Poet seemed to be doing easy business as people stopped by to load up for a weekend of clubbing. He moved further along the bar, slipping into a free spot near the far end, away from the door traffic, then waited impatiently for the staff to notice his upraised hand.

"Any time you're ready love, over here."

At last one of the girls decided she couldn't ignore him any longer and came round to Eddie's part of the bar.

"Yeah?"

"I'll have a pint of lager, love. And tell your governor I'd like a word with him if he's free. It's about Sid Miller. Tell him it's Shaun Gregory who wants to talk."

She looked him up and down a couple of times, appraising him for potential trouble. After a moment she just nodded, then went over to the pumps and poured him his lager. Handing him his change she then disappeared out the back.

She took her time, and Eddie had almost finished his pint before she'd finally returned, the landlord in tow. She pointed to Eddie, then went out the back again, taking a packet of cigarettes and a lighter with her.

The landlord came over and looked hard at Eddie for a moment. "What's this all about? Megs says you wanted to talk to me about Dusty Miller? I've already told you, the bastard's dead."

"I know that. I want to know who took over his business, and his stock."

He stood his ground as the landlord gave him another long stare. "Why do you want to know? You looking for a piece?"

"I might be, otherwise why would I be asking?"

"If you're going to get cocky, you can fuck off right now." He gestured towards the door with his thumb.

Eddie just glared back at him. "So who do I talk to in order to pick up a fairly clean piece? Nothing fancy, just a straight thirty-two or thirty-eight, none of that automatic crap."

"How much you willing to pay?"

"Five hundred, up front, small notes." Eddie patted his pocket where the top of an envelope was clearly visible. It had been a bit of a gamble, but he'd used one of the credit cards issued to Operation Gold Dust in order to get the money out of a hole in the wall machine. The card hadn't been cancelled, so it was easy to pull the funds out. The landlord just nodded, then disappeared out the back again.

The first half hour seemed to drag, and by the end of it he felt ready to snap. Only one thing for it. Outside, near the bus shelter, he pulled out his tobacco pouch and lighter. After the second puff he realised he'd accidentally flashed up one of the spliffs, instead of a natural. Not that it mattered outside. Anyway, he could do with a little chill waiting around for the bloody armourer to show.

With Cookie gone, and no one to watch his back any more, the only alternative he had was to carry something. Just in case. There was no point in carrying unless you intended to use, but it would only be if he really had to. Self-preservation. Nothing more.

Behind him a slow trickle of office bods were leaving the pub, most of them heading back to wherever it was they worked. He finished his smoke then walked back inside, feeling more comfortable now that there was room to move and breathe again. He paid for another pint of lager, then sat down at one of the tables towards the back. A few moments later a large guy, wearing a cheap and cheerless zip-up rainproof jacket, sat down opposite to him, putting his pint on the table.

Eddie looked up at the guy. He was chubby, with one of those instantly forgettable nerdy faces. Through the open half of his jacket a polo shirt hung loosely around his neck, but strained against a beer gut which probably hung over the top of his supermarket jeans.

A regular Man at Primark, thought Eddie as the guy smiled inanely back at him. *This is all I need. A visit from the local village fucking idiot.*

The stranger's smile broadened, and he leaned in towards Eddie. In a confidential tone he said, "I understand from Archie that you might be in the market for something I might have."

"Archie?" Eddie's mind was starting to jitter up on the remains of the amphetamine and the new rush of adrenaline.

"The governor." The stranger turned in his seat and looked back at the bar, singling out the landlord and shrugging his shoulders questioningly. The landlord just glared back, nodded a couple of times, then went off to serve another customer.

He turned back to Eddie, now happy he had the right guy. "Archie says you can be trusted, and you've got the cash for the deal. For five I can let you have a nice little thirty-eight revolver, or a twelve shot twenty-two, depending on what sort of work you intend to do with the piece. The revolver is a good all-rounder, but limited to the number of bullets. It could be that the two-two is better suited, if you intend working at close range – say taking down a street gang member or two. Ammunition for either is five pounds a round, by the way."

Eddie looked at him a little incredulously.

"Are you for fucking real?"

Pushing himself back from the table a little way, the stranger unzipped his rainproof jacket further. Underneath it Eddie could now see the butts of the two guns, sitting in shoulder holsters, and what he'd taken as a beer gut was a padded pouch strapped to the guy's stomach. Zipping the rainproof back up, he looked over to Eddie.

"Now, show me the money."

*

The WPC quietly knocked on the office door, waited for Raynolds to call out, then let herself in, closely followed by a relaxed and curious Jean Turner.

Gentleman that he was, Raynolds stood up when the two women entered. "If you'd care to take a seat?" Jean Turner smiled appreciatively. It looked like DCS Raynolds had been brought up right. *Shame he was a copper, though.*

Raynolds turned to the WPC. "Could you get us some coffee." Then, to Jean, he asked, "How do you take it?"

She thought about it for a second then shook her head. "Thank you, but no. Hopefully this won't be long. I'm assuming this is about the letter I gave the young sergeant when I came to collect Victor?"

Raynolds waited for the WPC to leave before opening the file on his desk. "I'll not beat about the bush, Mrs. Turner. You've supplied us with some interesting information. However, I understand from various members of my team you might not have been entirely honest and forthcoming in the past? I'm talking about various other activities which Victor Carlton may have been involved in."

Jean settled back in her chair. "I thought you said you'd get to the point? Victor had several choice phrases he liked to use, and the one which springs to mind at the moment involves urination and pots."

Raynolds coughed a little at her adept bluntness. *Okay, time to start pissing then.*

"You've effectively given us an account which potentially puts a known London organised crime leader here in Manchester on a certain date. You connect him with Victor Carlton who was later shot dead while trying to hijack a consignment of Class A drugs and a large holdall of money. If you're prepared to testify as to what happened that evening, and go so far as to identify the person you refer to in your written document, there is a very good chance that we can do something about it."

Jean Turner thought for a moment, the tip of a middle finger unconsciously rubbing at a tiny blemish by the corner of her mouth.

"And if I'm not prepared to testify? What then?"

Raynolds picked up the photocopied sheets from the file. "Then this becomes so much waste paper, and the person who set Victor up gets away with killing him."

"You know for sure he was directly involved with Victor getting shot like that?"

"I'm pretty sure he engineered the whole thing. Except for the police presence, of course."

The comment sounded a little too rushed. She had been around professional liars for most of her life, and although Raynolds was good, he wasn't in Jean's league. She thought it over as the WPC returned with Raynolds' coffee.

"I'm not a fool, Mr. Raynolds."

"I never thought you were."

Again, just the slightly wrong edge to his voice. He was a climber and slimy with it. Still, she'd been prepared for something like this when she'd handed the envelope over to the nice looking sergeant at the morgue. She'd gone home, packed a couple of suitcases, and even told Maureen and Frank next door she was going away on holiday for a while. The question now was what to hold out for in regard to negotiations?

"I'm only prepared to discuss this particular business of Victor's. I'm not going to go back over anything that happened in the past, and that includes anything you might think he was involved with. What's dead stays dead, and that includes my Victor."

Raynolds sucked on a tooth for a moment. "Okay, that's fine. But you've got to be prepared to deal with us straight. I've got to say it, there is a lot riding on the fact you can identify the other man again, and not just this case either."

She cocked her head slightly to one side. "Then I'm assuming you'll be placing me under protective custody?"

Raynolds picked up his coffee. "We would place you in a safe house for twenty-four to forty-eight hours. At least until officers from London's National Crime Agency unit can arrange to transport you to another secure location somewhere else in the country. They won't tell us where, and we certainly don't want to know."

"Saves you any further embarrassment if things go wrong again, doesn't it."

You bitch! But Raynolds left the thought unvoiced. "There is that, I suppose. However, do we have an agreement or not? If you're prepared to testify, then we can give you full, round the clock protection. If not, then I'm sorry but I don't have the level of resources to allocate that amount of specialist manpower."

Jean Turner let out a quiet chuckle. Underneath he was a conniving old bastard, despite his airs and graces. "Well, Mr. Raynolds, having already lost Victor, I don't think I've got anything left worth losing." She leaned forward in her seat and smiled demurely at him. "Is this where you spit into the palm of your hand and offer to shake on the deal?"

*

The weight of the revolver felt odd in Eddie's jacket pocket. He'd handed over the five hundred, and an extra twenty-five quid from his own pocket for the bullets. He'd had to go back to the Mondeo before he could check out the piece properly, and was relieved to find it wasn't some crappy conversion job with a fucked up firing pin. Scrabbling around in the glove compartment he'd grabbed his makeshift pill box and popped a couple of red and blue moodies. According to the guy who sold them, they were supposed to ease his tension for longer than the spliffs he'd been using. To help them kick in he'd gone back to the Cat & Fiddle and sunk another lager.

Feeling a little more mellow, he moved to a deserted corner, pulled out several of the phone record sheets and thought about who the various initials belonged to. The easy answer would be to phone the numbers, except it was best to keep his regular phone off for the time being. That way he wasn't likely to take any calls from that stuck-up IPCC bitch. He pulled out the iPhone he'd found in Cookie's flat, and checked the battery. Still a fair amount, and the phone came up with a connection immediately he'd turned it on. Tapping through the called numbers list, the first couple he didn't recognise at all, but the one after he certainly did.

Simone answered with a cautious "Hello?"

Eddie didn't speak, but sat listening to her confused voice.

"Who is this? I don't know what's going on, but it's not funny!" She was starting to sound scared, which made him feel good inside.

"It's me, Babe." His voice sounded quiet and detached against the background noise of the jukebox and the fruit machines.

"Eddie? Eddie, what the hell are you playing at?! Where did you get Tony's phone from?"

Still sounding cold and distant, he said, "What's your number doing in Tony's call list?"

"Because he called me."

"On a regular basis?"

She sounded a little exasperated. "Yes, on a regular basis. It's not a crime for me to talk to other men, is it? You're not the only man in my life you know."

"Is that all you two did? Just talk?"

"Christ, Eddie, just take a moment and bloody listen to yourself. You're sick, you know that? We just talked, about anything and everything. We talked because," she paused for a second before taking the final step. "Because Tony felt he couldn't talk to you anymore."

It caught him by surprise. "What? Why? Tony could always talk to me."

"No he couldn't, Eddie. He said you'd been losing it of late. He said you were getting way too unstable. You always have problems keeping reality separate from those make believe undercover fantasies. He said you were becoming dangerous, Eddie."

He remained silent for a moment, subconsciously grinding his teeth as her words bit into him. Then, "Of course he could talk to me. We were a team, Babe. We were a damn good fucking team as well."

"Maybe at the start, Eddie, when you didn't believe in all your own bullshit. Did you know he was looking to get out? Did he tell you he hated all that undercover stuff? All those fake IDs and the stress of trying to remember who the hell he was supposed to be from one week to the next? That was why he was putting together something of his own. It was something to do with what the two of you had been working on. Tony said if he could get together enough of a case, then hand it over to some department down in London, then maybe he could swing a position down there. Maybe even add some weight to his promotion prospects."

She stopped as she realised she was crying. "Anything to get out of working with you again."

Eddie felt as if someone had just kicked him hard in the balls, and he had to take several deep breaths before he could actually speak again.

"And you didn't think to tell me?"

"For Christ's sake, Eddie! If Tony couldn't talk to you, what chance did I have?" Her voice softened a little. "You need help, Eddie. You've been at it for too long without a break. You need to talk to someone professional about it all."

Eddie rubbed his eyes with a knuckle, feeling the pressure in his head. "I love you."

There was a strange pause, then Simone said, "I love you too, Eddie. But not like this."

"I just need to sort some things out with some people, Babe. Once I've straightened it out I'll see about a proper holiday, go somewhere nice for a change. Just me and you, Babe."

"No Eddie. Whatever it is, it can wait until you're well again."

But he knew it couldn't. He had to know if Tony had been behind the failure of Gold Dust or not. The easiest way to do that would be to confront this Paul Duffley outright. Face him up with the fact that Tony had been running a file on him, probably even recognised who he was from the start. And he was going to ask the bastard if Tony had been in on the deal from the start.

"I've got to go, Babe. Things to see, and people to do."

He turned the iPhone off and stuck it back in his pocket.

*

It had taken the uniformed patrols a while, but just after 4 p.m. Hansen had received a call from Dispatch saying that Wilson Merrillies had been picked up and was being brought in. An informant, with more balls than brains, had told a foot patrol where they could find him, and the patrol had called it in with a request for backup.

Merrillies had been at one of his backstreet nightclubs. He owned several, though none had been linked to any kind of money laundering activities. However, when the patrol had picked him up, he'd supposedly been entertaining a private party. But with only two other people in the club with him – and both had tried to slip away the first chance they got – the whole thing looked more like business rather than pleasure. Merrillies himself had put up no resistance, even smiling and joking with the officers bringing him in. The happy go lucky guy, pleased to be helping the police with their investigations, even though he'd never once asked why he was being taken in for questioning.

Now, under the florescent light of the interview room, the scars around his eyes and across the bridge of his nose showed up whiter than the rest of his face. A small section of his hairline was shaved back and a couple of butterfly stitches were visible across a gash in his forehead – the wound still angry and red.

Hansen leaned forward. "That's a pretty little trophy you've got there."

Merrillies forced a smile. "Perils of working in a garage. Had an old MG up on the lift. Turned around a bit too quick and caught the end of a bolt."

"You like to keep your hand in then?"

"When there's something special to be done, I like to give it the personal touch. Sets an example to the rest of my mechanics."

Fennick looked directly at Merrillies. "Is that why you paid a visit to Gary Tang's flat? Looking to give him the personal touch?"

Merrillies glanced down at his fingernails as if distracted by one of them. "I don't know what you're talking about."

Fennick shook his head. "Won't work this time, Wilson. Forensics went back over the crime scene at Tang's flat. Found a whole mass of your prints. Trouble is, they were on top of those the SOC team had already logged. In other words, we have you at the scene. Post murder."

"Has Gary been murdered then? I don't know. What is the world coming to?"

Hansen brought the questioning back on track. "What were you doing at Gary Tang's flat? And what do you know about this?" He pulled out a crime scene photograph showing the body of a small child, bent and twisted at odd angles, lying in a stairwell between two floors.

Merrillies licked his lips a little before he spoke. "I've no idea about how that might have happened. Looks like the poor little boy fell down some stairs."

Fennick put the photograph back in the file. "So you've never seen the child at all?"

"No, now can we move this along? Some of us have businesses to run." There was an undertone of anger in his reply. Not rattled, but certainly annoyed.

Hansen again. "So what were you doing in Gary Tang's flat? Your prints were inside, and on the front door. A bit careless were we?"

The smug smile was back in place. "I'd heard Gary had been involved in some unsavoury business activities with a bunch of Londoners. I'd intended on paying him a visit, just to see what all the gossip was about. Gary used to work for me, and I didn't want to see him get himself into trouble."

"Going to give him a beating for buying gear from another source? Or for getting involved with an undercover operation?"

Again, the half blank expression. "I don't know what you're talking about. I would never hurt Gary. He was like a son to me. As for any undercover operation? I hope it was more successful than the one still in the news. That looks to be a right mess. Again, can we move this along a bit? I visited Gary's flat, used my own key – which he gave me a while back – found he wasn't home, then left. That's all there is to it."

Fennick and Hansen remained silent, both intently watching Merrillies, trying to spot any slight changes in his body language. Nothing. Stone cold and emotionless.

After a minute Merrillies stood up. "If that's all you have, gentlemen, then I'll be going. I know my rights, and I volunteered to come here of my own free will to answer your questions. We're now done."

Both officers stayed silent and unmoving until Merrillies finally started to walk out of the interview room. Pausing in the open doorway he looked over his shoulder and said to no one in particular, "Well, someone make a bloody move, because one of you *cuntstables* is going to have to escort me out, aren't you."

Fennick nodded to the PC. "See the gentleman out."

When the door had clicked firmly shut, Hansen said, "Do we let him get home before we pull him in again?"

"No. Let him think he's somehow gotten away with it. The line about the key is bullshit. It's far too new and feels recently cut. We've just got to sit tight and wait for forensics to come back on the boy, then we'll see what trace the bastard left – DNA, fibre – there has to be something. When we've got that, then we can pull him in, knowing we've something which will actually stick this time."

Hansen sounded curious. "You think he's the one who killed the boy?"

Fennick nodded. "Too much of a coincidence. They've already matched the kid's prints to the scene of the robbery. Comparing the original scene photos has given the SIO a pretty good idea of what's been disturbed or taken. I don't know what he was looking for, but I suspect it might have been something the boy took. They found nothing near the child, except one of the pillow cases from the flat was missing. And how the hell did they get into the flat without any signs of forced entry?"

"You don't figure Wilson Merrillies for some kind of Fagin, do you? Christ, have you seen the intelligence file on that guy? He's a certified, one hundred percent, Moss Side nutter."

Fennick stood up and walked out into the corridor, Hansen close behind him.

"No, I don't think he's running some kind of crime school for kids. I also don't think his visit to the flat, and the child ending up dead, are unrelated. There's also a set of prints unaccounted for."

"Another kid?"

"Not sure. They could just be from someone with small hands."

The two of them were headed towards the booking desk when they caught sight of Wilson Merrillies, going through the final stages of security prior to being signed out.

Something about Merrillies immediately struck Fennick as odd. He seemed nervous, almost a little too eager to get away, which peeked Fennick's curiosity. He couldn't see any cause for anxiety on his side of the protective glass screen, and beyond it was the station reception area. A curved mirror up in the corner of the ceiling gave a contorted reflection of the area. All Fennick could see was a young woman, maybe late teens or early twenties, just sitting and waiting. She was holding tightly onto something which looked a lot like a bear, and she kept fidgeting nervously, eyes darting around at the merest noise. But some people always got twitchy when in the presence of the police, regardless of whether they were actually innocent or not. Somehow he doubted it was the general station atmosphere which was making Merrillies more than a little nervous.

Fennick moved in closer and spoke quietly to the uniform PC, who was watching as the desk sergeant processed Merrillies.

"Who's the visitor out front?"

"Some girl, sir. Said she wanted to talk to someone about an incident that happened today, but won't tell the desk sergeant what it's about. Says she wants to talk to a detective. Sarge doesn't know what to make of her, but he thinks she looks a bit too young to be interviewed on her own. He's left a message with the on-call welfare bod to sit in with any interview, just in case."

Fennick absently nodded, still watching Merrillies as he finally opened the front door, glanced angrily at the visitor, then quickly left.

As soon as the door had started to close, the young woman jumped up and franticly wrapped her knuckles on the glass screen.

"That was him! He's the one! He killed Mousey!"

15

Saturday Morning

"Julius, it's Jack Telford. Not too bad; yourself?" Telford looked around the incident room. Still too early for most of the staff to be in, especially once word had gone round that everything had been handed over to the NCA and the Met. Some people were pissed off, and rightly so when you thought about the amount of time and effort they'd put into it. Others were fed up with it and were glad it was all going down South. Still, eight a.m. wasn't particularly early, when you considered some of the other high profile cases he'd worked on in the past.

The voice in his ear finally stopped chattering inanities long enough for him to break in without seeming rude. When you want a favour it pays to listen now and again. And Jack knew all about that. He'd made a point of always saying 'yes' and 'no' in almost all the right places for years. His career and pension fund were witness to that.

"Julius, I need a bit of a favour. There's been a change of requirements.... No, we still need some safe accommodation, only now it's two guests: one male, one female. Also it's not quite as simple as it was before. What? Okay, so maybe it wasn't as simple as it could have been to start off with, then. All we want to do is upgrade the security as there's an additional requirement. The people we're looking after will now be protected by an Armed Response team. Yes. Yes, I know all about the restrictions and the public safety issues, believe me. Yes, especially with the recent crap in the papers about people getting shot."

Why the hell do you have to make such a bloody song and dance about it? All you have to do is call one of the yokel stations and tell them to provide us with something out in the sticks. It's not as if we're going to need it for long, come the finish.

Jack sighed understandingly into the phone again. "No Julius, the DCS hasn't told me when he intends to look at your budget figures. He tells me many things, but that's not one of them. What? No, I'm not being facetious."

Look, find me a bloody place and then we'll both be free of this crap.

"Yes, I'll be on this number for a while." Then, just before Julius hung up, Telford added, "Look, I can't tell you much, but SDC7 are coming up from London to collect these two. Not sure when, but they should be gone by Monday at the latest. So if it helps any, you don't have to tick all the boxes when it comes to armed guard requirements. See if you can find something closer to hand, or even near the airport. I'm assuming they'll be flown out. Yeah, I know, but you usually come through with something."

As he put the phone down two statement readers walked in, coffee cartons in hands, along with magazines to help pass the time. Hopefully, by Tuesday, it should be over and done with. He could start the paperwork now, requesting all evidence be boxed and escorted down to London. Also talk to I.T. and let them know they could start shutting down some of the workstations. Unless Fennick and his sergeant were going to be around? That could make a right bloody mess of things. And cleaners. He would need to talk to the cleaners once this was all over. How fucking humdrum could you get? There had been times in the past when job satisfaction actually happened at the end of an investigation. Now the only thing he had to look forward to was filing down work orders, sorting out any borrowed equipment, and signing off the timesheets for the contracted civilian staff brought in to help ease the paperwork processing.

Hum-fucking-drum.

He checked the time again. He didn't have anything to call in yet; best give it another hour, see if Julius could work his magic – and hopefully he'd taken the hint that Jack was prepared to overlook any deficiencies in order to make Julius' job easier. Jack would deny it later, of course, safe in the knowledge that he'd worked long and hard on his reputation. Good old Jack Telford, always by the book. No, give it another hour or so and then hopefully he'd have an address.

*

In the evidence booking office, PC James Stebbings looked at the mass of pictures the Scene Of Crime photographer had taken. That was one of the sad joys of living in the digital age. Take a picture, then print it off almost immediately. There was a message from the previous shift about a late Friday night delivery. Some evidence had been shipped over from Esterleigh, and needed to be augmented with the boxes for the Gary Tang investigation.

It didn't look much, to be honest, but at least the child's backpack had helped to provide some ID – though why rip a page out of a valid passport? It gave his name as Paul Spencer, but there was also a note from Jackie on the nightshift to say that at least 35 other boys, all roughly fitting Spencer's description, were on the Missing Persons database within the GMP area alone.

If the passport the page had come from had been a fake, or if the parents had changed their names, or if the boy had wandered in from outside the local area then there wasn't much hope of immediately finding any family, unless by luck. Which was saying that Paul Spencer had been reported missing in the first place. Even the girl who'd brought the backpack in had no idea who he really was.

Stebbings took another look at the photographs. In death the child looked almost angelic. At least the trauma had left few external signs, and the broken neck had been quick and clean. It hadn't left anything sharp poking through the boy's skin, and in the stairwell photograph Peter appeared as if he were asleep.

Maybe, after he'd registered and filed the Friday night backlog, he'd put in an hour or two checking through Missing Persons himself. With a date of birth he could refine the search better. It was probably going to be a laborious task, but if he didn't do something then he'd end up feeling guilty. Though having seen what sometimes got put into the evidence containers, guilt wasn't always the first emotion he felt.

He put the photographs in clear plastic folders, made sure the DVD of the crime scene was safely in its case, then did one final muster of the evidence before getting ready to shelve the box.

The boy could certainly draw, at least judging from the work in the A4 pad. He put it on top of the Paddington Bear backpack then picked up the various things the SOC team had found on him. Several brass animals, like a menagerie or a zoo, and the ever-present mobile phone. There was a couple of bus tickets, plus what looked like a well-worn small toy which might once have been a rat, or a mouse?

He picked up the clear evidence bag with the old mobile phone in, and turned it over several times in his hands. He'd had one like it six, seven, maybe even ten years ago now. In fact, the phone might even be older than the boy himself. That struck him as being more than a little odd.

As he kept rolling it over and over in his hands, Stebbings heard the clatter and chink of something loose rolling around inside the case. Deliberately he shook it again, listening to the rattle. Obviously there was more than one thing bouncing around and it clearly didn't sound right. Absently he tried to take the back off through the plastic of the evidence bag – but the back cover seemed stuck. He tried again, but it still refused to budge. With a hint of frustration, he gave it a sharp rap on the table top and felt the plastic finally move under his fingers.

As the cover slid down and came away from the body of the phone, a dozen or more small gemstones fell out from the battery compartment and settled in the bottom of the plastic bag.

*

Listening to the kitchen radio in the background, Ramesh screwed the cap back on the milk and looked down at his bowl of muesli bran – already savouring the sausage and egg bap he'd decided to get from the canteen later. Mrs. Bashani was, undoubtedly, turning into her mother – a creature even Kali would refuse to poke with a stick, regardless of its length. No doubt his wife meant well, and had his best interests at heart. But a man should be allowed a transgression from time to time.

And he'd certainly transgressed last night that was for sure. To the tune of four hundred and fifty pounds to be precise. All of it to the owners of the Lucky Legs website and their live feed from the Sacramento racetrack. It would certainly have helped his ego if at least one of the nags had come in first past the post, but even spreading the bets to places had failed to pull anything back. Next time would be better, but next time was going to have to be after the salary was in the bank.

Still, with the weekend overtime for playing nursemaid to Duffley and Turner, the impact wasn't going to be too bad.

The music stopped as the radio station broke for the news. A glance up at the clock over the kitchen door did nothing but confirm it. Time to be off to the armoury and sign out his Kevlar jacket and personal firearm. The Met's SDC7 team had video briefed Raynolds and himself, emphasising the need for a strong element of armed cover, as Penstone was known to be aggressively protective and proactive against perceived threats. With connections to Gordon

Lemon, it was odds-on he'd already got wind of developments and was almost guaranteed to act accordingly. Hence the Treat As Hostile status the DCS had immediately put on the assignment.

Bashani had decided to work a standard protective configuration, independent of the terrain around the house. Run it on a twelve hour shift cycle, two pairs, plus two on standby for sick cover. All in all, Raynolds would have to spring for seven extra hits on his budget, not forgetting the armoury, but at least it would get his *ghanta* out of the mangle. It would also put the spotlight on the NCA and the boys from the Met.

From the armoury, the drive over to the Slinger Road station wasn't too bad, even for a Saturday. After parking up, he rang through to see if Raynolds was in. Unfortunately he was.

"Ah! Ramesh! Where the hell are you?" Raynolds voice was tinged with the usual touch of aggression, or so it seemed to Bashani.

"Just coming up past the canteen, sir. Why?" Ramesh could smell the sausage and almost taste the processed white bread.

"They're already starting to set up the safe house. It's over in West Colton, out in the sticks. Jack Telford says he thinks it backs onto a bloody railway line of all things. I need you to go over there ASAP and see if you can spot any problems with it before we move the two witnesses. If you've any doubts – any at all – then I want to know about them. Whatever happens, I don't want this turning into another bloody confrontational protective custody farce, especially with the likes of Human Rights, Civil Liberties, or any other bloody group that might get offended."

Ramesh swore under his breath, West Colton wasn't close, and it wasn't a safe house he was familiar with at all. Raynolds was right to call him in to do the feasibility check, as it would be his team and his responsibility to defend the place should anything untoward happen. Yet Julius Brell was an old hand at assigning facilities, and had never failed him in the past. He thought about stopping off at the canteen before heading out again. What the hell, there was bound to be an opportunity to stop off at some little café on the way there.

With the imagined smell of saturated fats and the promise of excessive amounts of carbohydrates, Ramesh said, "Okay, sir, I'm on my way. Text me the details and I'll stick them in the satnav."

*

"Sorry we had to keep you here overnight, only a Franklyn Street squat isn't really classified as an official place of residence." Hansen's apology was genuine. There had been no way they'd have let her out of the station after her declaration. Especially with Merrillies and his organisation – and she being the only potential witness to a double killing.

He put the fried egg sandwich in front of her. As she ate, he ran his mind back over the previous night.

The whole thing had been very much a damage limitation situation, given the circumstances. After her reaction to Merrillies leaving the station, Hansen had immediately found a room, taking a chance on the lack of a social worker being present. He'd initially immediately interviewed her to find out as much as they could before one of the patrols pulled Merrillies back in.

Barely five minutes into the interview and she'd dropped her second bombshell when she stated she could also identify Merrillies as being Gary Tang's killer. It had taken Hansen about fifteen minutes to run off several stills from the CCTV footage, and even in some of the grainier shots she was easy to match up. The other pictures showed Jason Stubbs, and the boy she called Mousey.

She'd then dug around in the worn out back pack and eventually pulled out a page torn from a passport. Then Mousey had become Paul Spencer.

With her validity as a witness confirmed, it had taken time to process her into the system. Initially she'd maintained the pretence that her name was Mikka. Then later she had eventually admitted that her name was Madeline Churchman, and that she'd run away from Newcastle when she was thirteen.

The next hour had been an emotional tsunami as other pieces of her life came up from the depths of her repressed memories.

By 10 p.m. Madeline had finally calmed down enough to have given a fairly accurate account of the whole Arkendale business. She'd admitted they'd followed Gary Tang – but the CCTV evidence already proved that. In a detached way, she'd then described how the three of them had seen Tang getting strangled, and watched as Wilson Merrillies got out of Tang's old Volvo.

Later, the three of them had gone looking for Gary Tang's flat, in order to try and boost what they could. Only Merrillies had turned up and surprised them as they were about to leave.

Fennick looked at her from across the interview table. She was as tidy as could be expected after a night in one of the cells. Although not officially charged with anything, technically she'd left the scene of a crime, and also failed to report the death of Gary Tang. Plus there was also the B&E, and the death of Paul Spencer.

He cleared his throat and said, "Okay, if you could tell me again, why did the three of you decide to go to Gary Tang's flat."

"We went looking for stuff we could sell – anything we could shift without too much hassle. We knew there wouldn't be any gear left around the place, so we figured on just picking up some of the easy bits."

"And was this part of the haul?" He took a sealed evidence bag out of his pocket and put it on the table in front of her. She saw the old mobile phone Mousey had picked up, along with a load of loose gemstones. She remembered Mousey smiling happily as he flashed it to her, then stuffing it back into his pocket again.

"Were they in the phone?" There was an edge of curiosity to the way she asked the question. Then, shaking her head, she said, "No, we didn't know anything about them. We were only going to be there for ten minutes, then off again. If we'd known about those," She flicked a finger at the evidence bag, "Then we wouldn't have hung around looking for other stuff."

Forensics and several uniforms had gone back over the flat but had failed to find any more mobile phones. What they did find at the bottom of the sideboard drawer was a stack of papers – certificates of authenticity to a whole collection of gems. All in all, from the face value on the paper, there had to have been close to eighty thousand pounds worth.

Hansen came into the conversation. "And you say Merrillies turned up just as you were leaving?"

"Yeah." She paused, then, "I thought we'd shut him in the flat, but he still came after us. He tried to push me down the stairs." Her breathing caught for a moment and she blinked back her emotions. "But Mousey went over instead."

Her face became cold, her voice sharp with anger. "I kicked the old bastard as hard as I could in the guts. Stopped him chasing after us. Then got away as fast as I could." She bit at one of her fingernails. "I don't know what happened to Jason, though. He never came back to the squat. I don't think the guy got him but…." Her voice trailed off into silence.

Forensics had found Stubbs' prints in the flat and on the sideboard drawer, but as yet there'd been no sign of Stubbs himself. There was also another call out for Wilson Merrillies, though this time the warrant was for the murder of Tang, and the death of Paul Spencer.

Fennick had gone back over the video and photographs of the flat and had seen the contents of the drawers. No one had thought to check the old mobile phones at the back of the sideboard. So when the team finally went back into the flat, they found the other three phones were also missing. Whoever had them was anybody's guess.

Maybe Merrillies had gone to the flat looking for them, and had ended up disturbing the mini home invasion instead. Maybe Jason knew more than he'd let on, and had gone back to collect the others once Mousey had found them for him, hiding himself away until Merrillies had left after the girl. Or maybe Madeline had snatched up the pillow case, stashed them somewhere else, and was such a good actress she was able to fool the pair of them without even trying.

She looked up at Fennick and Hansen.

"Are you going to send me to prison?"

Fennick shook his head. "If you're prepared to help put Wilson Merrillies away for two murders, then I doubt it. Question is, are you prepared to give an official statement and then appear in court?" He knew it wasn't going to be that easy, but the less she knew at this stage the better. One way or another they would have to give her up, along with their case documentation, now that their part of the investigation was coming to a close. It would be nice to get back to home ground again, and while Sugden was a bit of a bastard, he didn't get himself side-tracked by internal politics too much. Plus, he'd be able to spend more time with Jan, workload permitting.

The sound of Madeline breathing heavily made him refocus.

"If I do give evidence, do I get a new name and things?"

Hansen took over. "It's not like on TV. It's going to take time, and you're going to have to stick at it. I won't lie to you, it'll be like running away from home again, but this time you won't have any choice about going back if you can't hack it."

She looked down at her hands and smiled a little. "Done pretty well so far."

Cautiously Fennick asked again. "So you're prepared to help us put Wilson Merrillies away?"

Madeline remembered the moment she'd looked into Mousey's dying eyes. No Jason, no Mousey, no squat. What had she left to lose?

"Just so long as I don't get sent back home."

Fennick nodded. The request would be something else to add to their turnover list. Switching on the recorder, he said, "Okay, for the official record then, let's start with Gary Tang going out of the Arkendale shopping centre and heading for the car park."

Later that afternoon, as Madeline was going over her statement for what seemed like the umpteenth time, word came that Wilson Merrillies had been apprehended by a motorway patrol on the M62. Inside his hurriedly packed holdall had been a one way ticket for the Liverpool to Dublin ferry.

*

On the coffee table in front of him, Eddie's mobile started into life.

Thankfully the IPCC didn't seem to work on weekends. At least the smug bitch of a secretary had stopped leaving voice messages on his mobile phone. Typical bloody non-coms. Perhaps if they weren't so eager to shop their own, then they'd be more likely to get some respect. Eddie had known some good coppers who'd been beaten into submission by pressure from the IPCC, all for doing their job and keeping the public safe.

Without touching the phone, he peered at the display. It was showing a new number, one he didn't recognise, so he let it go to voicemail. It was obviously another mobile phone. Maybe Simone had another number? His hand reached out, but his paranoia immediately jerked it back into his lap, and he let five minutes pass before calling his voicemail.

Instead of the soft voice of Simone, it was a bloke. That bloody sergeant again.

"This is DS Hansen. We'd like you to come into the station as soon as possible. It's regarding the death of a dealer, Gary Tang. We're not sure how it's connected to the Gold Dust operation, but DC Cooke and yourself seem to be the last official contacts anyone had with Tang. We also want to know about what you might've heard regarding Tang and a stash of gemstones he had in his possession. Call me direct," Hansen reeled off a number which Eddie didn't bother writing down.

Deliberately he pressed a button and erased the message. Gary Tang wasn't his concern. He needed to talk to Duffley or, better yet, Penstone himself, and try to find out what the fuck Cookie had been up to. The material in the box seemed chaotic, and made little sense to Eddie. Yet it did confirm what Simone had said. Tony had been gathering information and intelligence, then he'd put it into some kind of solo project to get himself out of undercover ops.

In which case why not tell Eddie about it? They'd been more than just mates, for fuck's sake. Unless Simone had got it all wrong and Cookie had been gathering police info for Penstone?

A quick glance down at the lid of the box file and his hand went out to pick up a couple of red and black capsules. He couldn't remember what they were supposed to do, but anything would be good if it helped take away the feeling of betrayal he was experiencing. He quickly washed them down with several mouthfuls of bottled water and waited for them to settle. Then he checked his watch and picked up the mobile phone again. A flick through the address book turned up the landline number he wanted.

"Detective Constable Falkirk, how can I help?"

"Mal, it's me, Eddie."

Falkirk's voice dropped to a half whisper as he tried not to attract attention from the people around him. "Where the hell are you? People are looking for you, man. At the watch brief we were told to keep an eye out for you. If we make contact we're to tell you to come in to the station. Word is that Wilson Merrillies killed one of your informants; Gary Tang."

"The least of my worries at the moment." Eddie absently rubbed his fingers through the growth of beard on his face. "Look, Mal, I need a favour."

Falkirk was immediately on his guard. It was one thing talking to Caradine, but totally different if he was caught helping him in whatever he was up to.

"I don't know, Eddie. What is it you want?"

"I need five minutes with Paul Duffley. Alone."

"But Eddie –"

"Five minutes, Mal. I've found some new info and I really have to talk to him about it. Five minutes is all I'm going to need, Mal. All you have to do is let me know when it's quiet, then let me in the cell with him, and make sure no one disturbs us."

"But, Eddie, as I was trying to tell you, Duffley's not at the station any more."

Like the time when Simone had slapped his face, it took seconds to finally register what Mal had said.

"You saying he's been released? No fucking way, Mal!" Part of him realised he was shouting down the phone, but somehow he couldn't seem to lower his voice.

"He's not been released, you stupid twat. The DCS had sold him to the NCA. At least that's what I've heard. Shiny-arse has done a deal with one of the Met's special groups – SDC7 – and they're going to be coming up to collect him. Probably some time tomorrow afternoon. The Major's been tasked to look after him and some other witness – Armed Response cover at that. But, hey, what the fuck do I know?"

Before he could stop himself, Eddie asked, "I don't suppose you know where they're keeping him, do you?"

"Too bloody right I don't. The least I know, the better I like it, and what makes you so fucking sure I'd tell you if I knew?" There was a touch of anger in his voice.

"It's okay Mal. I'm not thinking straight at the moment. Still on some pills from the hospital."

And fuck you very much for asking.

Mal's voice sounded sympathetic. "Look, Eddie, it's none of my business, but the sooner you come and talk to someone the better.

Then maybe take a break or something. I mean, c'mon mate, even I can hear you're not yourself at the moment."

Eddie just nodded his head, then said, "Yeah. Thanks, Mal. I'll think about it. Goodbye."

He broke the connection before Mal could say anything more, and tossed the mobile onto the coffee table. Think, think, think. His fingers drummed the top of the box file several times before he snatched up the mobile again. A rapid thumb dance and then a voice in his ear said, "Dispatch. PC Colly."

"It's PC Edwards, motorcycle courier. I need the location of Chief Inspector Bashani. I've got," he paused as if counting, "Two, no, make that three Intel and Update files relating to his current ops. There's an urgency tag on this as some of the intel is of a sensitive nature. It's a by-hand delivery as he hasn't been able to activate his Airwaves secure handset yet."

If you sounded like a tired and harassed biker with a five second fuse on his anger, you sometimes got what you wanted. But Dispatch wasn't happy.

"How come you're not coming in on Airwaves yourself?"

"Because it's fucked as well! Now, can you give me the details, or just pass me up to your shift Sergeant? I've got a tag on this and it's already getting close to deadline – and I'm not going to be the one held responsible for contributing to a late show."

"Hey!" Colly snapped back at him, "You're not the only one stuck using crap kit you know. Hold on."

There was a pause, then the dispatcher passed over an address in Gascoigne Road, West Colton. It wasn't any of the regular safe houses Eddie was familiar with. Not that it made any difference, just that it seemed more out of the way than usual.

Nodding to himself, Eddie sat back on the sofa. "Thanks, I owe you." He broke the connection before the dispatcher could ask any more questions, and turned the phone off for good measure.

Closing his eyes, Eddie felt a rush of fatigue creep over his body. The last couple of capsules didn't seem to be doing much. Only one thing for it. He pulled out his tobacco pouch and fished out one of the Moroccan loaded cigarettes. Soon he was slowly exhaling the first of several long drags on the roll-up, and five minutes later, with the roach haphazardly stubbed out in the ashtray, Eddie closed his eyes. Best to catch some sleep for now. All the better to be prepared for talking to Duffley after they'd settled into the safe house for the night.

16

Saturday Night

Paul Duffley sat in the darkness of the sparsely furnished bungalow lounge. A forgotten cigarette still smouldered in the crowded ashtray as he stared at the blank television screen, his mind in turmoil.

Half was occupied with the upcoming meeting with the people that the NCA and SDC7 would be sending up to collect him. Some of the organised crime teams were almost like old friends – family even. As perverse as it sounded, he felt he could genuinely trust them. Well, trust them more than some, that was for sure.

His anger flared again. It was clear that Ren had obviously set him up. Putting him in the line of fire with that psycho Carlton hadn't been part of any bloody plan at all. It should've all gone down in the hotel room, not out in the fucking car park of all places. Bounce the two buyers, then walk out with the moody gear and the cash. He'd been set to pick up a car Ren wanted dropped off in Essex, while the two Colombians should've headed back to London on the next train down south.

In a way he could appreciate why Ren had done it. It still didn't make things any more palatable, but at least he thought he knew why.

Ren had lost a shitload of cash, gear and respect when they'd been raided the last time. The cartel was understandably mucho pissed off, along with the Russian and the Chinese. Everyone who'd invested wanted to know how come they'd lost out, and rather than blame each other, they'd turned on Ren. Well, on the firm in general.

The annoying pricks who'd done most of the shouting said they suspected there'd been a leak, which must have been from somewhere inside.

The accusations were followed up with a spate of quite nasty killings, mostly small time dealers disappearing, then turning up days later. The bodies – parts of them anyway – had been dumped in various locations around the UK.

It was enough to cause friction and uneasiness within the firm, and that was always bad for business. That was when Ren came up with the fundraising scam.

All they had to do was set up several big deals. When everything was in place, come exchange time just hijack the lot and head home. It might've been dirty money, but Ren could start paying back some of the investors without being out of pocket himself. Do the whole thing a couple of times, using someone else's turf to help cover your tracks; should've been as simple as hell.

Then, right out of the blue, they'd been hijacked themselves by Psycho Sid and a pair of local goons. It had totally confused him at first. Then when the shooting kicked off he'd totally lost it. No one had expected the two Colombians to go schizo and kill people in public, and even he hadn't realised he'd actually set the ruddy scam up with a pair of bloody coppers.

Finding out he'd also been set up made him wonder just how much Ren actually blamed him for the raid. He'd been the negotiator, organised the venue, hospitality, and generally kept everything running smoothly. At least up to where they'd gotten word that an NCA team had gone hot and a raid was in progress. Most had been able to get away, but it still cost the gear, the money, and a few of the hired help.

Ren blaming him for the raid was a complete load of bollocks, but being set up by another squad to snatch the lot from him, made him realise Ren was quite literally gunning for him. Well, fuck him! He'd never turned on Ren in the past. But if he'd wanted to, then by fuck he could have. He knew where the skeletons were hidden – quite literally, in some cases – any one of which would put Ren and most of his other lieutenants away for life. Or even longer, ideally.

The legal bastard, Lemon, that Ren had set him up with? He'd been in on the deal, continuing the scam by telling him Ren had already built up a nice little prison fund, should poor little Paul need to go away for a stretch. Lemon was also supposed to pull some strings in order to take the heat off, and put it on that fucking insane Colombian. And he'd happily gone along with it. Almost.

Then, in the interview room, when Batman and Robin had told him about the remand centre killing, along with Ren's double cross – complete with times and dates, no less – that had been the final straw.

The National Crime Agency already had a witness protection programme which seemed as bullet proof as anything when it came to a defence against the wrath of Renton Penstone. Plus he'd obviously want one of those letters of immunity the Home Office had been sending out to those bastard Irish. He'd also see if they couldn't find him some little place in France, or Holland maybe. Certainly no country where the fucking local wildlife or bugs were out to kill you every chance they got.

The lounge door opened and Jean Turner walked in, packet of cigarettes and a gold Dunhill lighter in one hand, unlit cigarette in the other. With the pair of them being the only smokers, they'd all decided the lounge would be the smoking zone. She sat down and lit up, then held the packet out to him.

"No thanks, love. It's getting to the point where it feels like I'm chain smoking the bloody things."

She smiled in silent agreement as she put her cigarettes and lighter on the chair arm.

Tense and restless, he stood up and grabbed a discarded newspaper. As he headed towards the door, he asked, "You don't want to use the toilet for a while, do you love? What with all this excitement I don't know how long I'm going to be."

Jean Turner shook her head and blew out a thin stream of smoke. "No, I'm sure I can hold it for a while longer."

In the kitchen, Ramesh sat at the table while one of the Armed Response team stood by the closed back door, his MP5 holstered but unclipped and ready. Outside the bungalow another express train shot past as it headed down south, the low level rumbling vibrating the cups resting on the draining board. He would have to talk with Julius Brell at SecOps as to why the hell he'd allocated a safe house by a railway track. Although the bungalow was fairly well isolated from its near neighbours, the noise of the trains passing by so often was bloody distracting.

At least the two witnesses had agreed to the no lights blackout routine. The windows already had more than enough nets, blinds and curtains, and the street lighting out front gave the lounge, master bedroom and hallway enough of an orange glow to move around by. There was a torch in the master bedroom's en-suite bathroom, but that was unavoidable. The bathroom was located at the back of the bungalow, so was naturally pretty dark. However, the torch was low power, and the frosted glass in the window was also masked by a particularly vicious pyracantha with three inch long thorns. All in all, it seemed secure enough.

They'd even double checked the flare from the cigarette lighters. Miller, one of the Armed Response personnel, had been outside earlier to confirm there was enough street lighting reflecting off the double glazing as to make the flames invisible to anyone passing by. As it was, most of the time the two of them used the separate toilet-cum-cloakroom that was off the entrance hall, just before the kitchen.

Thank Christ it was only going to be for a short time. If the babysitting had been planned to go on any longer than a day or two, then he would've strongly petitioned for a change of venue. Still, according to Raynolds, it would all be over by Sunday evening. Just enough time for him to shit, shower, shave and be back at the station, nine o'clock Monday morning. The overtime money would come in handy, especially as it would be paid in before the first of the credit card bills came through the letterbox.

As Duffley shouted that he was going to be in the loo for a while, McManus came through from the hallway and rested his backside up against the sink. Wiry, he had a tall and gangling frame, and was on his first real ops since transferring to Armed Response. Like many of the AR team, he'd been in the Army, even served some time in the second Gulf War. But when he'd gone from there straight into the mess that had been the Afghanistan theatre, it had been enough for him to stick his notice in.

"Any idea how long before we can put these two to bed, sir?"

Ramesh shook his head. "If they've any sense then they'll try and get some sleep, but we're not here to tuck them in."

McManus looked at him expectantly, but Ramesh shook his head again. "Nope. No idea when they're going to be off our hands, but hopefully before tomorrow afternoon. Trouble is, we can't stand down until we've got a proper ETA."

McManus grimaced a little. The shift wasn't due to change over until two a.m. which was still another six hours away, and the last four had dragged like hell.

Jackson, his partner, grinned. "You'll get used to it. Most of the time it's all just hanging around and waiting. It's only the rare occasion things kick off."

He patted McManus on the shoulder and had started to head out into the hallway when the seven pound club hammer smashed through the kitchen window. Thrown with a massive amount of force, the hammer head hit McManus hard on the side of his face –

the sound of his jaw breaking was one of the few things Ramesh could remember with any clarity later on. Attached to the wooden handle by a short piece of string was a CS gas grenade.

*

Eddie's fingers tapped erratically against the Mondeo's steering wheel as he squinted out into the darkness. The nearside headlight had died, and driving into West Colton was like riding into the Wild West. Nothing but patches of greenery and the occasional street light – it was a fucking mugger's paradise. According to the satnav, the safe house was only another eight and a half miles. But he didn't trust it. The maps themselves were okay and up to date, but despite trying to change it, the voice always sounded weird, so he'd ended up driving with the sound off.

Whatever, he still needed to talk with Duffley about the stuff in the box file. He'd thrown it onto the back seat, now every time he took a fast corner he could hear it sliding around.

Pulling into a deserted bus stop, he put the hazard lights on and snatched up Cookie's iPhone from the passenger seat. Simone's number was almost at the top of the favourites list – something that'd been played on his mind and distracted him while driving. The remains of the Moroccan hash had kept his anger down to a controllable level, but it still niggled all the same. With his index finger he stabbed several times at the screen, bringing her details up.

It rang half a dozen times, clicked, then diverted over to her voicemail, and he bit his bottom lip as the message played out. Then came the beep, and he took a quick breath.

"Hi Babe, it's me. I wanted to let you know I'm out chasing something down tonight, but I've also been thinking about what you said. I just need to do this thing, get some answers, and then that's it. I've decided to jack this undercover stuff in and find something else. I don't know what it'll be just yet, but it's going to be well away from the Force. I want to be me again, Babe. I want to start over and see what I'm good at. Get us a bit of security as well, because I know it's what you want. And I want us to do it together, Babe. I realise I need someone with me, someone who believes in me for me, not just for what I do. I love you, Babe, I –"

The voicemail system ended the recording with a short message before it disconnected, and Eddie nearly bounced the iPhone off the dashboard in frustration. There was little point in ringing her back now, and if she didn't realise that he really did fucking love her then maybe she didn't deserve him after all.

He pulled out the little Ziploc bag and checked what was left in the bottom. Enough for a quickie now, then another quickie later on, after he'd had a chance to talk to Duffley. He licked his finger tip and dipped it into the powder, then sucked it off his finger, grinding it a little between his teeth. It tasted more than a little chalky, but after a minute or so he could feel his heart rate pick up, and he was eager to be off.

A check on the satnav showed a convoluted route to the safe house, through what looked like a maze of backstreets. Still, it wouldn't be long, if he drove carefully. Even quicker if he drove the way he wanted to, but that would be risking too much. All he had to do was take it steady, then talk the Major into letting him interview Duffley for five minutes. What could be simpler than that?

*

As Bashani pushed himself backwards and away from the table, he felt the chair collapse beneath him, sending him sprawling to the floor and hitting the stone tiles hard with his right shoulder. The pain was immense, making him cry out, then an uncontrollable coughing fit as some CS got down his throat.

Rolling onto his side he tried hard not to breathe as he wormed his way across the floor. Without stopping, he crawled over the motionless body of McManus, then blindly carried on out into the passageway. That was where Jackson had retreated to the moment the hammer had come crashing through the kitchen window.

The original plan in the event of an attack was for Bashani to fall back and cover the witnesses, leaving the two AR men free reign to proceed as they saw things develop. Through watery eyes, Bashani could see Jackson, crouched down on one knee in the doorway to the main bedroom, weapon drawn and pointing towards the kitchen. He wanted to tell Jackson to open a window and create a cross draft, but he knew doing so would help give their positions away. He also wondered if their attackers were going to wait for the CS to force them out into the street, or come in and try to finish the job as swiftly as possible.

Regardless of how things were supposed to have gone, Bashani kicked out with his foot, catching the kitchen door with his heel and slamming it shut behind him. It wasn't much, but it would certainly help slow the spread of the gas.

He did his best to get to his feet, then crouched low and scurried into the lounge. A quick scan of the room showed Jean Turner had not been slow in reacting. She'd created a makeshift barricade by pushing the sofa around so its back now faced the door.

Coughing to clear his lungs, Bashani said, "Where the hell is Duffley?"

Turner put her head around the side of the furniture. "He went to relieve himself."

"What?"

"He's still in the toilet! Look, what the hell is going on?"

As if to answer her question, from down the passageway came the muffled sound of the back door being smashed open with a battering ram.

*

Hansen closed the door to the interview room and joined Fennick in the corridor. All he could do was silently shrug his shoulders.

"There's nothing else we can do for the moment, sir. If Merrillies is going to stick to his story that Madeline pushed the Spencer boy off the stairs in her haste to get away from him, then it's going to be down to his word against hers. There's trace and fibre from both of them all over Spencer's body, but neither are denying close contact with the child. I doubt forensics will turn up anything useful from the stairs outside Tang's flat as the area's been compromised at least half a dozen times."

They started walking back towards the lifts.

Fennick asked, "What about the Tang killing itself? Can we nail him on that, independent of the girl?" There was enough to put Merrillies in the vicinity, but it was only the girl's testimony which was actually convicting him. What with their later encounter at Tang's flat, any defence worth their fee would try to taint her credibility.

Hansen shook his head a little. "I doubt it very much, sir. Although I know they're good at their job, I doubt forensics'll be able to turn up anything useful as the Volvo was a shit tip. Merrillies could easily dismiss any trace DNA by saying he'd ridden in the car on a regular basis. All we really have is the statement, plus some stills from the CCTV, but those are likely to be dismissed as well."

Fennick grimaced. Provided they could get the jury to believe Madeline Churchman, then things would be okay for winning the case. With a grunt, he said, "It's not whether you win or lose, but how you submit the paperwork."

"And, speaking of paperwork, I've still got a load of duplicate material regarding Gold Dust."

"Same here. All indexed and referenced. The originals need to be countersigned by the Major, but the duplicates will have to be couriered over to Westwitch sometime. I've no idea what Molly's up to – more internal buggering about I suppose. Still, we can't piss off from here until we've got someone's official seal of approval. We could drop by Raynolds' office now, and if he's in we could see about talking to the Major tonight. Apart from the official stuff, I still have to mend some bridges. He's going to be on guard duty, so he'll probably be glad of the call."

"If we could square that away before we get stuck into Merrillies, all the better."

As they approached the lifts, the doors opened. Out came DCS Raynolds, and behind him the neatly be-suited figure of DCS Suneel Peterson. Catching Raynolds' eye, Fennick said, "Sir, would it be possible to have a quick word?"

*

Jean Turner had sense enough to keep herself down low, hidden behind what protection the sofa gave her. Meanwhile, Bashani had positioned himself by the doorframe of the lounge, but was still having difficulty with his right shoulder. It was throbbing like hell, and the fingers of his right hand felt numb and doughy, painful when he tried to move his arm.

Hopefully just dislocated rather than fractured.

With his good hand he reached across his Kevlar vest and worked his sidearm out of its holster. It felt awkward and clumsy, and he seriously doubted his accuracy. He'd never fired the thing left handed before, not even for a bet down the range when re-qualifying for his firearms certificate.

Across the passageway he could see Jackson. The man was already in the classic shooters position – down on one knee, using the doorframe for support, almost rigid with concentration, even though Bashani could see a trickle of snot running from his nose and his eyes were watering.

Probably standard exercise conditions for the ex-Army guys.

But Ramesh still wondered if he was going to be able to provide support when it counted.

From behind the dim outline of the kitchen door came the sound of scuffling and movement, then silence again. Seconds later it was rapidly pushed open, and arcing out into the passageway came something popping, snapping and jumping around as tiny explosions spat little tongues of yellow and white flame. It was a long Chinese New Year firecracker. With it came a crouched figure in black, wearing a gas mask, and carrying a lightweight machine pistol – releasing bursts of sporadic fire.

Jackson didn't even flinch. In a loud voice he shouted out above the noise, "Halt! Armed Police!"

But before he'd finished the rest of the obligatory verbal warning he'd put two rounds into the attacker's body, and another through the gas mask eyepiece.

From his left Jackson heard Duffley cry out in alarm from the toilet, then thankfully he went silent. If the bastard just kept his mouth shut then they stood a good chance of saving him. Have him step out into the line of fire and they were all going to be fucked.

Still professionally calm, he fired another couple of rounds at the closing kitchen door, close to the handle – the bullet damage showed white against the dark painted woodwork. The noise of its slamming was closely followed by something heavy on the opposite side falling to the floor.

Two down? Ramesh had no idea how many were in the raiding party, but for a hit like this there wouldn't be too many, would there? The house seemed to shake as another heavy express train sped down the tracks, the sound all the more louder now that the back door had been smacked in.

Ramesh fumbled clumsily for his mobile phone, then remembered putting it next to the Airwaves handset at the back of the kitchen table, long before things had kicked off. He knew Jackson wouldn't be carrying anything on him for sure. It was part of the AR tradition. They all believed it was bad luck if you carried a phone on you when you went on an Op. Even if it was turned off, AR locker room myth probably said it could still end up getting you killed.

A snap glance at his watch showed there was at least another twenty minutes before the next check-in call via the Airwaves handset. Even if he'd remembered to pick up one of the hands-free adaptors, it would never have worked at this distance. The only good thing had been the draft created by the smashed window and the broken back door. Despite his stinging eyes, he knew the air was getting cleaner by the minute as he watched the cordite smoke from the fireworks getting sucked back under the kitchen door.

There was movement up ahead and Ramesh caught sight of the toilet door opening slightly. A confused and wide-eyed Duffley stuck his head around the door jam. He'd soaked a hand towel in water and had wrapped it around his nose and mouth in an attempt to combat the effects of the CS gas.

Frantically Ramesh waved at him to get back inside and shut the door, but Duffley just stood in the doorway looking at him blankly. Without breaking his concentration on the kitchen, Jackson said slowly, "Get back behind that fucking door. Now!"

Duffley yanked the door shut and remained silent. From behind Ramesh, Jean Turner whispered, "I've tried my phone several times, but I can't seem to get a bloody signal."

As he turned his head to answer her, the kitchen door flew open again, banging against the wall. In the doorway lay the limp body of McManus on his side, legs pulled up to his chest, with a black clad body pushed up behind it. At first nothing seemed to happen, but then the barrel of a large automatic appeared just above the bodies and half a dozen shots were snapped off blind, in quick succession. They seemed to be aimed at everything and nothing, the bullets gouging out chunks of the wall, punching holes into the ceiling and tearing splinters of wood off the toilet door frame.

Distracted by it all, Jackson failed to hear the sound of the master bedroom window breaking, until it was too late. The bullet from the forth gunman punched its way through his thigh, shattering the bone, before he could move and return any fire at all. As he fell back into the bedroom he desperately looked around for a target, but all he saw was the arm sticking through the broken window, pointing the gun at him, squeezing the trigger, and shooting him square in the chest.

Survival overriding fear, Ramesh brought up his own MP5. Firing wildly at the bedroom window left handed, he was amazed to see the body of the fourth attacker fall through the broken glass, slumping motionless over the window sill. To Ramesh, the sudden rush of cold air had felt as though a departing soul had touched his skin in passing. Then his attention was dragged back to the hallway and the kitchen.

From behind the prone form of McManus, the gunman stood up and started to advance down the passageway, the black automatic pointed directly at Ramesh's head. It was the thing he dreaded the most, in all the years he'd been involved with Armed Response teams. Would he chance swinging his arm round and taking a shot, or drop his own gun and hope for the best?

But the decision wasn't his to make.

As the gunman came level with the toilet door, Paul Duffley turned the handle and put as much force and weight behind it as he could. In one rapid movement, the pinewood door flew open, catching the gunman off guard. The force of the impact had been enough to deflect the gun up and away, at the same time sending the door panel smashing hard into the black masked face, breaking his nose, along with several teeth.

Duffley, feeling the resistance, pulled the door towards himself, then slammed it back open again, knocking the gunman senseless to the hallway carpet. In a blind, animalistic rage, Duffley slammed the toilet door shut behind him and immediately dived on top of the wounded attacker. Yanking the gun from the attacker's hand, Duffley held it firmly by the barrel and started to mindlessly beat the gunman around the head with the butt, three, four, five times before Ramesh finally realised what was happening.

"For fuck's sake stop it! Otherwise you'll be up on a manslaughter change!"

Duffley looked down the hallway at Bashani, eyes blazing with a mixture of fear and adrenaline, his hand held in mid-air. Ramesh tried to smile reassuringly. It was already a bloody shambles. The best he could hope to do now was to try for as much damage limitation as possible. At least before the back-up support turned up. What with the isolation and the bloody trains, he wasn't sure if any of the neighbours would've reported the gunfire.

Duffley looked at the battered face of the unconscious gunman, then back over to Ramesh. Finally he lowered the gun gently, wiped the blood off the butt, then turned it around so he was holding it loosely in his hand.

Getting up, he walked over to Ramesh and held out his free hand to help the Major up. As Bashani pulled himself to his feet, he could feel all the obvious signs of stress and shock starting to set in. He'd never been involved with a close combat action before, and no amount of training and simulations had prepared him for the harsh reality of it all.

As the two of them walked into the lounge, Jean Turner got to her feet, picked up her cigarettes and lighter from the back of the sofa, and lit one up.

Smiling weakly, she said, "I take it it's all over then?" There was a little tremor in her voice. Even when Vic had been alive she'd never really been conscious of any of the criminal violence she knew he'd been involved with. All she wanted right then was for someone to give her a hug and tell her it was all over. But all she had to choose from was Bashani with his lopsided shoulder, or a blood-splattered Paul Duffley. She took a deep breath, sighed, and took another long drag of her cigarette. It just wasn't her bloody day at all.

*

If it wasn't the screwed up satnav, it was the fucking council digging up the fucking roads. Eddie only realised he'd shot past the diversion sign as he rounded the corner and was forced to slam down hard on the brakes. The Mondeo slewed, skidding to a stop in front of the flashing yellow hazard lights hanging from the barriers, and Eddie pummelled on the steering wheel in mindless frustration. He got out, wrenched open the back door, then leaned in to collect the box file from the back seat. Slamming the car door shut again, he swung several kicks at the barriers before heading off towards the safe house on foot. According to the AA map, it wasn't that far away.

He'd thought about bringing the gun, but on reflection he'd decided against it. After all, he just wanted to talk to Duffley, and maybe get a second opinion from the Major. He'd obviously carry the weapon when he started after Penstone – they might be Cookie's notes, but no bastard was going to take the glory away from the pair of them. Especially when he finally collared the head of a big London firm. Not after all the work they'd put into it. No, it was Eddie's job to finish this for the pair of them.

With the box file under one arm he ducked down a side street, then off another bloody street, onto what looked like an estate of old nineteen-thirties bungalows. Retirement Country.

It sort of made sense in a way. Old people usually knew each other, and anyone aged fifty or under was bound to be a stranger. Anyone like that would certainly stir up curiosity from the window scratching curtain twitchers. Odd place for a safe house though.

But as he came down the road, he got the feeling something wasn't quite right. There was a large 4 x 4 parked up in the shadows between the safe house and its neighbour. Its dark, blacked out windows made Eddie immediately suspicious. Plus, there didn't seem to be any sort of life in the bungalow, either. He'd been on a couple of nursemaid operations before, and even the most hairy had never felt like this.

Then, on the wind, came a whiff of something peppery. CS gas. Surely the Major wouldn't have issued CS? Then the acidic smell of cordite made him stop short on the path leading up to the front door. Something was very badly wrong.

Feeling exposed under the street light, Eddie moved across the front garden, along the side of the bungalow, and positioned himself to one side of the large picture window. It had to be the lounge, or a dining room of some kind. A snap glance showed him nothing but reflected street lights and maddeningly opaque net curtains. Could it really get any fucking worse? There was no point in trying to listen for any movement. There'd have to be bloody elephants walking around before any sound stood a chance of escaping through the solid brick walls or the heavy double glazing. He was going to have to front up and look into the room directly.

He paused, took several deep breaths, then made his move. Careful not to touch the glass, he shielded his eyes from the glare of the street lights and peered into the room beyond. It wasn't a reassuring scene. The sofa had been pushed up close to the lounge door, and as he watched, a woman he didn't recognise was starting to pick herself up off the floor. Even at this distance he could still see the fear on her face.

Over by the lounge door the Major was being helped up by the bastard who'd gotten them into the mess in the first place. Something had happened, that much was bloody obvious, but the fact the three of them were standing up, rather than defending themselves, seemed to indicate it was now all over.

If he could just talk to Duffley, and maybe the Major, then he could be off to see if he could patch things up with Simone one last time. She might not be perfect, but she really was one of the few people he still felt affection for. After that it would be down to London to start in on Penstone.

Without giving it a second thought, Eddie brought his arm up, and with the flat of his hand he slapped it hard on the glass several times, so as to get their attention.

As he peered through the lounge window again, the last thing he saw was Duffley frantically pointing the big black automatic at him. Then the bright muzzle flash as Duffley snatched at the trigger and shot him twice in quick succession – the sound almost lost as the 20:55 to Glasgow sped past the back of the house.

For once it was on time.

17

Early Sunday Morning

"I can't really talk now, sir."

Holding the mobile phone tight to his ear, Fennick walked away from the collection of police cars and ambulances that had converged on Gascoigne Road a handful of hours earlier. Didn't the bastard ever sleep?

In his ear, Molly Sugden said, "Don't be bloody stupid, Michael. With everyone else running around, of course you can talk. It's what's called delegation."

Absently Fennick wondered how the hell Sugden had managed to get wind of the disaster so quickly. He was like a frigging octopus, tentacles all over the place. Obviously something else was also going on, otherwise Molly wouldn't have called him directly.

"This is all I have at the moment, sir, and to be frank the whole thing is a fucking mess. There's four dead including – so help me – DC Caradine. Two of the attackers survived, but are on the critical list. The Major shot one, and one of our star witnesses tried to remove the other's face with the aid of a toilet door. When that didn't work, he tried again with the blunt end of an automatic pistol."

"Well, that'll look good in the final report. What the hell was he doing with a weapon in the first place?"

"I have absolutely no idea. By the time we had an inkling something was happening it was probably all over."

When both he and Hansen had met up with DCS Raynolds, they didn't know DCS Suneel Peterson from the NCA had already arrived. Earlier Peterson had made a snap decision to come up in advance of the SDC7 team – "In order to talk to Jean Turner personally."

It was supposed to be an introductory meeting, but Fennick thought it was probably more to evaluate her potential for reliable intelligence. Peterson knew Duffley of old, so was more than happy to throw him to several members of the SDC7 who'd been assigned specifically to Ren Penstone. But Jean Turner was a potentially new source of information.

It had been Raynolds' subsequent call to Dispatch that'd started the bad feelings. They'd turned into serious concerns when the Ops Room PC came back to tell Raynolds that Bashani wasn't answering his Airwaves handset, or even his mobile phone.

Raynolds had then acted pretty swiftly. He'd immediately called out the contingency Armed Response team, who'd been on standby support for the operation. Then he'd press-ganged Fennick and Hansen into the incident as they were the only available resources within grabbing distance. Reluctantly he'd also agreed to Peterson coming along, even though it probably wasn't going to look good when they finally got to the scene.

As it was they'd arrived just as the AR and Scene of Crime teams were cordoning off the area – starting a boundary search while waiting for Forensics to finish screaming at the ambulance crews for disturbing the bodies in their search for vital signs.

Out of the three left standing, it was only Jean Turner who seemed the most in control and communicative. Bashani had been sitting on the sofa, facing the doorway, just blankly staring through into the master bedroom where one of his team lay dead.

Duffley had gone into a corner of the lounge and just sat down with his back up against the wall. He'd been starting down at the automatic pistol in his lap, quietly muttering to himself, when the medical team were finally allowed to enter the building and gather up the walking wounded.

Fifteen minutes later two Armed Response personnel found Eddie Caradine.

One of them had found the trail of blood spatter leading away from the broken lounge window. With a buddy for backup, the two of them had followed the trail around the side of the bungalow, and into a mass of overgrown shrubs. In amongst the overgrown branches they'd finally found the body of Eddie Caradine. Curled up in a foetal position, he'd been hidden from view by a mass of Rhododendron leaves. He'd been shot twice: the first round went through the palm of his hand, but the second caught him in the neck. Although the wound didn't look much, despite Eddie's best efforts to staunch the flow, he'd bled out long before any of the medical teams arrived on the scene.

As if that wasn't enough, to add to the confusion was the contents of the box file he'd been clutching to his chest when he died.

Sugden broke into Fennick's debrief. "What was in the box?"

"It looks like a mixture of files. Some relate to Penstone and Duffley, along with a bunch of other key players in Penstone's organisation. There's even paperwork concerning our friend, Gordon Lemon, and a couple of other legals. The rest seems to be telephone records, old surveillance photographs with copies of old case logs. Most of the stuff is covered with fresh handwritten notes and comments. If I didn't know better I'd say Cooke and Caradine had been planning on going after Penstone and his organisation. Only there's too much of the stuff, some of it going back too far, to even guess what they were up to. It'll take time to sort it all out and make sense of it."

There was a touch of concern in Sugden's voice. "What's happened to all of that?"

"DS Hansen is entering all of it into the Scene log. He's also making a couple of duplicate copies of everything as he goes."

"Well tell him to bring me a copy tomorrow. Once you're sure he's got those copies safe, then let me know and I'll officially pulling the pair of you off this."

Fennick's frustration finally got the better of him. "Would you care to tell me what the fuck is going on." Then, belatedly, "Sir."

"Ask yourself this, Mike. How did anyone know about the safe house, let alone so bloody quickly? Penstone probably had that assault team on standby for a while, just waiting for an address." Fennick heard Sugden sigh heavily. "Mike. For the moment just be satisfied with what you've achieved so far. You've taken a long time piece of shit down for at least one, probably two murders, and there's a London villain running scared enough to try and kill off two witnesses."

Sugden paused to let it sink in. After a moment, he said, "Not everything ends in an immediate result, Mike. You know that, yourself. And if it's any consolation, then I'll make sure Jimmy Raynolds mentions you in the final wash-up. That's if you really want to be associated with the whole Gold Dust fiasco?"

Fennick grimaced. "Yeah, well, maybe not. What time do you want us back, sir?"

"Once I've got a copy of those papers I don't want to see either of you until Tuesday. By then I expect the pair of you to brief me on the buggers doing all the lifting and shifting over in Northwich. Oh, and before I forget, tell Jimmy Raynolds he's to contact the ACC as soon as he's got a spare minute. If he asks what it's about, tell him it isn't an invite to the bloody Summer Ball."

"Okay, sir, will do."

Well, at least he had Monday off. Unless, of course, DCS Raynolds was in the habit of shooting messengers...

18

Two Months Later

Outside the café, Peter Wainwright put his polystyrene cup of coffee down on the small pavement table, and pulled out a chair.

"Oh, I do like to be beside the seaside. What about you, Jack?" He was dressed in an up-market Hawaiian style shirt, tailored knee length shorts and, for once, the August bank holiday sun was being kind to Blackpool. He sat down next to Jack Telford. Remaining silent for a while, he seemed content to watch the traffic driving by while, over the road, the listless clumps of holidaymakers milled around on the beach beyond.

Jack picked up his plastic cup of tea, took a sip, then said, "This will do me and Susan until I get around to retiring. Speaking of which...." He glanced at Peter, an expectant expression on his face.

Wainwright smiled. "There's a little bonus in the envelope for you this time, Jack. You did us proud. It looks like Mr. Penstone is having to fight his battles on several fronts these days. He's got problems with his suppliers, pissed off the NCA, and his right-hand man is going down better than a bus load of strippers at an Ellesmere Port Social Club."

Telford looked out to sea and slowly shook his head. "Well, don't expect me to keep you informed of things when you start moving down south. That's something I can't do without putting myself right in the spotlight, and you know that, Peter."

Wainwright smiled. "Don't worry, Jack. It's not in my nature to be greedy. Not with Wilson now safely tucked away for a long stretch. That really was a piece of luck and no mistake. Shame about that little bastard Stubbs, though. Still no sign of him, I suppose?"

Telford continued to look out to the horizon. "Not as yet. I'm pretty sure the little toe-rag has made off with most of Gary Tang's prize gemstones. Mind you, some are going to be difficult to shift without their certificates, especially as they're likely to have registration numbers etched onto them somewhere."

"Oh I don't know, Jack. The old Eastern Block still has a healthy taste for that kind of bling. It's certainly where I'd start heading if I were going to shift them. Any idea how much he might have run away with?"

Telford glanced across to Wainwright, a wry grin on his face. "According to the assessors it could be as much as seventy-five to eighty thousand, without really trying."

"Well, I say good luck to him, and I hope he gets away with it. The lad could do with a bit of luck after what he's been through."

The two of them sat, silently taking in the sights and sounds for a while longer, until Wainwright had finished his coffee. Getting up from the table, he said, "Here you are, as promised."

His hand went to his back pocket and pulled out a small, slim envelope.

"Don't go spending it all at once, Jack."

Handing Telford the envelope, Wainwright didn't hesitate. In less than a minute he'd vanished into the steady flow of pedestrian traffic moving along the sea front.

Telford tapped the edge of the envelope contemplatively on the table top, smiling as the outline of the bus station locker key slid down to the corner. Maybe he'd get Susan something nice this time.

Perhaps a little bit of jewellery.

Standing up to leave, Telford dropped the empty plastic cup into a bin as he moved off, heading towards the bus station.

*

Across the way, parked up by the sea wall, a member of the surveillance team in the large panel van radioed ahead that Target Number Two had now moved off from their location and was heading back towards the town.

As he watched Jack Telford walk away on the screen, Mike Fennick wondered just how long Jack had been selling information to Wainwright. According to notebooks found in Caradine's box file, Tony Cooke made the mistake of asking Jack to get some archived police reports, along with a stack of telephone records. He'd told Jack he was after background information concerning several local villains, including Peter Wainwright and any known associates.

Now that others had been going through the pile of material in Cooke's "Work in progress" box, it had taken a little while to realise that the annotated 'JT' wasn't as first thought, Jean Turner, but Jack Telford.

As soon as Cooke had requested the files, Telford had gone to Wainwright, and told him what the likely outcome would be if Cooke continued his unofficial investigations. Coupled with years of careful fudging and tweaking, the last thing Jack wanted was someone digging around in old case files and putting all the little misdirections together.

Not knowing about Jean Turner, or her incriminating written statement, Eddie Caradine had gone off on a mad crusade to put Penstone away single-handedly. But that wasn't important any more. The important thing had been trying to prove that Wainwright had taken a chance and deliberately set things up. Even to the point of talking Ren Penstone into helping with the hit on Cooke and masking it with the hijacking by Carlton.

Proving it wasn't likely to be difficult once the arrests had been made. It was just a case of letting Jack collect his reward before a couple of Cheshire DCs arrested him.

Fennick pushed himself away from the surveillance screens and thought back over the past couple of months.

Not long after his unofficial chat with ACC Richardson, Jimmy Raynolds had announced that he would be stepping down from the position of DCS:

"I feel police work is now, more than ever, about younger perspectives. So I intend on taking an early retirement in order to give the new blood a chance."

Fennick had asked Sugden if he'd given any thought about moving up to the dizzy heights of DCS, and was strangely gratified when Sugden told him to "Fuck off!"

Chief Inspector Bashani also contemplated taking an early retirement package. However, after several months of home confinement medical leave – coupled with Mrs Bashani expressing a strong desire for them both to visit family and relations in Mumbai – he'd decided that maybe a move from Armed Response to a less energetic, more desk-bound position would be financially preferable. If not essential.

Once released from hospital, both Paul Duffley and Jean Turner had been spirited away to another part of the country. According to Joyce Obletta, they were still giving the National Crime Agency team more than enough information to attack Penstone's organisation, with SDC7 gradually dismantling it despite the best efforts of Gordon Lemon.

Meanwhile, Madeline Churchman had celebrated her eighteenth birthday by successfully testifying against Wilson Merrillies. Thankfully the press took her request for anonymity seriously, keeping her face and name out of the papers during the course of the trial. Several weeks after the start of Merrillies' 15 year sentence, she'd quietly relocated to the West Country, adamant that whatever happened, her parents were not to be informed.

On the down side, Jason Stubbs was still missing, along with Gary Tang's gemstone collection. Last seen on a ferry heading towards Spain, the vessel had already docked by the time the authorities had boarded it – with Stubbs being one of the first down the gangplank and away.

But that's the EU for you, I suppose. The gateway to opportunity, after all.

Steve Hansen slid open the side door of the surveillance van – bringing with him the strong smell of cigars and a burst of bright sunlight.

Standing on the pavement, he looked hopefully up at Fennick. "I don't suppose you want us to hang around until they bring Telford and Wainwright in, do you sir?"

Fennick looked at his watch, then thought about giving Jan a call. Maybe there was a chance the two of them could enjoy some of the Bank Holiday after all. Stepping out of the van, he sniffed the air. "Not unless you can think of any other good reason to stay?"

Hansen shook his head. "None that spring to mind."

"Then I think it's time we called it a day and headed on back to our own patch."